VISIONS

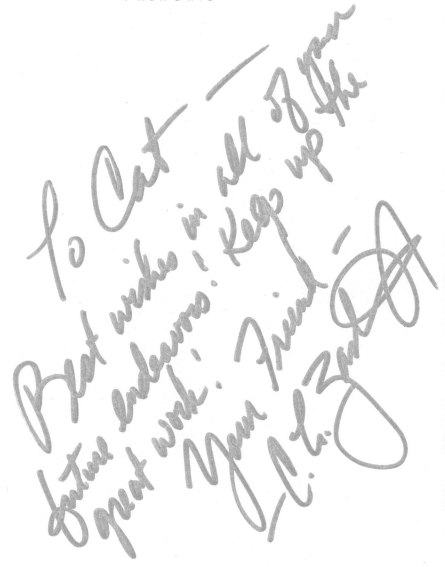

To Cat —
Best wishes in all of your
future endeavors! Keep up the
great work! Friend —
Myra

VISIONS

C. L. Zastrow

iUniverse, Inc.
New York Lincoln Shanghai

Visions

Copyright © 2005 by Cindy Lou Zastrow

iUniverse books may be ordered through booksellers or by contacting:

iUniverse
2021 Pine Lake Road, Suite 100
Lincoln, NE 68512
www.iuniverse.com
1-800-Authors (1-800-288-4677)

ISBN-13: 978-0-595-35429-0 (pbk)
ISBN-13: 978-0-595-79924-4 (ebk)
ISBN-10: 0-595-35429-7 (pbk)
ISBN-10: 0-595-79924-8 (ebk)

Printed in the United States of America

PROLOGUE

▼

Chris lay sprawled across Devon's chest, gently stirring…

"Mmmm…this is my favorite way to wake up."

"How's that—you mean hair all rumpled, no makeup, with a definitive case of dragon breath?" Devon said, sarcastically.

"No!" Chris yelled—taking the pillow from behind her and smacking Devon across the face.

Devon smiled.

The pixie-like woman rolled over onto Devon's chest…gently kissing the nape of her neck, and looking at Devon lovingly.

"Waking up next to you…feeling you with me…it's the best feeling in the world."

God how I love this woman…

FLASH

The lights and sirens…all something that Devon was used to…but not this time.

Lights. Spinning. Long hallways…

"Detective?"

"Devonnnn?" Chris moaned.

"Chris…baby…I'm here!" She said, running alongside the gurney as they rushed into the emergency room. "I'm here…and I love you, baby…I love you…"

Suddenly, an arm against her chest stopped her.

"Detective, I'm sorry…you'll have to stay out here."

"But…no! I have to be with her…she needs me!"

"Detective…Detective!"

Devon snapped out of her daze and faced the nurse.

"You need to stay out here and let us do what we need to do. She's in good hands…"

But they're not <u>my</u> *hands…mine…*

Devon watched helplessly as the gurney disappeared through the double doors…Chris disappearing with it.

FLASH

"Detective McKinney?"

Devon jumped out of the chair "Yes! How is she??" she said, spilling her coffee as she ran to the nurse.

"Detective, the doctor would like to talk to you."

Devon's heart jumped into her throat and she felt as though some mystical hand wrapped itself around her chest, squeezing the very life out of her.

The nurse led her down the long corridor with its stark white hallways...so cold...to a small room across from the nurse's station.

"Please have a seat. The doctor will be with you in a moment."

Devon pulled a chair away from the table and eased into it...setting what remained of her coffee on the table in front of her.

What is taking him so fucking long?? Why won't they let me see her??

Just then a tall man dressed in scrubs walked into the small room, behind him, a chaplain.

...the collar...no...

...and then the panic set in.

"Chris...is she...?" She couldn't say it.

"Ms. McKinney, I'm Dr. Gallagher, and this is Chaplain Royal." Chaplain Royal nodded.

"Ms. McKinney...Chris has sustained a very serious injury to her liver and her spleen."

"Well...y-you can fix it, right? So she'll need surgery..."

"Ms. McKinney...she's bleeding very badly and we can't seem to get it stopped. She's not stable enough for us to take her into surgery."

"But...you're just going to leave her die? You have to do something!" She said, rising out of her chair and grabbing the doctor by the top of his scrubs. "Do something!"

"Devon, I know this is hard...but you've got to calm down...you're not doing Chris any good by doing this..." The Chaplain reasoned...trying to get her to release her vice-like grip on the doctor.

"I'm sorry…it's just…" she choked on her words as the tears welled in her beautiful blue eyes.

"We've done everything we can for now—made her comfortable…all we can do is wait…" said Dr. Gallagher.

"Can I see her?"

"Sure. I'll take you down there now." he said, extending his hand to Devon.

They once again headed down the blinding white hall, coming to a stop at Trauma Bay 3.

"She's in and out of consciousness, but she'll know you're here." He said, gently squeezing her shoulder.

Devon hesitantly entered the room…not sure she was ready for what she was about to find. A familiar smell permeated the room—it was one that Devon knew well—it was the hot coppery smell of blood…only this was Chris' blood. Chris still laid on the trauma bay gurney—tubes coming from, and going into what seemed to be every part of her body…the color drained from her face…she had always been petite—but now, she looked so small…so fragile…so…broken.

"Dev…?" she whimpered.

Devon walked to her side, taking her hand in hers, careful not to disturb the IV's.

"Hey you." she said, forcing a smile.

"Hi." She winced…obviously in extreme pain.

Devon winced with her.

"Boy…the things people will do just to…" Devon couldn't finish…she broke down.

"Shhhh…shhh…Baby." Chris said, running her thumb along Devon's hand.

Another wave of pain hit Chris, she sucked her breath in, trying to stifle it.

"I want you to…I want you to listen to me…"
Devon sobbed, her head hanging down. Chris reached out, placing her hand under Devon's chin, lifting it up ever so slightly.

"That's my girl…gotta see those baby blues…"

Tears flowed down Devon's cheeks forming little rivulets on her face—dripping onto the blackness of her favorite leather jacket.

"I want you to promise me you'll find love again…after I'm gone…"

"No, baby…no—you're not going anywhere! You just need time…that's all…time to heal…"

Chris stopped her.

"Dev…promise me…please?"

"No…I won't…I love you! Only you…it's always been you—it will always be you!"

"Don't…" she gasped.

The pain was becoming unbearable…she swallowed hard…trying to stay awake.

It was time.

"…promise…me…."

BEEEEEEEEEEEEEEEEEEEP…………………………………

Devon bolted upright in bed, covered in a cold sweat. Her chest heaved, but the air was thick…she couldn't breathe…she couldn't anything…

It was dark. But it had been dark since she'd gone, hadn't it?

Devon pushed back the covers, swinging her legs to the side of the bed, sitting up…looking for some reason to go on with life, with everything.

Times like this, she didn't know if she was alive or dead.

She glanced over at the nightstand. Among the empty bottles of vodka and candy wrappers, she reached over for the one thing that she had left. The simple frame, it's glass long broken, held the one thing that kept her fine line to reality still intact. Chris.

That was the day they had gone to Disney World. Chris had never been there before—and she was absolutely giddy…especially when Goofy wrapped his arms around her for the picture…good times. Gone now.
Devon opened the drawer, taking out the all-to-familiar brown bottle where she found her comfort these days. She took two of the pills, throwing them to the back of her throat—swallowing hard.

Pretty fucking bitter pill to swallow…

She smiled at the irony of the thought as she collapsed onto the bed once more…

CHAPTER 1

▼

Pagers suck.

Devon rubbed the sleep from her eyes and reached over to the crowded nightstand, knocking an empty bottle off as she grabbed the beeping pager.

HOMICIDE—4453 N. MASON—M.E. ON SCENE—CALL WITH E.T.A.—MIKE.

Picking up the cell phone laying on the floor, she dialed…

"Morning, beautiful!"

"Hey."

"You okay?"

Devon cleared her throat "…rough night."

There'd been a lot of rough nights lately. Mike knew how bad things had gotten for his partner since Chris had died.

"Well get your butt over here…I've got a large black coffee and a box of Krispy Kremes with your name on it."

"Give me thirty minutes. I'll be there."

"You've got twenty." Mike said, hanging up. Deadlines seemed to be the only way to motivate her these days…if you didn't give her one, nine times out of ten, she'd stroll in hours later, if she showed at all.

Devon sat up, swinging her legs over the side of the bed. She took a deep breath, choking on the stale air, coughing. She hurt…every inch of her, inside and out.

Her pager went off a second time…it read simply "19".

"Son-of-a-bitch…I know! I'm coming!!!"

She grabbed a pair of jeans from one of the many piles of clothes on the floor, pulling them on and tucking in her shirt…pulling her hair back into a ponytail. She walked out the door, snagging her shoulder holster and jacket on her way out.

The air was heavy and damp, a thick layer of dew covering everything in a blanket of shiny wetness. Devon climbed into her SUV, reaching up to turn the keys that she had left in the ignition.

She always hated that…how many times didn't she tell me not to leave them in here…

The engine knocked a bit, but eased into a heavy purr as Devon peeled out of the driveway and down the dirt road. Mason Street was in what the uniforms referred to as 'the Zoo'—stating that you could find just about any kind of animal there…hookers, drug dealers, pimps, junkies, gang-bangers, you name it, the Zoo had it. She pulled up to the scene, running the SUV tires partially up onto the curb, catching the attention of a group of officers waiting near one of the cars.

"Looks like my partner's here." Mike grabbed a coffee and the box of doughnuts and walked toward Devon.

"Hey…thanks." She said, taking the coffee. "What have we got?"

"The neighbor was going for her early morning fix and saw blood on the sidewalk. Looked like it was coming from the bushes nearby, so she decided to investigate. She saw the body and called 9-1-1 on her cell phone."

Devon took a sip of the coffee, wincing "Geezus! What is this?"

"Coffee, black…brewed fresh yesterday…just the way you like it." He said with a smile.

"So the victim?"

"We haven't got an ID on her yet…little girl, white, looks to be about six or seven…"

"Any signs of sexual assault?"

"Can't tell…she's in pretty bad shape, Dev. Somebody gutted her like a deer."

"Great." She said. Tasting the bile coming up in the back of her throat. She grabbed a pair of booties from one of the crime scene techs, pulling them over her shoes—she ducked under the tape and made her way to the body.

Death was nothing new, she'd seen a lot of it in the past four years in the VCU (Violent Crimes Unit), but kids were never easy—for anybody.

A man, dressed all in Tyvek hovered over the girl's body, placing a thermometer probe into what appeared to be her liver—or whatever was left of it.

"Hey Doc…what's the word?"

"Well hello, Devon. Just trying to get a liver temp here…don't know how much good it will be, seeing as the gut's been exposed…she's basically been eviscerated."

He looked back at the temperature gauge "…nope, that's what I thought…we're just going to have to try to estimate based on lividity." He stood up, giving Devon her first full glance at the girl's body.

She was a small girl, no more than six or seven years old…dirty blonde hair, laying in mattes, partially stained red with her own blood. Her tiny hands had been covered with paper bags, wrapped at the wrist, to protect any possible evidence that she may have under her fingernails…skin, hair, anything. Whoever did this was in a hurry…they didn't even bother to unclothe her before slitting her open from her pubic area to her sternum. The teddy bear t-shirt she wore was torn up the center in much the same fashion as the rest of her body. Her lifeless eyes stared up into space, mouth agape in a permanent scream.

What did they do to you, baby? Give me something…help me catch this bastard…

Devon began doing what she knew best…working the crime scene. She knew there was nothing else that could be done for the girl…nothing except doing the best job that she could do to put whoever killed her behind bars. Care without caring…she wasn't part of the problem…she was part of the solution.

Devon looked down at the body once again…this time paying particularly close attention to the blood pooled around it…

She grabbed the mini-recorder from her pocket, pressing the record button…

"Victim is a Caucasian female, approximately 5 to 7 years of age, wearing blue shorts and white t-shirt with teddy bear pattern. Victim has large laceration with evisceration from the pubis to the sternum. T-shirt appears to have been cut up the center, possibly in accordance with the central wound to the torso."

Devon pushed pause on the recorder…looking to Dr. Brown, the Medical Examiner.

"What would you say on the blood loss…around 2-2.5 liters?"

Dr. Brown smiled. "You always were one of my best students…yes…I'd say it's around 2 to 2.5 liters…her entire blood volume, I'd wager."

"Any pettichial hemorrhaging? Ligature marks?"

"No on the pettichial hemorrhaging…I haven't found any obvious ligature marks as of yet…but I'll know more after I get her on the table."

"Was she…" Devon hesitated…she always hated the thought of someone being violated sexually…especially a child.

"I'm not sure yet, Devon…she's pretty torn up. I really can't tell without doing the internal examination."

"Yeah…I know…anything else unusual?"

"Not that I noticed as of yet."

"Okay…thanks, Doc. When do you think you'll get to her?"

"I'd like to get her first thing in the morning…say…9:00am?"

"I'll be there."

Devon's rough appearance did not escape Dr. Brown's notice.

"How about you meet me for breakfast before…say 7:30am…we can talk…my treat." He said.

"Not much into eating these days…"

"I can see that…we'll talk…you'll eat…at 7:30am…at Frost's…that's an order."

"Well…if you put it that way…"

"I do…and you will be there…" he said, grabbing his case and walking back towards his vehicle.

"Okay…see you later."

Devon pressed the red record button once again.

"Estimated blood loss at this scene 2 to 2.5 liters…total blood volume. Victim was alive here…this is most likely the primary crime scene."

She pressed pause once again...looking around the entire scene...a crowd of 'goose-neckers' was starting to gather.

Her eyes scanned the crowd...

Where are you? Are you out there...watching us? Watching her?

Faces in the crowd...faces that she would etch in her memory...anything unusual...out of place...

These were the faces of the night. Death was no stranger to this community...it visited here on a regular basis.

Each person standing on the other side of the yellow crime scene tape was waiting and watching...hoping that the victim wasn't family or friend...

Devon knew the routine well. She'd been there so many times before...a nameless body...laying cold on the ground...until someone from the crowd notices something...a shirt, perhaps...or hat...and then the scream...the sound of someone realizing that their loved one will never be coming home again.

But the scream never came.

Devon pressed record once more...

"Predominantly black neighborhood. Victim is white...maybe mulatto...or maybe not from this part of town..."

She paused again...changing her venue, she moved to the outskirts of the taped area...beginning to walk a spiral to the center of the scene...examining everything carefully...up and down...

She remembered what Dr. Brown had always said...

A crime scene is not only what appears on the ground in front of you...it is three-dimensional...you need to treat it as such.

Meanwhile…Mike had his hands full trying to canvass the locals for information. Seems no one had seen anything…a familiar story in this neighborhood…

"Ok…you live in that house, right there." He said, pointing to an old house that was only about thirty feet from the body.

"Yeah." The woman answered.

"Pretty hot out…did you have your windows open?"

"Yeah."

"But you didn't hear anything at all…no screams…nothing?"

"I told you before…I didn't hear nothing…"

"That's what I thought…" Mike said, exasperated.

This is going nowhere and getting there in a hurry…

"Thanks." Mike said, walking back towards the scene.

Devon walked over to the edge of the tape…

"So how's it going with the locals? Anything?"

"What do you think?" He said, sarcastically.

"That good, huh?"

"I seriously doubt that we're going to get anything out of these people…how's the scene going?"

"Nothing much yet…think we're looking at the primary…so that's something…but other than that…not much. I'm going to sit in on the autopsy. Hopefully we'll get something to work with there."

"Better you than me."

Although he was a seasoned homicide detective, Mike had never gotten used to sitting in on autopsies. The sights were one thing…the smells were another. More than his stomach could take most of the time…that was Devon's job. For some reason, no amount of blood and gore ever seemed to get to her…in fact…she seemed fascinated by it…by how the human body worked…how it functioned…in life…and in death.

"I'll page you when we're done…give you the information then."

"Sounds good. I'll go start the paperwork on this…let me know if you need anything…"

"I will." Devon said, turning back to the scene.

She worked the scene over and over until daybreak…hoping that the sunlight would help to reveal something that she may have missed in the cover of night.

Nothing.

Maybe that, in and of itself, is a clue…

Devon watched as the assistants from the M.E.'s office bagged the body and loaded it onto the gurney.

Hopefully we'll turn up something at the autopsy…whoever did this isn't going to stop with just one…

CHAPTER 2

▼

Devon sat at a small booth inside Frost's Café, going over her notes from the scene while she waited for Dr. Brown to arrive.

Victim is found in highly populated area. It's a hot night…most people have their windows open, yet no one heard anything…no immediate material evidence procured at the scene…

Why am I not liking the sound of this?

"Penny for your thoughts?" Dr. Brown said, sliding into the bench across from Devon.

"…a penny doesn't buy much these days…" Devon joked.

"So…find anything promising at the scene?"

"Not so you'd notice…I'm hoping we'll turn something up today…"

Just then the waitress appeared.

"What can I get for you two today?"

"Diet Cola." Devon said.

"That'll rot your gut, Dev...for God's sake, I use that to clean greasy engine parts!"

Devon smirked "Yeah...seems like you've told me that a few times before..."

"I'll have tea...thanks."

"Can I get you anything for breakfast?"

"Can you give us a few minutes?" Dr. Brown asked, looking at the menu.

"Sure thing...I'll be back shortly...take your time."

"Okay! So what's it going to be...pancakes? French Toast? How about a big farmer's omelet?"

Food. Just the thought of it made her stomach queasy. She wasn't much into the whole eating thing lately...an occasional doughnut here and there...or maybe some chips...but nothing really sounded good...it hadn't in a long time...

"Nah...think I'll just stick with the diet Cola for now..."

"Dev...you look like shit...you've got dark circles under your eyes, your cheeks are starting to sink in...need I go further?"

"Doc...I'm fine."

"Yeah...sure."

"Seriously...I eat!"

"Hon...a two liter of diet Cola and a package of Ho-Ho's does not constitute eating."

"I don't even like Ho-Ho's..." Devon said, pouting.

"Come on...humor me...pancakes?" He said, smiling.

"You're not going to shut up until I agree, are you?"

"No."

"Okay…pancakes…no meat."

"You need some protein."

"Hey…I'm eating the pancakes…don't push it, alright?"

The waitress arrived just in time with the drinks to cause a well-needed time-out in the action.

"There we go…one diet Cola…" she said, placing the glass and a wrapped straw in front of Devon "…and one tea."

"Thanks." Devon said, drinking directly from the glass.

"Now what can I get you for breakfast?"

"I'll have the farmer's omelet with wheat toast, buttered…and a side of bacon…"

"In other words…give him a heart attack on a plate…would you like a side of lard with that?" Devon added sarcastically.

"The lovely lady here…and I do use the term loosely…would like a double stack of your buttermilk pancakes…"

"No m…" she started to remind him.

"Yes…no meat…I know…" he added.

"Ok…got it…shouldn't be too long." She said, writing down the order on a green pad of paper and walking to the kitchen.

"So…from the look of the whites of your eyes…or should I say the 'reds' of your eyes…I'd gather eating isn't the only thing you haven't been doing much of lately."

"Sleep is optional…" she said, taking a drink of the cola.

"Since when? Last time I looked…the human body kind of required a bit of it now and then…"

Always so smug…

"Doc…I'm sleeping…"

A look of doubt spread across the doctor's face…

"Seriously…I am!" Devon said, defensively. "Just not so good sometimes…" she said, looking down into her glass, studying the intricacy of the ice floating in the fizzy liquid.

"Dev…you want to talk about this?"

"Not really…do I have a choice?"

"Not really."

"Yeah…that's what I thought."

Devon took a deep breath…hoping that it would in some way make talking about this easier. Instead, it just made the muscles of her chest wall tighten further…tears started to cloud her eyes.

You are not going to do this! You are not going to cry in front of him!

"Dev?"

"Yeah."

The doctor stretched his arm out, placing his hand on top of Devon's.

"I'm here."

"I know, Doc...it's just...you know...tough." She said, swallowing hard.

"I know...hell...I don't know...who am I kidding? I don't know what it's like to lose the love of my life...I don't. But I do know about death...and pain...and grief."

Devon's eyes were still trained on the glass in front of her...

"We deal with it every day, Dev...every goddamned day. I know how rotten I feel sometimes...and they aren't even people that I know!"

Devon took a breath...still not raising her eyes...knowing that if she did, her last remaining protective wall would crumble.

"Yeah...did you ever wonder why, though? Why this person is picked to die...and this one isn't? I mean...what made them so different? Why were they the one? Why wasn't I..."

Her tears betrayed her...running down the soft curves of her face.

"Why weren't you the one to die instead of Chris?"

Devon looked up, her eyes finally breaking the plane of the table, looking at her mentor for answers...

"I don't have a good answer for you, Dev. I don't...I wish I did...maybe it's because your mission...whatever reason you were placed on this earth...it's not complete yet...I just don't know..."

Devon sniffled, breaking contact with the comfort of his hand...wiping the tears from her face.

"Yeah...well...whatever."

"You're not going to bring Chris back by killing yourself like this...you know she'd be the first one to be kicking your butt right now."

Yeah...you would be, wouldn't you, baby? Never thinking of yourself...always of me...

"Can we just not talk about this right now?"

"You need to talk to someone about this Dev...if not me...then someone else..."

"Okay...listen...I'll be fine. I just need some time, okay? Now...how about we get over to the office and see what our girl has to tell us."

Dr. Brown knew that Devon was on a downward spiral. It was no longer an 'if'...it was when she would crash...it was only a matter of time. He really hoped that she would eventually let someone within the confines of those protective walls of hers...but just like life, there were no guarantees.

"How about we eat...then go..."

"I'm fine...seriously."

"Well, I'm not...I've got to get something in my stomach before I waste away to nothing..."

Looking at Dr. Brown's rotund stature, she highly doubted that he was in any danger of that...the thought did elicit a slight smile from her, though...

"...and you've got to get something in there to keep that battery acid you're drinking from eating a hole in your gut."

"Okay...whatever you say, Doc..."

"I'm glad you haven't totally lost your senses!" He said, as the waitress delivered their food.

Devon looked at the plate of greasy eggs, cheese, bacon, hash browns and but-ter-slathered toast that sat in front of her friend...

"You're seriously going to eat that?" she said, pointing at the plate of food.

"You betcha."

"…and you yell at me?"

"What?"

"Ugh…never mind…disregard…"

Devon looked on through the stack of jellies on the table…

"Damn…no peanut butter."

"Peanut butter?"

"Yeah…peanut butter…can't have pancakes without peanut butter!"

Devon remembered the first time she had tried the weird concoction. It was the first time she had stayed over at Chris' place when they were in college…Chris had made her breakfast in bed the next morning…pancakes…

Devon lay in the bed, still dreaming of the night before…she and Chris…their first time together…how soft her skin had felt against hers…safe…warm…

Chris tip-toed in to the room…trying her best not to wake her love…but one of the floorboards betrayed her…waking Devon with a squeak.

Devon opened her eyes…

"Morning…" she said, smiling.

"Good morning, sleepy-head!" Chris said…sitting on the edge of the bed…tray in her lap…

"Wow! What's all this?"

"I just thought you might be hungry…after last night and all…" she said, blushing slightly.

"Hmmm…let's see what we've got here…pancakes…yum! And juice…milk…Lucky Charms…ooh…they're my favorite! This looks great, hon."

Devon reached for the bottle of syrup on the tray…

"Oh…wait! I forgot the peanut butter!"

"Peanut butter?"

"Yes…peanut butter…you can't have pancakes without peanut butter!" She said…running back to the kitchen. She returned momentarily with two jars…

"Which to you prefer…creamy?" She said, holding up one jar."…or crunchy?"

"Um…crunchy?" Devon said, hesitantly.

"Crunchy it is! You're a girl after my own heart!" Chris said, unscrewing the lid on the jar…

"Dev…Dev? You okay?" Doc said, snapping her out of the daze.

"Wha…What did you say?"

"Did you want some peanut butter…for your pancakes?"

"Oh…yeah…sure."

Doc raised his hand…waiving to the waitress.
"Ma'am…could you please get us some peanut butter?"

"Sure thing, hon. Be right back."

The waitress returned with three white plastic packets…

"Here you go…" she said, sitting them on the table.

Devon picked them up…reading the package…

Creamy…it figures…

CHAPTER 3

▼

God…was it always this cold?

It was the first thing that came to Devon's mind when she walked into the morgue.

The pungent combination of antiseptic and death hung in the place like a spring storm…waiting to burst open at any second…drowning her in the downpour.

This wasn't her first trip here…she'd haunted these halls many a night…so why was this any different?

Chris. They took her here after she…after she…

There it was again…that familiar tightness that started deep within her chest, creeping up into her throat, welling up in her eyes…

This was where they had taken Chris after she died. Devon didn't want to think about it, but she knew it was true. State law required all traumatic deaths to be autopsied, and Chris' death was nothing if not traumatic…

"We've got about twenty minutes before the theater doors open…did you need anything, hon?" Devon asked.

"You know…it's pretty warm out tonight. I thought I was going to need my jacket…but I think I'll just toss it into the car before we go in."

"I can take it over there for you." Devon said, outstretching her hand to take the jacket.

"That's okay, baby. I can get it. Just need you to unlock it for me."

Devon reached into her pocket, grabbing the keys and remote.

'Click-click'. The remote locks chirped as she hit the button twice.

"Hey Chris…why don't you throw mine in there, too." She said, handing the black leather coat to her. "Thanks, hon."

Chris draped Devon's signature coat around her shoulders. Devon watched as Chris made her way through the parked cars and out into the street…

The moonlight bounced off of Chris' delicate features…Devon didn't think that anything could possibly be more beautiful. She stared at her love in amazement…this woman…this beautiful creature chose her to be with…she could have had anyone…but she chose her…

Devon's thoughts were interrupted by the scream of tires gripping the blacktop…an engine speeding…

She looked just in time to see the Black Cadillac turn the corner and accelerate towards the figure crossing the street in front of her. It took her only a split second to react…but that second seemed like a lifetime as Devon sprinted towards Chris…

"CHRIS!!!!!!!!!!!"

Devon reached her just before the car impacted…trying to push her out of harm's way…but it was in vain…and both were sent flying, landing on the harsh blacktop with a thud.

Devon looked up, seeing the car speed away. Still stunned from the impact, she was unable to move. Her eyes scanned the street, finally coming to rest on Chris body lying battered and bloodied in the gutter. Everything went dark...

It had been dark ever since...

"Dev?" Doc said.

No reaction.

"Devon, are you okay?" he said, laying his hand on her shoulder.

"Yeah...sorry."

"Listen, Dev. You don't have to do this, you know. I've done plenty of these by myself...I think I can handle it." He said, trying to give his young friend an easy way out. He knew that this wouldn't be easy for her...not now...

"I'm fine, Doc. Let's get in there and see what she can tell us, okay?"

Devon didn't know who she was trying harder to convince, Doc, or herself.

"Okay...lets suit up." Doc said, pushing his way through the heavy steel door into the prep room.

Doc grabbed a gown, cap, booties, and mask for Devon, handing it to her...then taking one for himself.

"Thanks." Devon said, taking the items.

"No problem."

"No...I mean for...for everything." She said, looking intently at Doc.
He knew how stoic his young protégé could be...and how difficult it was for her to accept that she might need someone to talk to...

"Anytime, Dev...anytime you need to talk...I'm here."

"I know." She said, tying the back of her gown and slipping her booties on. She reached into the glove box, pulling out two pair for herself. "Ready to do this?"

"Let's do it." He said, stretching his second pair of gloves onto his hands with a snap.

The autopsy suite was not unlike a hospital Emergency Room suite. It's smooth tile walls and stainless steel fixtures gave it an icy look. The air was a queasy mix of antiseptic, formalin, and death. The centerpiece of the room was a stainless steel table with drains at both ends. A large tray of shiny stainless steel instruments, a camera, and a small pocket tape recorder sat nearby. The small figure shrouded in white sheets lying on the table made it look like a sacrificial altar…

Normally there would be a diener on hand to assist with the actual autopsy; however, Devon was more than qualified. She had been trained personally by Dr. Brown, and had assisted him on many occasions.

"Well…shall we get on with the external examination?" Doc said.

"Let's do it."

Dr. Brown pressed the record button on the mini-recorder and placed it in the breast pocket of his gown.

"External examination of female Caucasian, approximate age 5 to 7 years old. General appearance, child is well nourished with no obvious signs of disease or malady. Tape measure, please."

Devon handed the tape to him.

"Height is 101.6 centimeters…and weight is 24.484 kilograms." He said, looking at the scales on the table.

He rolled the tape back up, handing it to Devon. She laid it on the tray with the rest of the instruments.

"Subject has large ventral incision with somewhat ragged edges extending from the pubis to the xyphoid process with complete evisceration of the abdominal contents. Let's get some pictures of that."

Devon grabbed the camera, making sure there was film in it, and began taking pictures of the body from different angles.
"Make sure you get close-ups of the edges of the wound…" Doc reminded her.

"I know, Doc…you trained me well." She said with a smirk.

"Doesn't appear to be any pettichial hemorrhaging…but let's get a picture of the eyes, just in case."

Devon snapped the picture, setting the completed prints and the camera back onto the tray.

"Could you hand me the magnifier?"

"Here…" Devon said, handing him the tool.

She stood watching as Dr. Brown made his way across the young girl's body…searching for anything…fibers, stains, anything that might give them some clue as to who may have snuffed out this innocent life.

"You want to give me one of those small specimen jars?" Doc said, stopping over the girl's left arm.

Devon handed him the small jar, opening the lid for him.

"What have you got, Doc?" she said, moving in to look over his shoulder.

"Can't tell for sure…looks like some kind of animal hair…" he said, picking up the hair with a pair of tweezers and holding it up to the light before placing it into the container.

Devon squinted, trying to make out what type of hair it was.

"What is that? It doesn't look like cat…"

"I'm not sure…we'll let the state lab figure that one out…let's go ahead and remove the clothes…"

Devon started at the feet, carefully removing the shoes without untying them, then the socks. Each piece of clothing was placed into a plain paper bag, sealed, and initialed for processing at the crime lab.

"Ok…ready to turn her?"

"Yeah…let's do it." Devon said, log rolling the body onto its side, hoping that the intestines wouldn't fall out onto the table.

Dr. Brown handed her a pair of EMS shears.

"I take it I'm doing the scissor-stripping, huh?"

"Do you mind? If you'd rather not…"

"No…I'm fine." She said, slipping the shears underneath the blood soaked fabric of the girl's shorts…slitting the legs up the back to the waistband. She repeated the process with the t-shirt.

"Okay…let's roll her back."

Devon held onto the clothing while Doc rolled the body over once more onto it's back.

"Got it?"

"Got it." Devon pulled the shorts and shirt out from underneath the body, placing each one into separate paper bags and sealing them.

"Let's go ahead with the internal exam."

Devon rolled the tray of surgical instruments closer to the table, and both she and Dr. Brown removed one pair of their gloves and replaced them with a new pair from the box on the wall. Not wanting to transfer anything from the clothing that they had just bagged onto the body.

"I think what we'll do, since she already has the large ventral incision, we'll just complete the Y and bring it down to the wound itself."

"Yeah…looks like he pretty much did our cutting for us, didn't he?" Devon said sarcastically.

"Devon…you're making assumptions…"

"Oh come on, Doc! Are you going to tell me that you think that a woman is capable of this?" She said, pointing at the gaping wound in the child's abdomen.

"I know…but you know as well as I do that truth is sometimes stranger than fiction."

"I know…"

"All I'm saying is that you need to keep an open mind about this, Dev. Are you sure you're ready for this? It could turn out ugly…"

"My whole life's ugly, Doc…what's a little bit more, right?"

Just as they were about to start, the door to the room opened and a short, African American woman dressed in scrubs entered the room.
"Doc…sorry to interrupt you two…but we may have a possible ID on the little girl."

"That's alright, Karen. Do we have someone to make a positive identification?"

"The parents are waiting outside."

"We've got some pretty good shots of the face over there on the table. You can take one of those to show them if you'd like." He said, motioning to the table.

"Doc…they want to come in and see for themselves…"

"I really don't think that's a good idea…" Devon said, given the severity of the injuries.

"Detective, do you want to come out and talk to them?"

"Not really, but I will…give me a second, okay?"

"No problem. I'll tell them you'll be out in a minute." Karen said, closing the door behind her.

"Dev…why don't you let me do this…if it is their daughter, this isn't going to be pretty."

"It's my case, Doc. I said I'll do it." She said, turning and walking into the prep room.

Devon could feel her chest tightening in anticipation of facing the couple waiting outside. Times like these, she hated her job…but she was good at it…and this was her duty.

She peeled the soiled gown, cap, mask, and gloves off, throwing them in the red biohazard bin, straightened her clothes, and walked into the waiting room. Karen was waiting with the couple. She stood up when Devon entered the room…

"Detective McKinney, this is Mr. and Mrs. Hingerman…I'll be in with Dr. Brown if you need me."

Gee…thanks for the support, Karen! God, I hate this…

Mr. and Mrs. Hingerman looked like the typical working-class young couple. It was evident from their appearance that they didn't have a lot of money, but they were well kept and took pride in themselves and their appearance.

Okay McKinney…time to put on your game face…take a nice deep breath and just do it…

Devon sat down in the chair adjacent to the Hingermans. The young couple sat quietly…looking to Devon for some kind of an answer.

"I'm sorry that we have to be meeting under these circumstances. Karen tells me that you think that one of our…patients…may be your daughter. Could you tell me a bit about her? What she looks like…when did you last see her?"

"I have some pictures of Hallie…if you'd like to see them." Mrs. Hingerman said, sniffing back the tears.

"That would be very helpful, thank you. When did you last see Hallie?"

"Last night." Mr. Hingerman answered. "It was when we put her to bed. It was so hot…and we don't have air conditioning. I opened the window…" The emotion welling up in his throat brought his explanation to an abrupt halt. Mrs. Hingerman continued…

"We never heard a thing…but when I went in to wake her up for school…she was gone. We live over in Wagerville…the police there said that it looked like someone had cut the screen…" Mrs. Hingerman said, handing the pictures of Hallie to Devon.

It didn't take long for Devon to realize that the girl in there on the slab was, in fact, Hallie Hingerman. Her heart sank at the thought of what was coming next. She'd seen it before…the denial…the pain…the pleading…she'd done it herself, not too long ago.

She didn't have to say a word…they could see it in her eyes…their daughter was gone.

"Oh God…NO! Not my baby! It's not her! Not her!" Mrs. Hingerman cried, collapsing into her husband's lap.

I know…God, I know…I wish there was something I could do…but there's nothing…nothing that can stop the pain.

Mr. Hingerman held his wife, trying to be strong…but also wanting to make sure…his little girl was gone. "Can we see her?"

"Mr. Hingerman…I really don't think that would be…"

"I need to see her." He said, solemnly.

How do you tell someone that their little girl is laying cold on a slab, gutted like a deer? What am I supposed to say?

"I'll go tell Dr. Brown. If you'll just wait here for a moment. Is there someone that I can call for you?"

Mr. Hingerman shook his head no…his wife sobbing in his arms.

Devon walked through the prep room and into the autopsy suite.

"Doc…it's her."
"Are you sure?" he asked.

"Yeah…it's her…and they want to see her."

"Damn…okay. You're going to have to give me a few minutes. I don't want them seeing her this way." He said, laying the girls chest plate back onto her body. "There's some extra sheets in the prep room, can you grab them for me? We're going to have to drape everything except her face."

"Yeah…sure." Devon said, walking back to the prep room. She took three clean sheets off the shelf.

"Will three be enough?" She asked.

"That should work…I just don't want the blood soaking through while they're in here…" said Doc. "It's a damned good thing I didn't get to her head yet…"

The words echoed through Devon's head…it's not that it wasn't upsetting before…seeing the young girl in on the table…working on her. But things were different now…now she had a name…people who loved her…she had a past…and now, no future.

It wasn't fair…but then, life rarely is.

Dr. Brown repositioned the body into a more natural position, removing the body blocks. The tray of instruments was placed at the foot of the body. He then carefully draped the sheets over the table, covering the worst of the injuries to the girl.

"Okay…it's not great, but it's as good as it's going to get right now."

"Okay." Devon said, walking out to the waiting area. "Mr. and Mrs. Hingerman? You can come in now." She said, holding the door open for the couple.

"Baby…I'll be right back." Mr. Hingerman said, rising from the chair by himself and walking through the door.

Mrs. Hingerman sat crumpled into a pile on the chair, rocking back and forth, sobbing uncontrollably…just as Devon had done the night of Chris' death.

You could hear the air leaving the young man's lungs as he entered the room and saw his only child lying on the cold metal slab in front of him. He was a broken man…

"Oh baby…" he said, walking slowly toward the table. He placed his hand on hers underneath the sheet. "Daddy's here…and Daddy's sorry, baby…Daddy's so sorry."

He looked up at Devon and Dr. Brown, tears streaming down his face. "She never liked her window open…she said that the Boogey Man would get her…Oh, God!!! Hallie!!!" He screamed, collapsing to the floor.

It never gets any easier…

CHAPTER 4

▼

It had been a long night...and an even longer day. By the time they had finished the autopsy on the Hingerman girl, it was just about one in the afternoon, and Devon was exhausted, both physically and emotionally.

"You okay, Dev? You're looking pretty rough..." Doc said.

"Yeah...I'm fine...just tired."

"I'll take care of the paperwork...why don't you go home and get some rest."

"You're sure you don't mind? That's a lot of paperwork..."

"I'm sure...now get going, before I change my mind, okay?" he said, smiling.

"Okay...I'm going." Devon said, tossing her soiled gown into the biohazard bin.

"...and get something to eat...you look like 'Mr. Bones' hanging up in my office..." he said, eying her up "...no...I take that back...you're skinnier than he is."

Devon looked at him, annoyed not only because he had the gall to say it...but also because she knew he was right.

"Anybody ever tell you you're a real pain-in-the-ass?" She said, pointedly.

"Gluteus Maximusitis…that would be me! How'd you know?" He said with a grin.

"This little bird told me." She said, flipping him the 'one-finger wave' and grinning.

"Hey…have you got a license to fly that thing?"

"Yeah…as a matter of fact…I do…it's right here…" she said, patting the holster inside her waistband.

"Oooh. Okay, you win this round…now get out of here."

"Thanks, Doc…I'll talk to you later." Devon said, turning to walk down the hallway.

Heavy, hot and humid, the air outside hit her as she opened the door to the parking lot…sending a wave of nausea through her body. She swallowed hard, hoping to keep what may have remained of her breakfast, down.

Okay…that was just unpleasant…

Devon's feet dragged as she made her way across the parking lot to the Jeep Grand Cherokee parked across from the morgue. She hit the remote, unlocking the vehicle with a chirp. Climbing into the seat, sliding the keys into the ignition, she leaned back with a sigh. She reached down, turning the air conditioning full blast…closed her eyes, and waited for the cool air to slide over her body…

"Out…out! Why won't you come out?" the voice said. Hands rubbing furiously under the water…pink rivulets flowing down the silvery drain…

FLASH

"Please…please…I just want to go home…I won't do it again…I promise…I want my Mommy…please?" Hallie pleaded.

"No…she has to pay…do you know how she made him feel? Do you know how many nights he cried?"

Knock, knock, knock!

The knock on the window of the SUV startled Devon, waking her abruptly from her twilight sleep state. She reached over, pushing the button to lower the driver's side window. Outside, a young man with short dark hair and glasses, dressed neatly in khakis and a button-down shirt stood near her door.

"Ma'am? Are you okay?" He asked as Devon's window rolled down.

"Yeah…I'm fine…just had a long night…I guess I kind of dozed off for a second." Devon said, smiling.

"Okay…just wanted to make sure…have a safe drive home!" He said, walking off into the distance.

Go figure…chivalry's not dead!

Devon shifted into drive, starting the long trek home. She struggled to keep her eyelids open…cranking both the stereo and the air conditioning in the hopes that one or both would keep her from falling asleep.

Gotta stay awake…

Before…Devon would have been looking forward to diving into her bed when she got home after a night like last night…but now, her cold, empty bed was nothing but a chilling reminder that Chris was gone…she was alone.

The majority of the drive was nothing but a blur, until she reached the familiar curve of her driveway. She pulled up to the house and parked the SUV.
Home.

She walked up, turning the key in the lock and opening the door…

"Hey baby…rough day?" Chris said.

Devon nodded "The roughest..." she said, taking off her leather jacket and tossing it onto the chair in the entryway.

Even in sweats, Chris was beautiful...her silky hair, every curve of her body...Devon knew them all.

"Aww...c'mere..." Chris said, crossing the room. She placed her arms around Devon's waist. "How about I kiss you and make it better?" she said, pulling her along as she backed up to the couch.

Their lips met softly as Devon lowered her down onto the cushions, easing onto her chest as the kiss deepened. She pulled back briefly, looking into Chris' eyes...a smile spread across her face as she brushed a few strands of hair out of her eyes...

"What?" Chris said, smiling.

"I can't take my eyes off you..." Devon said, lowering herself onto Chris' velvety lips...

She could almost feel it...Chris' lips on hers. The sweet smell of vanilla and jasmine...the softness of her skin...how perfectly their bodies fit together...

She walked over to the couch, lying down. She reached over, taking one of the pillows and clutching it to her chest...closing her eyes...she slowly drifted off to sleep.

I love you, Chris...

FLASH

"We are here today to celebrate the life of our dear sister, Christine. Chris believed in living and loving to the fullest...as demonstrated every day by her commitment to her work with troubled youngsters...and her loving relationship of six years with her partner, Devon..."

Devon looked at the oak casket in front of her...draped with forget-me-nots...Chris' favorite flower...

"Chris' work here on Earth was done, and so our Father saw fit to call her home, where she now bathes in glory and in light. Chris once told me of a Native American proverb that was special to her…she said that' when you were born, you cried—and the world rejoiced. Live your life in a manner so that when you die, the world cries and you rejoice.' Chris did exactly that…and although we cry for her today…she is rejoicing with her Maker in a much better place…"

Devon stood in silence…tears running down the curves of her face and falling upon the lapels of her jacket.

"…and so it is that we commit our dearly departed sister to the ground from whence she came…ashes to ashes…dust to dust…"

Devon looked down. She could see in between the railings and the casket…down into the vault. It's cold, damp depths sent chills down Devon's spine…

"Is she in a better place?" Devon said, the pain welling up deep within her soul.

Mike moved over to his partner, putting his arm around her waist, trying to lead her away from the gravesite.

"Come on, Dev…"

Devon twisted her body away from Mike "No! Seriously…how do we know she's in a better place? How can it be better? It's all cold…and dark…and wet…How can that be better than this? Better than being here with me?"

Devon's chest tightened…like someone was sucking the life's breath out of her lungs…

"Dev…"

She turned to the casket, the pain and anger boiling within her.

"How could you do this to me, Chris? We're supposed to be together! You promised you'd never leave me!" She said, collapsing on top of the casket in a heap, sobbing uncontrollably.

Mike walked over to the casket, taking her in his arms, leading her away…

"We were supposed to have forever, Chris...forever..."

Devon was rudely awakened as she rolled off the couch, hitting the floor with a thud. She sat up slowly, using the couch as a backrest. It hurt...it still hurt...just as much as it did that day. Would it ever get any better? How could it? She was gone.

Meanwhile, at East Central Elementary School...

Three young girls stood on the sidewalk in front of the school jumping rope, when a young boy walked by...

He wore hand-me-down clothes that were obviously too big for him...as well as being drastically out-of-style...his hair a mess...his tennis shoes in tatters...

"Can I play?" He asked, shyly.

One of the girls, dressed stylishly in bell-bottomed jeans and a t-shirt turned to him and laughed.

"Look at the way you're dressed! Where did you get those clothes? The local trash dumpster?"

The little boy hung his head in shame as the other girls laughed at what the girl had said.

"...and that hair! It looks like something's living in it!" she said, laughing hysterically.

The little boy walked off, head hung low, tears running down his cheeks...

No one noticed the man parked in front of the school, watching the scene unfold.

They'll pay...I'll make her pay...

He thought to himself...as the rage boiled up like a volcano waiting to erupt.

Slamming the car into drive…he moved forward, parking near the curb…

You'll never do that again…

How long had she slept? She wasn't sure…it was dark out. She slowly rose from the floor, stretching in an attempt to rid herself of the stiff muscles that she had developed from sleeping propped against the couch.

She walked to the kitchen, opening first the refrigerator, then the freezer…both were greatly lacking in the food department…

She grabbed a half-filled carton of orange juice and walked towards the sliding glass doors that led out onto the patio. She slid the glass door aside…walking out onto the deck. The night air was heavy…the soft glow of a full moon filled the yard and it's surrounding woods with light.

Devon sat on one of the weathered wooden chairs, taking a drink of the orange juice. Her senses seemed to be hypersensitive…her skin prickled with electricity as though a strong storm was approaching. The trill of the small tree frogs cut through the night like a knife…disturbing the comfort of the darkness.

She stared into the darkness…as if looking for answers to questions she hadn't even asked it yet…
"Chris…are you there? No…you're not, are you baby…you're gone…I miss you. It hurts…it hurts so bad…sometimes, I just want the pain to stop…and other times…the pain is the only thing that reminds me that I'm still alive…"

She took another drink of the OJ, hoping it would ease the tightness now creeping through her chest and into her throat.

"Am I alive? I don't even know anymore…it's all so wrong…it's so wrong without you…we were supposed to be forever…we were going to grow old together…remember? You promised…you said you'd never leave me…"

I didn't leave you, baby…

"Chris?" Devon said, not believing what she was hearing…was she hearing it? Or was it in her mind?

It's me, baby…I'm here. I'm always here…

"Chris…it can't be…you can't…" she said, hot tears streaming down her cheeks.

I can…

"Why…how did you…?"

You brought me here…

"None of this is making sense…I've lost it…I've finally lost it…" Devon said, rising up from the chair.

No you're not…you're finally starting to see…

"See what?! Blood? Pain? Death?"

That's all a part of it…yes.

"A part of what? Suffering?"

Life…it's all a part of life, baby…it's like a glass of fine wine…that first sip…it's bitter, has a bite…but it's that bitterness that makes the sweetness of the wine that much better…

"I don't have a life…it's nothing…it's all nothing without you, Chris."

I know it feels that way now…but it will get better…

Devon looked down "How can it ever get better? You're gone…"
I'm here…I'll always be here…as long as you have love in your heart…I'll be with you.

"You were my heart…"

Knock, knock, knock.

Devon awoke in her bed…her head throbbing…

Knock, knock, knock!

The knocking turned into a pounding as she struggled to lift her head from the pillow.

"Just a minute!" She yelled, pain shooting through her head.

She swung her feet over the side of the bed, her foot hitting something on the way down…a bottle of pills and an empty orange juice carton.

That explains a lot…

The pounding continued as Devon walked down the hallway, placing her hands along the wall to steady herself. She walked to the front door, looking through the window…it was Mike. She opened the door, turning her head away from the sunlight.

"Are you okay? I've been trying to get a hold of you for the past three hours!"

Devon ran her fingers through her hair, her eyes still open only in slits.

"I'm fine…just tired." She said, slurring her words.

The air in the house was stale. Mike glanced around the room. It was in a state of general disarray…an old pizza box…an empty fifth of vodka…paper plates…His friend was in trouble. He knew she had been on a downward spiral since Chris had died…but he had no idea it was this bad.

"Dev…come here…" He said, trying to get her to turn around.

"What? I'm fine…"

"Look at me." He said, grabbing her arm, this time physically making her face him.

She looked up at him…her pupils were blown.

"What did you take?"

"I'm fine…

"Devon…you're not fine! What did you take?!" He said, insistently. Walking around…looking for the bottle of pills.

"It's okay…they're prescription…I'm fine…I'm just tired!"

"You're not just tired…what did you take?"

"It's Deseryl…alright? The doctor gave it to me to help me sleep…"

"How many did you take?"

"I don't know…I might have taken a couple of extra…it's really no big deal…"

"No big deal? Dev…that stuff is strong…and dangerous if you take it with alcohol…"

"I took it with orange juice." She said, plopping down onto the couch.

Mike sat down on the opposite end.

"Dev…I know how rough things have been on you since Chris…"

"You know? How exactly could you know, Mike? Huh? Because last time I looked, your wife was still alive and kicking!"

"You're right…I don't know…and I hope I never do…but I did know Chris…and I know that she wouldn't want you to be doing this to yourself."

"Yeah…well…she's not here anymore…so I guess it doesn't much matter what she wants, does it?" She said, coldly.

"We both know that's not true, Dev. I know you care…if you didn't, you wouldn't be doing this to yourself."

"Whatever."

"Listen…I need you in top form on this Hingerman case…we've got to catch this guy…before he does it again."

He was right…and Devon knew it. This guy wasn't going to stop…

"How about we get you some coffee…"

"What time is it?"

"Twenty after eleven." He said, looking at his watch.

"Geezus…okay…just give me ten minutes to shower and I'll be ready." She said, getting up and walking slowly down the hallway to the bathroom.

"You've got nine!" He said, trying to add a bit of brevity to the situation.

The only response he got was her trademark 'one-finger-wave' as she disappeared through the bathroom door…

"That's my girl…" He said, smiling.

CHAPTER 5

▼

True to form, Devon exited the bathroom in her Mike-allotted nine minutes. She walked down the hallway in a pair of snug-fitting jeans and white tank. She reached for her pancake holster, tucking in the waistband of her jeans, sliding her .40 caliber Sig into position safe within.

"Coffee's ready." Mike said, grinning.

Mike's coffee tasted unlike any coffee you would ever have tasted—or would ever want to taste again. Devon always swore that it was, in fact, a lethal combination of battery acid and kerosene, with just a touch of drano for flavor. It came with a guarantee that it would sober you up in one cup or your money back.

"The question is…am I ready for it?" Devon said with a smirk as she walked around the house, gathering up her shoes and her jacket.

"It couldn't hurt…" Mike said, pouring her a cup of the black, viscous liquid.

"That's debatable." Devon said, reaching under the desk and grabbing her black boots. She pulled out the chair at the desk and sat down, wiggling her feet into the boots one at a time.

Mike sat the cup of coffee on the desk in front of her.

"Thanks…I think." She said, grabbing the cup and raising it slowly to her lips. The smell hit her before the taste…both were equally revolting…

"Ugh!" She said, spitting the concoction back into the cup and sitting it firmly on the desk. "I'm sorry…there's no way…I'm awake." she said, her eyes now wide open and all senses completely alert.

"See! One cup, guaranteed!" He said, proudly.

"Yeah…definitely. Let's go…I need some fresh air." She said, opening up the door and walking out, quickly.

"I'll drive…" Mike said, following close behind.

"You're gonna make me ride in the grocery-getter?" Devon said, semi-seriously. Mike had a wife and three kids, the picture-perfect domestic situation…including the classic mini-van.

"Hey…I'll have you know this is the top of the line in family vehicles…look! eather interior…heated seats…" He said, trying desperately to convince both himself and his partner that the vehicle had redeeming qualities.

"Yes…and so many of them!" Devon said, kidding him as she climbed into the passenger side.

Mike eased himself in behind the wheel, took a deep breath and let it out with a sigh. "God, I want a truck…not just any truck…a big truck…four-wheel drive…single cab…lift kit…short box…wheel flares…"

"Snap out of it, 'Ward'…face it, you're destined to drive a kid-mobile for the next, oh…I'd say 16 to 17 years…"

"Yeah…" Mike said, frowning.

"So…have we got anything new to work with?" Devon said, reaching into the pocket of her coat and removing a pair of sunglasses and putting them on.

"We've got to go by the Hingerman's house and interview them…"

"I was afraid you were going to say that...I was kinda hoping you would have done that already..." Devon said, knowing from her earlier encounter with the couple.

"Sorry...did you get much from them at the morgue yesterday?"

"Not much...they were pretty broken up...especially the wife...I don't know how far we're going to be able to push her."

"Great...well...we'll get what we can. I just hope they can give us something to go on. Have you run a check through FIA on the parents yet?" Mike asked.

"Nope, didn't get that far, sorry." Devon said, wishing now that she hadn't just gone home yesterday.

She hated letting Mike down...and she felt like she had been doing it a lot lately. He knew she was going through a bad time after Chris died...and he had gone out of his way to pick up the slack. She had to start pulling herself out of her self-proclaimed pity party...and soon. She knew that...it was just tough some-times...a lot of the time...most of the time.

"Listen...let me call one of the clerks at the station and have them run it quick...and then I'll do some more thorough digging later on after we get done at the Hingerman's...okay?" Devon said, hoping to take some of the stress off her partner's mind.

Her effort didn't go unnoticed.

"That would be great, Dev. Um...looks like this is it...guess we'll get that report later." Mike said, pulling up to the curb and parking the van.

The house was a small 1940's style bungalow...not unlike the one that Devon and Chris had shared in college. There was nothing special about it, other than the amount of cars parked in the driveway and on the street in front of the house.

"Holy shit...quite the crowd....this is going to be interesting." Devon said, looking around.

"Yeah…no kidding…we're going to have to find somewhere that we can talk to them in private."

"Definitely. Let's get the plates off of these cars while we're here…I'll run them when we get back to the station. See if anything interesting comes up."

"What are you thinking?" Mike asked, looking at Devon.

"Our guy…or gal…or whoever did this…they might be right under our nose…checking out their handy work…I just want to see who exactly is hanging around the family here. Ready to go?"

"Let's do it." Mike said, opening the door of the mini-van.

After walking slowly by the vehicles, copying down the license plate numbers, they continued towards the house. The two walked up to the porch, passing several people as they went. Each making a mental note of the faces they saw leaving and what cars they were leaving in.

Mr. Hingerman was standing in the doorway. He recognized Devon as she approached him.

"Detective McKinney? What are you doing here?" He said, somewhat confused.

"Mr. Hingerman…I'm sorry to bother you at this…difficult time…but we need to talk to you and your wife. This is my partner, Detective Mike Penaglio."

Mike stepped forward, shaking Mr. Hingerman's hand.

"I'm sorry for your family's loss, sir." Mike said, politely.

"Thank you…please, come in…" He said, stepping aside to allow them through the doorway. "Would you like something to eat? All of the family…neighbors…people from our church…they've all brought food over…since they heard about Hallie." He said, as the grief visibly spread across his face.

"Thanks, we're fine." Devon said, answering for the both of them.

Mike gave her an annoyed look…she knew how his stomach worked…and she also knew that he had been trying to lose weight…a veritable smorgasbord of home-cooked food would not help in that department.

Mrs. Hingerman was sitting on the couch, surrounded by her mother and sister, who were trying their best to comfort her.

"Honey…Detective McKinney and her partner are here…they need to talk to us about Hallie."

Mrs. Hingerman looked up at Devon through teary eyes, as if to plead with her not to put her through any further pain and suffering.

"I'm sorry to bother you, Mrs. Hingerman…I know how tough this must be for you right now…but we really need to ask you and your husband some questions…privately." Devon said, looking at the other two women, hoping that they would get the hint.

She slowly rose from the couch, coming face to face with Devon. A combination of grief, pain, and anger etched on her face.

"How could you possibly know how tough this is for me…for us? How could you know how much this hurts…how the only thing that I think about day in and day out is how I will never…EVER…get to see my baby girl again?" She said, shouting at Devon.

Devon swallowed hard…trying to maintain her composure. She did know…all too well how she felt. She looked at the angry woman with compassion in her eyes.

"Unfortunately…I do know how you feel…and I'm really sorry that we have to do this now…but we need your help to find who did this to Hallie…so we can keep it from happening to someone else's child."

Mike placed a comforting hand on Devon's shoulder…just to let her know that he was there for her—backing her up.

Mrs. Hingerman noticed Mike's actions and realized that Devon must, in fact, have been telling the truth…that she did know how this felt. She dried her eyes as best she could "We can go into our bedroom…no one should be in there."

"Thank you." Said Devon, stepping aside to allow her to lead the way.

Mrs. Hingerman stepped forward and was met by her husband, who wrapped a protective arm around her waist as they walked down the hallway to the master bedroom.
The bedroom was tastefully decorated in a lodge motif. The bed centered on the far wall of the room was partially covered with a layer of purses, jackets, and visitor's other belongings. Pictures of Hallie as a baby…her first day in kindergarten…a family vacation to Florida…were lovingly placed throughout the room.

"Please, have a seat…this may take a while." Mike said, motioning to the bed.

Devon pulled a chair from the corner of the room closer to the bed and sat down.

"I know this will be painful, but I need you to tell me about Hallie…what she liked to do…who she 'hung out' with…anything you can think of."

"Who she 'hung out' with? She was six years old, for Christ's sake! She didn't hang out with anyone!" Mrs. Hingerman said, starting to cry once more.

"I'm sorry, I really am, but we need to know these things. Did she have any friends that she mentioned more often that others…or maybe went to their house or something?" Devon asked, trying to be more cautious about her wording.

"She had lots of little friends…I can't think of one in particular." She answered.

"Was she involved in any groups outside of school…Girl Scouts or sports…or church groups?" Mike asked.

"She played soccer on the youth league." Mr. Hingerman answered.

"Do you remember what her coach's name was?" Devon said, jotting notes down on a small pad of paper.

"Sure…he was here earlier today. His name is Roger Torola. He and his wife brought some pictures of Hallie over to us today…I can get them if you'd like." Mr. Hingerman offered, rising up from his seat on the bed.

"That would be great, thank you." Mike said, continuing "Have you seen anyone suspicious in the area lately…cars that you didn't recognize?"

Mike's questioning was interrupted by the sound of he and Devon's pagers going of simultaneously.

Devon and Mike exchanged worried looks…this was not a good thing.

Mike pulled his pager from its case, pushing the button. It read: CHILD MISS-ING—POSSIBLE ABDUCTION—8734 N. PATTERSON.

He looked over to Devon "We've got to go."

Devon removed her pager, looking at the message. The color drained from her face as her instincts told her this was number two…

"There's been another one, hasn't there?" Mrs. Hingerman said, looking to Devon for an answer.

"We have to go. I'm sorry, we'll have to come back later." Devon said, trying to avoid the question. She rose up out of the chair, walking to the hallway, followed closely by Mike.

"You get this bastard!!!" Mrs. Hingerman yelled, in between sobs. "You get him before he does this again!"

"We're trying." Devon mumbled as they rushed out past the many visitors, finally getting to the mini-van. They climbed in, slamming the doors behind them.

"It's him, Mike…I can feel it."

Mike kept his eyes on the road…he knew that they couldn't jump to conclusions, but he also trusted his partner's instinct.

"We don't know that, Dev…let's just keep an open mind going into this, okay? For all we know, this kid could be over at a friend's house or something."

Devon remained silent. She hoped that Mike was right…that the child would be found at a neighbor's or a friend's house, but right now, her gut was telling her something else, and as much as she hated it, her gut was usually right.

The house couldn't be missed…the place was crawling with uniforms. Mike parked the mini-van and the two of them got out, walking towards the scene.

"Hey Paul…what's the scoop?" Mike said to one of the uniformed officers, Paul Donin.

Paul was what the uniformed ranks liked to refer to as a "Lifer". He had been on the force for the past fifteen years, passing up several opportunities to become a Desk Sergeant…or a Detective…preferring instead to remain what he knew he had always fit him best…what he was inside…a cop, nothing more, nothing less. His choices had made him one of the most respected officers on the force.

"Hi Mike…Dev…here's what we've got so far…LeAnn Ballister…9 years old…Caucasian with shoulder length curly brown hair, brown eyes. Scar above the right eyebrow. Mom's a broker…Dad's a lawyer…corporate-type. Last time Mom and Dad saw her was this morning when she left for school. She was wearing bell-bottomed jeans and a white t-shirt at the time…she also had a red L.L. Bean backpack with her name embroidered on it. We already checked with the school, she was there for the whole school day. Teacher said the last time she saw her, the kid was out in front of the school playing with some of her friends…jump rope or something."

"Have we got somebody contacting these kids' parents?" Mike asked.

"Yeah…the teacher…lemme' see…" Paul said, looking at the notes he had taken earlier "…her name is Mrs. West. She is getting together a list for us of these kids and their addresses."

Devon's eyes scanned the crowd…taking note of the faces of those people 'hanging around'.

"Where's the parents?" Devon said, her eyes never stopping their journey.

"Inside..."

"Do we have a Trailing team coming in?" Devon asked.

"State dog is on it's way...but they're coming from Lansing, so it's gonna' be a while." Paul answered.

"Okay...let's see what we've got...I want to get an 'Amber Alert' out ASAP if this is an abduction." Devon said, walking towards the house.

Paul led the way, followed by Devon and Mike, respectively. The house was a two-story cape cod...very well kept. It was obvious that the Ballisters had money...and lots of it. They walked in through a beautiful foyer with a terrazzo floor and marble furnishings. Everything was in light colors of white, beige, and pale yellow.

Not exactly a kid-friendly atmosphere...

Mr. Ballister was busily talking on his cell phone...sounding rather harried, to say the least. He noticed the two Detectives standing with Paul, and held his finger up, mouthing "Just a minute..."

He continued his conversation on the phone...

"What? Tell them I needed that brief yesterday! Mr. Anderson wants to proceed with the take-over tomorrow morning...I expect you to do whatever it takes to get the job done! (pause) I don't care if it IS your kid's birthday! It's not going to be much of a birthday when you lose your job, now is it? (pause) That's what I thought...just have a courier bring it over to my house tonight." He said, pushing the END button on the phone. "Sorry about that...business...couldn't wait."

What the hell? Hel-lo! Your daughter is missing...think the shop-talk can wait for a fucking minute or two? Bastard!

Mike sensed the anger building deep within his partner. It was no secret that Devon had a temper...but her fuse had been running a lot shorter than usual lately...and he wasn't about to let her mouth get her into trouble...even if the guy was a major-league asshole. He was a lawyer...and she didn't need that headache.

"Dev...why don't you take Mrs. Ballister...I'll take care of things here." Mike said.

Devon's blood pressure instantly rose...she knew what Mike was doing...but it infuriated her nonetheless...

Okay, okay...I get the hint...you don't want me going off on the lawyer...but Geezus, Mike! Did you have to make me sound like your 'little-woman'? Ugh...me man...talk with man...you woman...shit!

Devon smiled, cocking her head slightly "Okay...why don't I just go do that..."

Mike cringed inside...

Oh boy...I am really going to get it when we get back in the van...she's gonna kill me...

Mike smiled and cleared his throat nervously as Devon walked out of the room in search of Mrs. Ballister.

The whole house was so...organized, for lack of a better term. A place for everything and everything in its place. Devon weaved through the influx of people wandering through the house finally finding Mrs. Ballister sitting at a computer screen in what appeared to be a den or home office.

Geezus...it's her kid that's missing...you'd think she'd be looking for me!

"Excuse me...Mrs. Ballister?" Devon said, peeking into the room.

"What?" Said the woman, looking up briefly from her computer screen. "Oh...I'm sorry...did you need something?" She asked, calmly.

"I'm Detective McKinney…I need to ask you some questions about your daughter."

"Please…come in…I was just taking care of some last minute trades before the exchange closes…and it kind of keeps my mind off of this…" She said, calmly.

"I need to get some specifics on LeAnn…I know you've already told the responding officers most of it…but I do have a few more questions for you."

"That's fine…"

"How has LeAnn been doing lately…has she been a happy kid? Is there anything going on in the household lately that may have upset her?"

"No…not really…I mean…her father and I haven't exactly seen eye-to-eye on things lately…but…"

"Haven't seen eye-to-eye?" Devon asked.

"Yes…well…other than the fact that he thinks it's perfectly fine to fuck everything near him in a skirt…we get along just fine." She said, sarcastically…reaching for the double scotch on the rocks sitting next to her computer.

"O-kay…is there any possibility that LeAnn might have wanted to run away or might be hiding somewhere? Does she have a special place that she likes to go to…to get away from things?"

"If she does…I wouldn't know about it…she doesn't tell me anything. Guess you're thinking I'm a pretty shitty mother right about now, aren't you?" She said, taking another drink.

"Actually…I'm thinking about what I can do to find your daughter before something really bad happens to her…if it hasn't already." Devon said. The minute that the words came out of her mouth, she knew that she shouldn't have said them…but she never was one for candy-coating the truth…and that was the truth.

"Thanks so much for your comforting words…" Mrs. Ballister said, sarcastically.

"Ma'am...I'm not here to comfort you. I'm here to get whatever information I can...by whatever means I need to use...to bring your daughter home to you and your husband alive and in one piece. Now you can either get rid of the 'Mommy Dearest' act and help me, or you can continue to act like a cold-hearted bitch and we'll get nowhere in a hurry."

Oh boy...I'm seeing a definite trip to the Captain's office over this in the near future...

Mrs. Ballister sat her drink down on the desk and placed her hands over her face, pausing a moment before raising her head and looking at Devon with tears in her eyes.

"You're right, you know...I am a cold-hearted bitch. I wouldn't blame her if she did run away...God knows I'd like to..."

Okay...maybe I was a little hard on her...but if it will get me some useful information, it was worth it, right?

"So things haven't been exactly rosy here at home, I take it." Devon said.

"No...far from it...her father and I...we fight almost constantly. I know she's heard us...shit...the whole neighborhood has heard us..."

"Has she ever mentioned running away before...or wanting to go stay with friends or relatives a lot or anything?"

"No...surprising, isn't it? She's never said a word about it...spends most of her time up in her room...playing on her computer..."

"I'd like to see her room if I may." Devon said, softening a bit.

"Sure...I'll take you up there..." she said, pushing her chair away from the desk, rising up and walking towards the door.

The two women made their way up the main staircase to the second floor. This floor was decorated much like the other…very light colors…not exactly what you could see a nine-year-old running around in.

"This is her room." She said, motioning to Devon.

Devon walked in. The room was a stark contrast to the rest of the house. It's light blue walls covered in posters of the latest 'Pop Tarts', as Devon called them. Matching bedroom set…desk with computer…stereo…television…

Damn…this is better than my first apartment was!

"We're going to need to take her computer with us…just the CPU."

"Her computer? What for?"

"We'll have one of our IT specialists take a look at it…see what sites she's been frequenting…chatrooms…that sort of thing…"

"Oh…I don't think she's been chatting with anyone but her friends…and as far as websites…I mean…she is only nine…"

"You'd be surprised what we've found on kid's computers."

Devon's eyes scanned the room…the bed was neatly made.

"Do you have a cleaning lady or someone who comes in and does your house-work and such?"

"Yes…she's normally here on Mondays and Fridays."

"So she hasn't been here today?"

"No."

"Good…we're going to need a scent article for the Trailing K-9…preferably something that she's worn recently…or a pillowcase that she's slept with." Devon said.

Devon had worked with the K-9 units while she was at the academy. Trailing dogs were 'scent specific'—meaning that they would be pre-scented on an article that had the person's scent on it...and they would follow only that person, whether it was going through woods, groups of people, roadsides...anything. The best dogs for this purpose were without a doubt, Bloodhounds; however, German Shepherds and some of the other breeds of hounds also faired well.

"They'll follow her specifically?" Mrs. Ballister asked.

"Yes...it's actually pretty interesting...our scents are as unique to a K-9's nose as our fingerprints are to humans. Every time you take a step, you shed hundreds of microscopic skin cells...and those cells are what the dog smells...there are no two people who smell exactly the same...or so we think...it's not like the dogs can actually tell us or anything...and I'm rambling...sorry about that."

"That's alright...really..."

"Did LeAnn keep a diary?"

"I don't know."

"We'll see if we can find one later...right now, I really don't want to disturb her room any more than we have to. I'm going to unplug her computer and disconnect the CPU to give to IT...we'll get them going on that right away. Do you have some pictures of LeAnn that we could take with us...for circulation through our computer network...as well as flyers..."

"She just got her school pictures back the other day. They're downstairs in the study. I'll get you one."

"That would be great...and if you have a full body shot of her, that would be useful as well..."

"There might be one in our vacation pictures...I can check."

"Thanks." Devon said, following her out of the room. She turned back, taking one more look at the room as a whole...

The best of everything...top of the line computer...stereo...plasma screen TV...designer clothes...You didn't want for much, did you kiddo? Only the best of everything...

CHAPTER 6

▼

It didn't take long for Mike to figure out that he wasn't getting anywhere with Mr. Ballister. He met Devon just as she was coming down the staircase.

"Hey…I was just going to get some pictures…you all set with the mister?"

"Yeah…I think I've had about all I can take." Mike said, the aggravation in his voice coming across loud and clear. "I'll meet you out at the van."

"Okay…tell Paul to have them tape off her bedroom…I want to keep it as 'clean' as possible for them to gather a scent article."

"Got it." Mike said, heading for the front door.

"They're in here…" Mrs. Ballister said, motioning to Devon.

She walked over to a drawer in computer desk, pulling out a white envelope and handing it to Devon.

"I'd like them back…when you're done with them, I mean."

"That shouldn't be a problem…thank you." Devon said, turning to the door.

"Detective McKinney?"

Devon turned back, looking at Mrs. Ballister. For the first time she saw her not as an irritating, self-absorbed woman…but as a mother…a mother terrified that she had lost her only child.

"Please bring her home to me." She said. She was speaking to Devon…but it also came out as a prayer…asking God to spare her the grief of losing her daughter.

Devon nodded and walked out the door.

No promises…never make a promise you can't keep, McKinney…you learned that a long time ago…You'd want to tell her that it's all going to be okay…that by this time tomorrow morning, her daughter will be home safe and sound without so much as a hair out of place on her privileged little head…but that's not the way it usually works out…your gut's telling you that's not the way it's going to work out this time…sorry…

Devon made her way to the van, sliding into the passenger side's seat, she slammed the door beside her, letting out the breath that she hadn't realized that she had been holding since she walked away from Mrs. Ballister.

"You okay?" Mike said, noticing his partner's tensed demeanor.

"Yeah…just great." Devon said, sarcastically.

"Listen…about earlier…" Mike began, hoping to make amends for patronizing her earlier.

"Hey…it's no problem…I'm not mad. It's just…" Devon stopped herself. She knew how important it was to treat every case like this as if the person was still alive…until you knew otherwise…but something in her was telling her that there was no way that this was going to turn out alright.

"I know…I've got the same feeling. But we've got to get past it…both of us…we've got a job to do, Dev."

"I know…"

"So let's get on it...I got a hold of the K-9 Unit while you were still in there. They're going to stop by the house and get a scent article and then meet us there at the school."

"We can have one of the uniforms at the school fax one of these pictures to the station...get the Amber Alert going. I don't want to waste any time on this...if we do have a chance."

As they turned down the street leading to the school, they could already see members of the local TV stations gathering around the outside of the taped off area.

"Geezus...looks like the wolves are hungry tonight." Devon said.

Mike pulled the van over to the curb and the two of them got out and started walking towards the police line. They were met almost instantly by Brenda Stone...investigative reporter for WJLT TV-9. This wasn't the first time they'd dealt with Miss Stone...Devon liked to refer to her as the 'Stone-Cold Bitch'. She had a reputation for being one of the most cutthroat, bloodthirsty, publicity-hungry reporters in the state...and Devon hated her with a passion.

"Detective McKinney...we understand that one of the students here...a young girl...has been abducted...is this related at all to the murder of Hallie Hingerman?"

"Brenda...you know that we can't comment on anything right now. We'll let you know as soon as we're ready to make a statement." Mike answered, hoping to keep the attention off of his already tense partner.

"Mike...the public has a right to know! You can't keep something like this from them!"

"Don't you mean from you?" Devon said, pointedly.
"I'm just here to report the news...to make a difference." Brenda said, matter-of-factly.

That was it. Devon had been on edge all day, and Brenda had just conveniently provided the catalyst needed to shove her off that cliff...

"You self-righteous bitch…" Devon said, getting in the reporter's face. "…you don't give a shit about anything but being the first to get the story…to get your over-painted face plastered all over the Six O'clock News…You want to make a difference? Then get the hell out of our way and let us do our job!"

"Come on, Dev…take it easy." Mike said, stepping in between the two women.

"Yes…listen to your partner…he seems to be the one with manners here…"

With that comment, Mike turned to face the reporter.

"Miss Stone…you need to kindly remove yourself from our immediate area…before I shove that microphone of yours so far up your tight little ass that you'll need a dentist to remove it…do I make myself clear?"

"Crystal…" she said with an annoyed smirk as she stepped aside and let the two of them pass.

"You think she'll quote me on that?" Mike said, grinning as they made their way to the taped off area.

Mike ducked under the tape, holding it up for Devon as she passed through.

"God…I hope so!" Devon said, smiling.

They walked over to a tall young dark-haired officer, tapping him on the shoulder. He turned around, and a smile spread across his face as he recognized the Detectives before him.

There's something about him that's so familiar…that smile…where have I seen him before?

"Detective McKinney…Detective Penaglio…wow! This is a real pleasure finally meeting the both of you!" Said the young man enthusiastically.

Mike and Devon exchanged glances, each thinking the same thing…

Rookie.

"I'm sorry…I'm Patrick Donnelly…Chief Donnelly's my dad…"

That's why he looks familiar! Duh!

"Nice to meet you, Patrick…new to the force?" Mike said, shaking the rookie's hand.

"Yeah…couple of months, actually…I graduated from the academy in May." He answered.

He stretched out his hand to Devon, who gave it a reluctant shake.

"Devon McKinney…wow…you know, you're a bit of a legend around here…I mean in the academy…"

"Yeah? Well…don't believe everything you hear…" Devon said with a sly grin.

It was true. Devon was a legend at the academy. First in her class…moved up the ranks in record speed, making Detective within three years of graduation…there weren't many cops who could say that they'd faired that well…hell…there weren't any. She was good at everything she did…and she did <u>everything</u>…she'd spent all of her limited free time while at the academy helping out at the dog kennels…learning about the different types of training that the K-9 teams used. After graduation, she spent her off hours working at the Medical Examiner's Office with Dr. Brown. He had taken her under his wing and personally trained her in medico legal death investigation techniques. Her sense of 'hinky', as her fellow officers called it, was unreal. If Devon McKinney got a gut feeling about something…by God…you'd better listen to it, because more often than not, she was dead-nuts on.

It had been a while since someone had referred to her as a 'legend'…in fact, she was usually rather annoyed by it. But today…as shitty as she'd been feeling about herself, in general lately…well, this kind of added a little lilt to her step. Gave her ego some well-needed stroking.

"You ever worked with a K-9 Unit?" Devon asked.

"No...haven't had the chance to yet...but it's something I'd really like to try sometime."

"Well...that sometime is now. Stick around, they should be here shortly." Devon said, with just a hint of cocky superiority.

The young rookie's eyes lit up like a kid on Christmas morning. He looked at Devon like some kind of deity.

Mike smiled...it was good to see Devon acting a little cocky. That was Devon...or it had been...before Chris died.

Just then, the Blue Chevy Suburban of the State's K-9 Unit pulled onto the scene. Devon walked over to the driver's side of the vehicle as a man stepped out. "Jim! How the hell are you? I was hoping it was going to be you!" Devon said.

He walked over to Devon, wrapping his arms around her in a big bear hug. He was rather stunned at how frail she looked, compared to the last time he'd seen her. She had always been slim...but very muscular...athletic. Now...well...she was downright skinny.

"Hey you...you get any skinnier and you're going to blow away in this breeze out here!" He said, letting her go hesitantly.

"Always the charmer!" Devon said, sarcastically. "Who'd you bring with you?" Devon said, motioning to the back of the SUV.

"Hoover."

"Excellent." Devon said, feeling more confident by the moment. Hoover was a four-year old saddle-backed Bloodhound...the 'Cadillac' of the trailing dogs...

"Hoover...like the President?" Mike asked.

"...like the vacuum cleaner." Devon answered, smiling.

"So where's our PLS? That's trailer-talk for Point Last Seen?" Jim said, jabbing Mike in the ribs with his elbow...razzing him.

"The last time that she was seen, she was in front of the school…near the steps." Devon said, pointing to the area.

"Okay…does she normally walk home from school?"

"Yes, she has. She usually travels east on Park to South Oak…and then takes a right on Patterson. The last time she walked home was a couple of days ago…so that scent should be relatively cold compared to her trail from today." Devon said.

Much of what Devon and Jim were talking about was foreign to Mike and Patrick.

"Hey Dev, you want to put that into English for those of us who don't talk-the-talk?"

"Sorry, Mike…you're going to hear us refer to scent as being 'hot' or 'cold'. Cold scent is scent from a person who has been in the area usually over 12 hours ago…the older the trail…the colder the scent…it sticks pretty close to the ground, but it may be hard to find…real faint. A trail more fresh than, say…6 hours or so…is more of a 'hot' scented trail…you'll have those scent flakes we talked about close to the ground…but you may also still have some in the air…it's stronger…easier to find."

"Okay…that clears things up a bit. But with the scent still hanging in the air and getting blown around and all…doesn't that make it tougher for the dog to find the actual trail?"
"He may cast for the scent a bit…work a little wide…but we're not concerned with footprint-to-footprint type tracking. What we're looking for is the big picture…direction of travel…corners turned…people that may have come into contact with LeAnn…things like that." Jim explained.

"People that came into contact with her?" Patrick asked.

"Yep…anyone that may have something of hers…or maybe held her…they will all have her scent transferred onto them…so the dog should hit on them, kind of like a scent line-up." Jim continued.

"Wow...I had no idea that they were that good!" The rookie said in amazement.

"They are pretty amazing animals!" Devon said.

"Definitely...every one of them...I'm just the 'dope-on-a-rope'...they are the masters...so are you guys all ready to get this show on the road?" Jim asked.

"Oh! You know...let me run over to the squad and check in...let them know I'll be going with you...I'll be right back." Patrick said, walking quickly towards his patrol car.

"New kid on the block, eh?" Jim said, looking to Devon and Mike.

"Yeah...he's pretty green."

"Green huh? I seem to remember not too long ago when you were still a little wet behind the ears there missy!" Jim said, teasing Devon.

"I was never that green!" Devon said, sternly.

"Oh really? Well I seem to remember one time when you thought that..."

Jim was interrupted by the sound of Patrick running back to their location.

"Detective McKinney...sorry about this...but it looks like I'm going to have to take a rain check on working with the K-9 Unit today. The press is swarming over at the Ballisters...so they're sending all available units over to control the situation. I'm really sorry."

"Not a problem, kid...we'll catch you another time." She said with a smile.

"Thanks! I'd really like that!" He said, turning and running back to his squad car.

"Did I ever have that much energy?" Devon asked Jim.

"About three times as much...annoyed the fuck out of me."

"Hey!" Devon said, taken aback by the comment.

"Okay, okay…I lied…it was four times as much!" Jim said, he and Mike bursting out in laughter.

Devon's response came in the form of quick punches to both Jim and Mike's upper arms.

"Hey!" Mike said, rubbing his arm. "He was the one who said it, not me!"

"You laughed." Devon said, smirking.

"On that note…I'm going to go get Hoover out and potty him before we start this thing…Dev, you coming along?"

"After the potty part? Yes…definitely. Mike?"

"I'm going to pass this time. I'm not really dressed for it…that…and I want to get that photo into the system so we can issue the alert statewide."

"Sounds good. I'll give you a call on your cell if we come up with anything."

"Okay…be careful…" Mike said.

"I think I can handle it…" Devon said, rolling her eyes.

"I wasn't talking to you!" Mike said, laughing.

"Dickhead."

"Oh…you love me…and you know it!" Mike smiled, putting one hand into the air as he walked into the school.

Jim stood at the back of the suburban, opening the crate holding Hoover the Wonder Dog…

"Hey buddy…come on…time to ambulate and evacuate!" He said, taking the hound by the collar and easing him out of his crate.

"Evacuate...that's nice!" Devon said, laughing at Jim's choice of terminology.

"Call me crazy...but I think evacuate sounds a little better than 'come on, boy...time to take a crap.'"

"Good point." Devon laughed.
"Hey...can you grab his harness and lead out of the back...and I've got a can of freeze-dried liver treats up there...we're going to need them."

Devon rummaged through the containers in the back of the SUV, gathering the items that Jim had asked for...it had been a long time since she felt the smooth leather of the leads and harnesses for the trailing K-9's...it felt good...familiar.

"Hey Dev...I'm gonna need one of those baggies, too...umm...make it the big ones..." He said, grinning.

Ewww...great.

After getting Hoover situated with a drink of cold water...Devon kneeled down, taking the hound's head in her hands, rubbing his slobber-soaked jowls...

"Hey boy...how you doing?"

Hoover answered her with one of his patented super slobbery bloodhound kisses right across her mouth.

"Aww...thanks buddy..."

She stood back up...knowing that this would be her last contact with the dog until the trail was done. Once Hoover was into work mode...there would be no contact with anyone except Jim...and the victim, if they found her. He had to stay focused on her trail and her trail only.

"Ok, boy...let's get your working clothes on..." Jim said, slipping the sheep's wool padded leather trailing harness over Hoover's head, buckling the straps behind his shoulders. Hoover's tail began to wag, knowing he was going to be doing what he loved the best very shortly...trailing.

Mike walked him up to the PLS, dumping the scent article he had gathered earlier at the Ballister's onto the ground. He snapped the trailing lead onto the back of Hoover's harness and walked him to the article. Hoover's head immediately dipped into the soft cloth...snorting as he inhaled the scent...making an imprint on his olfactory senses that this little girl was who he was looking for.

Devon took the small notebook and an ink pen from her pocket and stood back, waiting for Hoover to take off on the trail.

Hoover lifted his head and gave it a good jowly shake, sending little slobber-rockets flying and sticking to those around him.

"Ready, boy? Let's find!" The magic word...find. The words had barely come out of Jim's mouth when Hoover's head dropped to the ground, sweeping back and forth, searching for the scent of the young girl. Suddenly, he hit something...the lead tightened, and they were off! Jim doing his part as the proverbial 'dope-on-a-rope', with Devon following about ten feet behind...keeping track of where the dog led them.

The team headed down the sidewalk with Hoover in the lead...they turned the corner with ease and continued on the sidewalk for about fifteen yards. Then, just as suddenly as the trail began, it seemed to have ended. Hoover raised his head, sniffing the air at different levels, trying to pick up the girls scent once more.

"He's casting...not sure what's going on here. Let's give him a sec and see if he works it out...if not, we'll take him back and start the trail over." Jim said, watching his partner intently.

"Sounds good...take your time." Devon said, watching the team work.

Hoover continued to cast...

"Hey Jim...do you think he's in a scent pool?" Devon asked, watching the dog's body language.

"I don't know...could be...he's acting like he's getting scent, but just can't pick up the direction of travel. Let's take him back to the article and start again...see what happens."

Jim leaned down, removing the lead from Hoover's harness and placing it on his collar. The team walked back to the start of the trail. Once there, the lead was replaced on his harness, and the command given once more...

Hoover started the trail, turning the corner with ease, and once again started casting in the same area as he had previously done.

"I don't know...I'm thinking we might have a vehicle trail here..." Jim said.

"Thinking somebody picked her up?"

"Yeah...we might be able to drop-trail it, though...I'm going to need a few more guys out here for that...and it would probably be better if we waited until the sun got a little lower."

Devon knew exactly what Jim was referring to. Scent has a tendency to stick to moist areas...with the sun pounding down on them, the moisture starts to evaporate, taking the scent with it...forming more scent pools. If they waited for the sun to go down, the scent would settle a bit more...making the trail easier to find.

"Okay...what are you going to need? We'll get it for you...a chase vehicle?"

"Yeah...definitely...and a couple of guys for traffic control. Are you gonna be able to stick around to map things out?"

"I'd love to...but I probably should get back to Mike. We're going to have a ton of paperwork to take care of...plus I've got some background information I need to get in line."

"Not a problem...I'll get Bob to come down here."

"Let me know if you come up with something...you've got my pager number, don't you?" Devon asked.

"Yep…got it…we're all set."

"Okay…I'm going to go see if I can round up my partner."

"I'll catch you later, Dev…you take care, okay? You know…if you ever decided to get out of the blood and guts business…we'd love to get you down at the State K-9 Unit…"

"I'll keep that in mind, Jim…and thanks…for everything." Devon said, walking back towards the school.

"No problem…any time." He said, hoping that Devon would take the offer seriously…

Mike was busy chatting on his cell phone when Devon walked up to him.

"Hey Karen? I've gotta let you go…Dev's back…you'll enter that into the system? Great. Thanks!" Mike said, pushing the off button on his cell phone. "That was quick…did you get anything?" He asked.

"I don't know…he took off like gangbusters for the first 60 yards or so…turned the corner…and got lost in a scent pool or something. Jim's thinking that maybe she got into a car…or someone took her in a car…"

"Okay…so where do we go from here?"

"Jim's going to see if he can drop-trail it."

"Drop trail?" Mike asked…the term being rather unfamiliar to him.

"Yeah…it's something that you can do if you've got a vehicle trail. We're lucky we're in the middle of summer…the person driving the car likely either had the windows down or the air conditioning on…either way…the scent will roll off of the vents of the vehicle…depositing on the nearest source of moisture…which will likely be the plants and grass on the side of the road…Jim will take Hoover and start checking intersections and exits…to see if he's got any scent of her…it should help us get a better idea of the direction of travel."

"Wow...I guess I never thought they could trail them once they're in a vehi-cle...you learn something new every day!"

"Yeah...they are pretty friggin' amazing...so where are we at? What needs to be done?" Devon asked.

"I just got off the phone with Karen...she's going to get the Amber Alert initi-ated...I'd kind of like to get back to the office so we can start running some checks on some of this information...I was talking to the girl's teacher...Mrs. West...I got that list...but she said something kind of interesting..."

"Like?"

"Like when I was asking about the Ballister's...I happened to mention that I was pretty impressed by the house...that they obviously have a substantial amount of money...and she said that I shouldn't let that fool me...something about Mr. Ballister agreeing to donate money for some new computers...and his check bounced."

"His check bounced? That's hard to believe." Devon said, thinking.

"That's exactly what I thought...I think it's worth checking into a bit more...don't you?"

"Definitely...I want to run that check on the Hingerman's, too...didn't get the chance to do that yet."

"Okay...so how about we swing through and grab a little Chinese and head back to the office." Mike suggested...his stomach now rumbling from having gone more than two hours without it's usual 'fix'...

"Grab a little chinese, huh? Don't you think he might get a little mad about that?" Devon said with a wink.

Mike grinned...it was nice to see a little bit of the 'old' Devon starting to peek through.

"Come on…I'm buying." He said, putting his arm around his partner and leading her towards the van.

"Hey…did they give out raises and forget to tell me? Since when are you buying?" Devon said, sarcastically.

"Since…it's good to see you smile again…" He said, seriously.

"Yeah? Well…how about a laugh? I could use a new set of tires on the jeep…"

CHAPTER 7

▼

A half eaten carton of Mu Shu and a can of diet cola sat amongst several stacks of paper on Devon's desk…

"Damn…I don't remember my desk being this messy!" She said, rather annoyed by the whole site of things.

"It wasn't…things have just been a little discombobulated lately…that's all." He said, taking her can of soda and replacing it with a carton of chocolate milk.

"Hey!" Devon said, reaching for the soda. "What the hell do you think you're doing?"

"Trying to keep my partner from getting an ulcer on top of everything else…I need you on this case, Dev."

"Ulcer? What ulcer? I feel fine! Give me that!"

"That stuff is like battery acid! It will eat the paint off a car…what do you think it will do to your stomach? Besides…you look like you're anorexic or something…you need to eat more calories than I need to lose!" He said, patting his somewhat round stomach. "Come on…just humor me…it's chocolate!"

He was right…she never could refuse chocolaty-goodness…

"Oh alright…just this once…since you bought supper and all." She said, opening the carton and taking a swig. "So…have you found anything yet on Mr. Ballister?"

"Yeah…actually. I ran a credit report on him…looks to me like maybe the Ballister's don't have as much money as they let on." He said, handing the printout to Devon.

She looked over the papers one-by-one…

"Thirty days late…ninety days late…geezus! This list goes on and on! How many cards does this guy have?"

"Thirty-seven…and that's if you don't count the gas cards. He's got a line of credit big enough to choke a horse on…but he's several weeks…if not months…behind on all of the payments…interesting, huh?"

"Yeah…very…I wonder…" Devon said, thinking to herself momentarily.

"Are you thinking what I'm thinking?" Mike asked, looking to his partner.

"Insurance policies." Devon said, flatly.
"I'll get a warrant for his bank records…it shouldn't be a problem."

"If he did this…there still might be a chance…"

"…that she's still alive. Yeah…I know…I'm hurrying." Mike said, grabbing his papers and leaving the office.

Devon looked at her computer, entering the information to run the background check on Mr. and Mrs. Hingerman…

Her eyes scanned the screen, looking for anything even remotely suspicious.

"Nothing big…couple of speeding tickets…MIP (minor in possession)…okay…how about you, Mrs. Hingerman?" Devon said, talking to herself. She input the information and hit RETURN.

As she was waiting for the information to come up, she took another drink of the chocolate milk…

He's trying so hard…poor guy…I know I'm not easy to work with…

Her train of thought was interrupted by the beep of her computer telling her that the search was complete. She scrolled down the page for Mrs. Hingerman…her eyes coming to a complete halt as they reached one line…

10-21-99   1—COUNT—MURDER III—NEGLIGENT HOMICIDE—AQUITTAL.

"Huh…wouldn't have guessed that…looks like we'll be needing to look at you a little closer!"

She looked at her watch…11:08 pm…"Time flies when you're having fun…" She picked up the carton of milk, bringing it to her mouth, only to have her pager go off…

BODY FOUND…2285 MOCABRO STREET…PLAYSCAPE.

She heard someone running down the hallway towards the office door…it was Mike.

"Think it's our girl?" Mike asked, breathlessly…reaching up to loosen his tie.

Devon slid her chair back, grabbing her jacket and her gun.

"I'd bet money on it." She said as they sped out the door.

The drive over to the Playscape was a quiet one. Neither Mike nor Devon relished the thought of what they were more than likely going to find at the crime scene. They hoped it wasn't the girl…but their gut feelings told them otherwise. Mike pulled up to the scene, parking behind what appeared to be an endless line of patrol cars. Several members of the Crime Scene Unit were busy taping off the area.

"Geezus...the place is lit up like a friggin' Christmas tree!" Mike said, as they climbed out of the mini-van.

"Yeah...no shit. Let's see what we've got..."

They spotted a familiar figure among the sea of uniforms...it was Captain Winters. He had been with Kent City PD for the last ten years. Making Captain three years ago. His background consisted of several years with the Criminal Investigations Division (CID) of the U.S. Army. He was a little rough around the edges at times, but he was well-respected.

"McKinney...Penaglio...looks like we've found your girl." He said, as the two Detectives approached him.

"You sure?" Devon asked as they reached the Captain.

"I'm not positive...but she fits the description...clothes, hair, everything...she's pretty messed up."

"How so?" Mike asked.

"Best to just see it yourself..." The Captain said, turning to lead them into the scene.

Captain Winters held the yellow tape up for the two Detectives as they entered the scene. The Playscape had been built the year before by volunteers in the community. Several local businesses had donated supplies and money for the new playground area. It had been the source of much happiness and joy for the people of this community...but now...it was marred not only by death...but by the senseless violence against of one of it's own...

Devon felt the bile raising up in the back of her throat as they approached the body. Perched atop the spokes on the merry-go-round was the figure of a young girl, posed spread-eagle. Not unlike the Hingerman girl, she had been ripped open at the midsection, her entrails hanging out of her abdomen for all to see. Where once there were beautifully soft brown eyes, there were now empty bloodied sockets staring out into the night.

"Oh man!" Mike said, covering his mouth as he turned away from the scene momentarily, attempting to keep his supper down.

"Yeah…I'll second that…oh man…" Devon said, taking in the entire scene.

"Okay you two…let's get this guy…preferably before he has the chance to do this again…" Said Captain Winters walking off toward the police line to face the looming members of the media.

Devon glanced back at her partner, who was still looking a bit 'green around the gills'.

"Hey Mike, you get the crowd…I'll get the scene." She said.

A look of relief spread across Mike's face. He knew that Devon was well aware of his problems with scenes like this…and he also knew that she was by far the better Detective when it came to death investigations. His forte was talking to people…getting them to talk to him. Perhaps this is why they worked so well together…

"Got it…I'll see you in a while…good luck."

"You, too…" Devon said, reaching for the mini-recorder in her pocket, she turned back to start surveying the scene more carefully.

She pressed the red record button and began her narration…

"Body is that of a caucasian female…approximately 9-12 years of age, brown hair…wearing bell-bottomed jeans…shirt…unable to discern the color of the shirt at this time…" Devon leaned closer, noticing what appeared to be faint bruising around the girls neck "Possible contusions around the neck consistent with manual strangulation. Unable to confirm peticchial hemorrhaging in the sclera as both eyes have been removed from the sockets. Large laceration to the midsection from the pubis to the xyphoid process with evisceration."

Devon pressed pause on the recorder as she looked around the merry-go-round…

She pressed record once again.

"Relatively small amount of blood found considering the extensive nature of the wounds found on the body…she wasn't killed here…it's not the primary crime scene. Clothing is still intact…unable to determine if sexual assault occurred."

Devon was intensely wrapped up in the task at hand and did not notice the person approaching the scene…

"Well…have you got everything all done for me here, Dev?" Dr. Brown said, sitting his case of equipment on the ground next to him.

Devon pressed stop on the recorder…

"Nope…not quite…" Devon said, stepping to the side so Dr. Brown could see the scene in full-view.

"Oh my…looks like our slasher struck again, eh?"
"I don't know…at first glance there are a lot of similarities…but a lot of differences, too…look…not a whole lot of blood for this kind of a hack-job, eh?"

The doctor glanced over the area around the body.

"Huh…nope…looks like you've got a primary scene to find." Said Dr. Brown, still looking over the scene.

"Exactly…and the way she's posed…the Hingerman girl was just dumped."

"Maybe he got interrupted…didn't have time to finish what he started with her…"

"Yeah…could be…I don't know…this just *feels* different…look…look here…" Devon said, noticing something around the girl's wrists. "He used clear plastic wire-ties to hold her onto the spokes of the merry-go-round…he posed her…picked this spot for maximum shock effect…"

"So what are you saying, Dev?"

"He's changing…from disorganized to organized…"

The first killing…Hallie Hingerman…had been done quickly. She had been killed on the scene, without much, if any, thought put into the actual act. The killer didn't use any special tools or props, he simply killed her and left her body out for all to see…this was known as being 'disorganized' in nature. This scene was much different. The killer had to have planned ahead. He (or she for that matter) had killed the girl in one place and then transported the body to the secondary scene, where they used items that had to have been obtained in preparation for the act, such as the wire ties, etc. They also chose the location ahead of time…looking for a place that would make a 'statement' when the body was found…all characteristics of an 'organized' killer…

"That's pretty rare, isn't it?" Doc asked.

"Yeah…from everything that I've read or been taught…really rare." Devon said, wrinkling her brow in thought…

"What are you thinking?"

"Huh? Oh…it's nothing…I'm going to start a walk-through of the whole scene…let me know if you find anything…"

"Will do…I'm going to go ahead with the autopsy first thing in the morning."

"I'll be there…"

"You really don't have to, Dev…I know you've got a lot on your plate right now with two high-profile cases and all…" he said, trying to be understanding. He knew how much pressure his young colleague had been under lately.

"Doc…I said I'll be there…and I'll be there…okay?" Devon said, pointedly.

"Great…looking forward to it…about eight?"

"Yeah…that'll work."

"How about breakfast…Frost's at seven?"

"I think I'm going to have to pass this time, Doc…I've got some things I need to get done at the office first thing…I'll just meet you over at the morgue."

"You have to eat sometime, Dev." He said, trying his best to be gentle with the reminder.

"Damnit, Doc! Between you and Mike, I feel like I've got two overprotective, nagging mothers following me around every minute!" She said, snapping at her friend. Before the words were out of her mouth, she already regretted saying them. She took a deep breath, and exhaled slowly, trying to calm the rage suddenly building within her. Her features softened as she went to apologize.

"I'm sorry, Doc…I didn't mean that…things have just been…well…tough lately…to say the least."

He patted her softly on the shoulder.

"It's okay, Dev…I know…remember what I told you before…if you ever need to talk…"

"I know, Doc…thanks…I'll be okay, really…I appreciate it, though."

Dr. Brown nodded.

Devon smiled and then started out for the edges of the perimeter of the crime scene. She spent the next few hours walking the grid, looking for anything that might be considered a clue…nothing. The whole area was covered in wood chips…for padding around the playground equipment…which made getting any sort of footprint next to impossible.

Fingerprinting the area was out of the question…with all of the heavy traffic in the area. Their only hope would lay with whatever could be found on the body itself.

Devon walked over to Mike, who was now waiting on the other side of the police line.

"Hey…did you find anything?" He asked.

"Not a damned thing…but we are dealing with a secondary scene here…she was definitely transported after the fact. We need to find the primary scene."

"That may be like finding a needle in a haystack, Dev."

"I know it…did you get anything?"

"Not a damned thing. Whoever did this picked a good place and time to do it…no houses really close by…and most everyone was in bed…nobody heard or saw a thing."

"Great…not exactly what I was hoping for…"

"Tell me about it…you just about ready to head out? I want to go home and catch a few Z's before we get started tomorrow…"

"You mean today." Devon said, looking at her watch.

"Oh…yeah…today."

"Can you drop me off at the station? I want to catch up on everything before I meet Doc for the autopsy at eight."

"Sure…but don't you think you should get some sleep, Dev? It's been a pretty rough day…"

"I'm good…if I get too tired, I'll crash on the couch or something…"

"You sure?"

"Yeah…let's get going…" Devon said, as she leaned over, going under the yellow tape.

Twenty minutes later, they pulled into the station's parking lot.

"How are you going to get to the autopsy?" Mike asked.

"I'll get one of the unmarked's…no biggie."

"Okay…I'll see you later."

"Watch out for those killer mailboxes on your way home…" Devon said, jok-ingly. The last time Mike drove home this tired, he took out three mailboxes before he woke up.

"Yeah…yeah…" Mike said, putting his window up as he drove away.

Devon made her way to her desk, stopping at the pop machine on the way for some well-deserved and definitely needed caffeinated goodness. She dropped her coins in and hit the diet Cola button…nothing…she hit it again…nothing… "Damnit…" she said, pushing the coin return…nothing.

"Son of a bitch…just my luck…" she said, giving up on the soda, she walked into the office that she and Mike shared, plopping down into the chair and turning the computer on.

She had needed the caffeine more than she thought…within a few minutes, the soft glow of the computer screen lulled her into a restless sleep…

It's night…the woods is so dark…where's the moon? I can feel my heart beat-ing…pounding…like it's going to break right through my chest…running…run-ning…what am I running from? Or am I running to something? The hair on the back of my neck stands on end…my hackles are up…someone or something is watch-ing me…what is it?

A voice…so familiar…so comforting…Chris…

"You have to do more than look…you have to see…" she says.

I look up…there's a huge oak in front of me…

"You have to see…" she says once again…

Up in the tree sits a great horned owl…looking down at me intently…it's yellow eyes piercing my very soul…

FLASH

I'm flying…just above the canopy…there's a clearing…a group of trailers…shacks, really…abandoned? What is this?

FLASH

I'm back on the ground…walking on a two-track through the woods…is this the same woods? There's a fork in the trail…there's a ghostly figure in the path to the left…small…pale…it's Hallie. My eyes glance to the right fork…another fig-ure…LeAnn…in the middle, up in the tree, is the owl…staring back at me once again…

BEEP

Devon sat bold upright, abruptly awakened by the sound of the intercom on the desk. She brought her hand to her face, wiping the saliva off of the corner of her mouth.

Okay…that was weird…damn…must have been more tired than I thought…

"Detective McKinney? You have a call on line one…Detective McKinney…line one…" said the voice on the intercom.

Devon reached over, picking up the phone and bringing it to her ear.

"McKinney." She said, drowsily.

"I know what you see…"

The voice was distinctively female…

"Excuse me?" Devon said, not clearly understanding what was said.

"I said my name is Brid…Brid Morrigan." Said the voice.

Breed? What kind of a name is that?

Devon wrote BREED MORRIGAN on the yellow legal pad in front of her.

"Okay...Miss Morrigan...what can I do for you?"

"I think I may be able to help you on a case that you're working on..."

Oh boy...psychic...here we go...

"Okay...you know we do have an anonymous tip line...I can transfer you..."

"No...I need to talk to you...I don't want to leave some message on a recorder...listen...the last body...the one you just found...she didn't have any eyes..."

Devon's ears perked up at the statement. That was a detail that had not yet been released to the press.

"Okay...you've got my attention...go ahead..." Devon said, leaning back in her chair eager to see what the woman would say next.

"Not on the phone...I need to meet you in person..."

Devon knew the procedure...they weren't supposed to meet with people for tips...they were to try to encourage them to give the information over the phone...but there was something about her voice...Devon *wanted* to meet her...she *had* to meet her...

"Alright...I'm really not supposed to be doing this...but when and where?"

"Houlihan's Pub...over on the South side...you know where it is?"

"Yeah...I know it..."
"Seven tonight."

"Wait...how will I know you?"

"I'll find you..." she said, hanging up the phone.

Okay…that was major weird…what the hell were you thinking? You're going to meet someone that you don't know…without backup…for a potential tip on a hot murder case…with the suspect still at large…not the smartest thing you've ever done, McKinney!

Devon looked at her watch…it read 7:23am.

"Shit…I'm gonna be late…" She said, getting up and grabbing her jacket as she sped out the door and down the stairs…stopping at the main desk.

"Hey Julie…can you give me keys for one of the unmarked? I've gotta be at the morgue in 30 minutes…"

The young officer behind the desk smiled, reaching behind her and taking a set of keys off of the hook behind her.

"Here you go, Dev…the black Chevy Caprice…" she said, handing the keys to Devon.

"Gee…do you have anything bigger?" Devon said, sarcastically.

"Nah…all of the limos were taken today…sorry…" she said, smiling back.

"Thanks, Jules…" Devon said, turning and walking out the door to the garage.

The parking garage was exactly that…nothing fancy…just rows of police cars, some marked…some not. Devon looked down the row…

"There it is…land barge ho!" She smirked, walking over to the car and climbing in. "Holy shit…could it be any bigger?" she said, turning on the car and driving out of the garage.

Even with the couple of hours that she'd snagged while at her desk, Devon was still suffering from a serious lack of sleep…

Coffee…I really need coffee…or a big huge diet Cola…like a bladder-buster 64 ouncer! Definitely gotta stop…

Devon pulled into every cop's best friend…the 24-7-365 convenience store…or as most police called them…the 'Stop-n-Rob'…or the ever popular 'Rob-n-Run'.

Devon was no stranger to this store…and was instantly recognized by the worker behind the counter…a young man by the name of Bob Ling. Bob had been working there when Devon was still a uniformed cop on the beat. She always made a point of frequenting these stores, especially at night…as the clerks were easy pickings for any scum-bag with a gun.

"Hey Bob…how's it going?" Devon asked as she worked her way around the aisles to the coffee pots.

"Dev! Haven't seen you in a while…where've you been hiding yourself?"

"You know…the whole Detective thing…not a whole lot of spare time any more…"

"Yeah…I've heard from a couple of the guys that you're on that big 'ripper' case going on…what kind of a monster does something like that to a little girl…I'll tell you…I'd like five minutes alone with the asshole once you catch him!"

Devon reached for the pot of regular coffee and the largest cup that they had in the holders…

"Yeah…I think a lot of people would, Bob." She said, pouring the steaming hot liquid into the cup.

The aroma of the freshly-brewed coffee hung in the air like a thick summer fog…and Devon was inhaling every last bit of it…the smell bringing her senses back to life. She reached for a couple of hazelnut creamers and several packets of sugar, peeling back the covers and dumping them in the cup creating a sugary-caffeinated concoction that would most definitely have woke the dead…

"Wow…rough night, Dev?"

"They're all rough…"

"Yeah...ain't that the truth..." Bob said, figuring that Devon was referring to the monotony of her job...

More than you know, Bob...more than you know...

"Hey...how much do I owe you?" She asked, reaching into her pocket for change.

"Nah...don't worry about it...it's on the house..."

"Bob...we're not supposed to do that..."

"Well I won't tell if you don't..." he said with a wink.

"I think I can handle that...thanks..." She said, smiling as she walked out the door and back to the car.

Back to the morgue, McKinney...it always ends there, doesn't it?

CHAPTER 8

▼

It was 7:55 am when Devon pulled into the parking lot of the county morgue. She climbed out of her seat, jumbo coffee in hand, and made her way to Dr. Brown's office. Once again, the smell of antiseptic and death met her head on as she hit the hallway.

Damn...ever heard of air fresheners?

It was a smell that permeated every pore of her body...and she knew she'd be smelling it long after she had left for the day...

Okay...personal note...leave early enough to shower before going to the pub. Smell of death? Never a good thing...

Dr. Brown was sitting at his desk, looking intently at his computer screen as Devon approached his office. She knocked quietly on the door frame to get his attention...he turned to the door, smiling.

"Good morning, sunshine! I see you've got your 'wake-up-in-a cup' there..." he said, pointing to the huge cup of coffee in Devon's hand.

"Yeah, well...seems the pop machine at work was in cahoots with you and Mike...I couldn't get my daily quota of caffeine there...so I had to resort to this!" She said, sarcastically referring to the defective pop machine from the night before.

"Yes…I have a lot of connections in the soft-drink machine industry…" Doc said, snickering. "You ready to get going on this?"

"Ready whenever you are, Doc…lead the way." She said, standing aside and letting Dr. Brown pass her.

The two walked down to the prep room, where the two of them donned their gowns and gloves.

Much like her last visit…it wasn't easy for Devon to be here. The feelings she had experienced the last time were still looming over her like a group of storm clouds waiting for exactly the right moment to erupt into a flurry of electrical activity. But there was something different this time…she couldn't quite put her finger on it…but she just felt more…focused.

"Oh…did I tell you we've got a new diener working with us today?"

"Nope…newbie, huh? Is this going to be his first autopsy with you?" Devon asked…not really liking the idea of having someone that inexperienced involved on such a high-profile case.
"I believe so…I mean, aside from the training that he's had…" Dr. Brown said. He could feel Devon's apprehension…and it wasn't entirely unfounded…this was a very important case. "Don't worry, Dev…I know what you're thinking…and I'll be watching him like a hawk…"

"So will I…" Devon said, pulling her second pair of gloves on as she hit the swinging door with her back, entering the autopsy suite. When she turned around, she saw the new diener standing near the table, his eyes transfixed on the sheet-covered body below. He looked up with a jerk as he heard them enter the room.

"Devon…this is our new diener…Frank Donnelly."

Devon nodded…

The jury's still out on you, Frankie…let's see how strong of a stomach you've got…

"Frankie here is Chief Donnelly's youngest."

Nothing like a little help from Daddy to get you into a job with the county...gotta love nepotism!

"Just met your brother, Patrick, yesterday."

"Oh r-really?" The young man said, taking a step back as if he suddenly became uncomfortable with the situation...

Huh...that's interesting...looks like I struck a nerve...there's something familiar about him...

"Yeah...you're both in the business, eh? I'm sure your old man's just thrilled..."

"Um...y-yeah...I g-guess so..." Frank said, nervously.

"Well...now that we all know each other...how about we get down to business here?" Dr. Brown said, walking towards the table.

"Sure thing, Doc...let's go." Devon said, taking her place at the foot of the examining table.

Dr. Brown took the tape recorder from the tray of instruments and pushed the red record button down, beginning the external examination. He nodded for Frank to remove the sheet that was covering the body.

Frank hesitantly moved forward, grabbing the sheet by the end, slowly pulling it off, revealing the bruised and mutilated body of LeAnn Ballister underneath.

Devon and Dr. Brown had both seen the body while it was still at the scene; however, seeing it in a well-lighted room brought new meaning to the word 'brutal'.

"Wow...he sure did a number on her..." Dr. Brown said, shaking his head in disgust.

"He's perfecting his style..." Devon said, eerily.

"W-what do you mean?" Frank asked, keeping his distance from the body.

"Look at her…there was nothing frenzied about this…" Devon said, cocking her head to one side as she surveyed the body further. "You're getting better at your work, aren't you?" She said, thinking aloud.

Frank's eyes opened wide as he took another step back, bumping into the tray of instruments and knocking them to the floor with a loud clang.

"You alright there Frank?" Dr. Brown asked, looking at the young man who was now feverishly trying to salvage the instruments that had ended up on the floor.

"Yes…I'm s-sorry…I'm so c-clumsy!"

Clumsy? He's wound tighter than a top! Talk about your first day on the job jitters! Geesh!

"Just relax, Frank…no need to be nervous…" Dr. Brown said, trying to calm the young man. "Why don't you get another tray from the storage area and we'll get back to work, okay?"

Frank nodded as he headed into the storage room.

"Wow…little nervous, eh? Was he like that when you hired him?" Devon asked, looking towards the door of the storage area to make sure that he was still safely out of hearing range.

"Oh, he was a little uptight when I interviewed him, but basically, he's a really good kid…you have to admit, Dev…this is a pretty hard one for him to break his cherry on…"

"Yeah…I suppose so…" she said, as Frank stepped back into the examination room with a fresh tray of instruments. He walked carefully, as though he had a glass full of water and was trying to keep from spilling a drop.

"Here you g-go…sorry about t-that." He said, sitting the tray on the stand.

"Okay…let's try this again, shall we?" Dr. Brown said, pushing the red record button once again.

"External examination of Caucasian Female, age 7 years. General appearance, child is well-nourished with no obvious signs of disease or malady…" he said, reaching for the tape measure.

"Height 105.3 centimeters…weight 26.758 kilograms."He said, handing the tape measure to Frank, who proceeded to roll it up and replace it on the tray.

"Subject has large ventral incision with smooth edges extending from the pubis to the xyphoid process with complete evisceration of the abdominal contents…visible contusions bilaterally on the sternal area…"

That's odd…don't usually see bruises on the sternum unless…

"CPR?" Devon asked, interrupting his narration.

Dr. Brown pressed pause on the recorder, looking at Devon.

"Could be…we won't know for sure until we get in there for the internal examination…check and see if there was any bruising on the heart…cracked ribs…you know…"

"Okay…sorry I interrupted…"

"No problem, Dev…it's nice to see you've remembered everything I've taught you and then some!" He said pressing the record button once more.

"Subject also has horizontal contusions to the anterior portion of the neck…unable to determine if petticheal hemorrhaging occurred, as both eyeballs have been forcibly removed." He reached into the mouth, pulling the lower lip down, exposing the soft flesh on the inside. There were dozens of tiny red hemorrhages no larger than a pin-prick lining the surface of the inside lip, close to the gums. "Petticheal hemorrhaging present on the inside of the lower lip, in close proximity to the gum tissue…probable manual strangulation." He said, stopping the recorder. "Okay…let's get some pictures…"

Frank stood frozen in place, his eyes fixed on the body in front of him.

"Frank? Can we get some pictures here?"

The bile raised up in the back of Frank's throat, causing him to gag uncontrollably...he ran from the room, holding his hand to his mouth in an attempt to keep from hurling his half-digested Egg McMuffin onto the examining room floor.

"Whoa...looks like things were a little too much for junior there, Doc!"

"I guess so...think I'll be needing a new assistant...at least for the rest of this exam...you up for the job?" Doc said, raising his eyebrows, waiting for an answer.
"I think I might be able to help you out...just this once." She said with a wink.

"Gee...thanks...I owe you one." He said, sarcastically.

"I don't think you'll ever end up owing me one, Doc! I still owe you about a hundred after everything you've done for me over the years!"

"One hundred and sixty-three, to be exact...but hey, who's counting?"

"Smart-ass!" She countered. "So...you think we should go check on him?" She asked, remembering how sick the young man had looked.

"Let's give him a second...maybe he'll be back once he gets a little fresh air." Dr. Brown said, grabbing the camera off of the tray and handing it to Devon. "Here...lets get some pictures of this." He said, pulling the bottom lip down, once more exposing the reddened pin-prick hemorrhages within.

Devon took several pictures, not only of the hemorrhages, but also of the wounds, the contusions, and the body as a whole. After they had completed the initial survey of the body and removed the clothing, they proceeded with the internal examination.

"Are we going to do the Y incision like the last one?" Devon asked, taking a scalpel off of the tray.

"I guess so...that would probably be the easiest. We'll be able to keep the edges of the laceration intact that way...go ahead." Dr. Brown said, removing one pair of his gloves and replacing it with a new pair from the box on the cupboard.

It had been a while since Devon had done the actual dissection part of the autopsy. Cutting into a dead body was never a 'pleasant' experience; however, having to cut into a child was decidedly worse than normal.

She pressed the blade of the scalpel onto the child's skin just below the right shoulder, drawing the blade slowly through the flesh...she could feel the sinew and muscle separating as the blade sliced it's way towards the sternum...the skin behind opening in a deepened channel, exposing the ruddy flesh beneath. A bead of sweat started to form on Devon's brow as she made an identical cut on the opposite side...

Dr. Brown noticed and moved closer to make sure everything was okay.

"Doing alright there, Dev?"

"Yeah...it's just been a while...I kind of forgot what it felt like...you know?"

"Okay...the viscera has already been removed...courtesy of our new resident psychopath. I've got it all separated and in the pan over there. Let's get a look at the chest wall here..." he said, as they laid the body open at the incisions. The flesh that had been covering the sternum had several areas where blood had penetrated the flesh, clotting throughout.

"Well...would you look at that..." Dr. Brown said, using a probe to manipulate one of the clotted areas. "Oh...he's special, our boy!"

"So he did do CPR on her." Devon said, thinking out loud.

"Definitely...and from the looks of it...maybe more than once...his hand placement changed on the sternum...see this?" Doc said, pointing to another area of clotting.

"Wouldn't he have to…when he gives the breaths in-between the compressions…no…wait! If he had CPR training…which, from the looks of it, he did…he would only be using one hand for the compressions with a kid her age!"

"Exactly…That's why we're only seeing a couple of different areas of contusion and clotting. Go ahead and open up the neck area…let's see if we've got deep tissue contusions there as well…"

Devon made the necessary incisions and peeled back the flesh, exposing the same type of clotting within the tissues.

"Looks like we've got a definite yes on the manual strangulation…" Dr. Brown said, looking over Devon's shoulder.

"I'd say so…just a second…almost got the hyoid bone exposed…there." Devon said, nodding to Dr. Brown to check the area.

Underneath the layer of flesh and sinew shone an extremely small and fragile bone, the hyoid. Dr. Brown gently tucked the probe underneath the bone, pushing slightly upwards, exposing what appeared to be a fracture.

"It definitely looks like it's broken. Let's go ahead and remove it so we can examine it a little better."

Devon carefully dissected the area, removing the fragile bone carefully and placing it on a specimen tray.

"Okay…lets get at the heart and lungs…here's the rongeurs…" he said, handing her a pair of what appeared to be something like pruning shears.

Devon took the shears, inserting them just under the lower part of the ribcage, slowly clipping her way through the bone and cartilage, finally removing the two anterior sections. Underneath laid the pleura…which surrounds the lungs…and the pericardial sac, which encases the heart.
The sac around the heart looked like a deflated balloon, and there were a few large blood clots lying around it.

"Looks like he must have gone a little deep with the knife...the left ventricle was perforated."

"So what do you think actually killed her...the wound, or the strangulation?" Devon asked, she had her suspicions, but she wanted to see what Dr. Brown thought.

Dr. Brown stuck his hand underneath the heart, feeling the texture underneath his gloved hands...examining the chest cavity closely.

"Manual strangulation...see this? Not much blood in here. If he had done this while she was still alive, the whole chest cavity would have been pumped full of blood. Nope...he did this after the fact."

"Okay...so he strangles her...brings her back with CPR...strangles her again...and then brings her back again...strangles her a <u>third</u> time...and then guts her and gouges out her eyes..." Devon said, trying to contemplate the order of events.

"Yep...that's pretty much how I see it...uh...bad choice of words, huh?" Dr. Brown said, making reference to the eyeless corpse before them.

"Any ideas on the eye-business?" Devon asked.

"Boy...you're really asking the wrong person on that one...psychology is not my thing..." He said, shaking his head. He loved pathology...it was all about science...like putting together the pieces of a puzzle...but psychology? Too many possible variants...like looking at an inkblot test...everybody sees something different.

Eyes...what was it about the eyes?

"I think I remember something about eyes in that profiling course I took...I'll have to check my books..." Devon said, making a mental note to check on the information later.

Within the next couple of hours, they had completed the internal examination and all of the clothing, swabs and samples were prepared to be sent to the laboratory for analysis. Devon and Dr. Brown walked back to the prep room, stripping off their gowns and booties and placing them in the biohazard bin.

"So...you want to catch some lunch? My treat..."

"Actually, Doc...if you don't mind...I'll take a rain check on that. I really haven't slept much in the last..." She looked at the watch on her wrist "...about 28 hours now. All I want to do right now is crawl into bed and sleep for like a week!"

Okay...so that's a bit of an exaggeration...I caught a couple of hours sleep at the office...but that doesn't really count!

He was actually relieved to hear that his friend was actually going to sleep for a change...

"No problem, Dev...do you need a ride home? Because I can drive you..."

"Nah...I'm fine...I've got one of the unmarked out there...I'll take that home and drive it back into work tomorrow...Mike can give me a ride tomorrow night."

"Well...sounds like you've got it all worked out then...I'll give you a call as soon as we get the results back from the lab on the swabs." He said, placing his hand on her shoulder. "Be careful on your way home, okay?"

"Will do, Doc..." Devon said, walking out of the prep room and into the hall-way, where she accidentally bumped into a young man dressed in scrubs. "Oh...sorry...didn't see you there." She said, apologetically.

"T-that's okay...it was my fault..." Frank said, looking down at the ground. He walked quickly down the hallway, away from the two of them.

Without the facemask on, Devon now understood why she had thought that the young man seemed familiar...he was the one who had waked her up in the parking lot that day...but he hadn't stuttered, then...had he?

"Looks like junior's still a little shook up..." Devon said, smirking.

"Yeah…guess so…I'd better go check in on the lad…"

"Okay, Doc…I'll talk to you later…"

"Take care, Dev…get some sleep!" He said, waving as he disappeared down the hallway.

"I will…" She said, walking out the door.

CHAPTER 9

▼

It hadn't really sunk in that she was as tired as she was until the drive home. Devon found herself zoning out momentarily as she would swerve on the road, only to be brought out of it when the tires dropped off the shoulder with a thud.

"Whoa!" Devon said, jerking the wheel, bringing the car back onto the road. "Okay…that was really not a good thing…time to crank the air and turn up the tunes…" she said, thinking aloud. She reached down, turning the air conditioning on maximum, and increased the volume until the whole car was vibrating to the bass line of Bohemian Rhapsody…

She turned into the driveway, letting out a sigh of relief at having made it there successfully. Throwing the car into park, she dragged herself into the house, tossed her keys on the desk, kicked off her shoes, and plopped down onto the couch.

Ugh…I seriously don't feel like going anywhere tonight…least of all to a pub to meet some woman who in all likelihood is some psycho-psychic chick…but then again…if I don't go, and she actually does have information…I'm fucked…

Devon reached to her side, removing her pager from its case and setting the alarm for 5:30pm.

That ought to do it…I'll have enough time to take a shower, grab something to eat, and then head over to the pub…smoke-filled pub…lovely…

Eyelids drooping, sleep finally claimed her mid-thought.

The time seemed to go by in an instant as the alarm on her pager sounded. Devon rolled over, wearily opened her eyes, and grabbed the pager from the floor, shutting off the alarm. Raising her hands to her face, she rubbed the sleep out of her eyes and slowly sat up, placing her feet on the floor. Pausing momentarily for the blood to make it's way back to her brain...

Ugh...head rush...not good...need food...

Slowly she rose from the couch, walking into the kitchen, her feet scuffing along the carpeting along the way. She leaned up against the cupboard, opening the refrigerator door...

Great...baking soda and something that looks like my fourth grade science fair experiment...lovely...

She closed the refrigerator door, reaching up to the freezer...

Let's see what we've got here...ice cubes...Rocky Road!
She grabbed the carton of ice cream, ripping the top off with a smile on her face...which soon disappeared when she saw the thick coating of ice crystals inside...

Damn it! I'm starving here! Where's the fucking food fairy when you need her...fridge whore...

But then...from behind the extra ice cube tray...it shone through like a brick of solid gold...one lonely bean and cheese burrito...her's for the taking.

"Yes!" She exclaimed, as she grabbed the burrito, throwing it wrapper and all, into the microwave and turned it on in one smooth motion. Two minutes later, Devon and her little bean and cheese treasure were heading into the dining room. The table was covered with stacks of unopened mail, empty pop cans, and various other assorted pieces of junk. Devon looked at the mess, disgusted with herself...

Damn, this place is a pit!...and to think...I used to be the clean freak! Funny how things change...

Devon hadn't been much into housekeeping since...well...it just didn't seem important any more. She smiled remembering how Chris had always teased her about being obsessive compulsive about 'a place for everything—and everything in its place'...

You're probably up there laughing at me right now about this, aren't you baby?

She took a bite of the burrito and promptly spit it out.

"Ugh!" She said, wrinkling her face at the rather distinct taste of freezer-burn.

Okay, eating is out...might as well get in the shower...

She said to herself, tossing the burrito in the trash as she walked down the hallway to the bedroom.

The bedroom itself, was not much better than the dining room table...the bed was a mess of mangled blankets and sheets that honestly hadn't been changed since Chris died...Devon had tried to several times...but she just couldn't bring herself to do it. However faint, she could still smell the scent of Chris' perfume on them.

The rest of the room was littered with piles of clean and dirty laundry sitting on the floor...even Devon herself, found it difficult to distinguish one pile from the other at times. She reached down, grabbing a pair of jeans from one pile and giving them a quick sniff...

Yep...clean.

She said to herself...digging back into the pile in an attempt to find a shirt to wear. Near the middle of the pile, she found a white button-down shirt.

Not great...but it'll do...not like I'm out to impress anybody...

She thought, tossing the jeans and shirt onto the bed as she peeled off her clothes and walked into the bathroom.

The tile on the bathroom floor felt cool under her feet as she bent over, turning on the water in the shower, adjusting it to just the right temperature before climbing in. She rested one hand on the wall of the shower, letting the water cascade over her face and down her body. Slowly but surely, the droplets of water flowing across her smooth skin brought her back to the world of the living…washing away the smell of death that had permeated her body earlier in the day. Ten minutes and two shampoos later, she pushed the shower curtain aside, reaching for the towel that she had laid on the countertop.

Drying her hair, she stepped out of the shower, tracking water onto the bath mat…she stepped over to the rug in front of the sink, careful not to slip on the wet tile. She looked in the mirror, not quite prepared for what she saw looking back at her…it was Chris…standing there behind her…her arms wrapped around Devon's midsection…a soft smile on her lips…

Devon stared at the image, her mouth agape…afraid to turn around or to blink, for fear that she would be gone…

"Remember…" Chris whispered as she pressed her lips lovingly to Devon's bare shoulder.

"Chris…" Devon managed to say, breathlessly, tears welling up in her eyes.

"Remember…don't just look…see…" she said, smiling.

Devon couldn't take it any more…she turned around, hoping…praying that Chris would be standing there behind her…but it was not to be.

Devon felt like her world had caved in on her…the tears fell down her cheeks and onto her chest as she sunk to the ground, bringing her knees to her chest…sobbing…

"It's so hard…going on without you…I try so hard…so hard, baby! But it doesn't get any easier…it hurts so bad!" she said, her breath now coming in gasps as she cried uncontrollably. "Nothing stops the pain…nothing!"

"In time…give it time…remember, Dev…"

Was she making this all up in her mind…was this her subconscious' way of deal-ing with the whole thing? She didn't know…all she knew was that it hurt…and that she was sick of hurting…beyond sick…it had to stop…and it had to stop now.

She walked out into the bedroom…opening the drawer in the nightstand. Inside, the light flashed as it hit the smooth stainless steel of her Ruger Security Six .357 Revolver. The gun had been a present from Chris…it felt only fitting that she use it to finally end the pain. She opened the cylinder, making sure it was loaded, and flipped it back into position with a click.

Raking her thumb over the hammer, she pulled it back into position…hearing the first click, and then the second, signifying that it was now in firing position. She sat on the bed, pulling Chris' pillow into her face…taking a deep breath…savoring the scent of Chris one last time and letting the pillow drop to the floor as she took the barrel into her mouth, the cold steel resting on her lips. Her finger on the trigger, she tilted the gun just slightly, making sure that the bullet's path would decimate her brain stem…it would all be over in a fraction of a second…she wouldn't even know what hit her…and the pain would finally be gone…

She slowly squeezed the trigger…waiting to hear the final 'pop' of the gun dis-charging…splattering her brains across the room.

Suddenly…visions of Hallie Hingerman and LeAnn Ballister and other little girls clouded her thoughts. What if this woman that she was supposed to meet was the key to it all…what if she didn't go…they'd never find out…and the killings would continue. More girls would die…and it would be her fault…

She slowly pulled the trigger, keeping her thumb on the hammer as she released it to its resting position. She removed it from her mouth, placing it back into the nightstand drawer…

The pain would end…but not tonight. Tonight…she had work to do…there were lives to save.

She reached for the jeans, pulling them on as she stood up…leaving them unbuttoned as she slowly returned to the bathroom to finish getting ready.

Hope she isn't expecting some spit and polished uber-bitch…'cause that's not what she's going to get tonight…

Devon pulled her still damp hair back into a pony-tail, brushed her teeth, slathered on her roll-on…and grabbed her shirt, buttoning it and tucking it into her jeans as she walked back into the bedroom.

Belt…I need a belt…if I were a fucking belt…where the fuck would I be?

She lay down on the bed, hanging over the edge and lifting the covers, looking underneath. There, on the floor under the bed, was her belt.

Ha! Works every time!
She grabbed the belt, weaving it through the loops, buttoning up the fly on her jeans, she walked out to the living room.

Grabbing her badge from the desk, she clipped it on her belt. Opening the desk drawer, she found her leather concealment holster, tucking it and her .40 caliber safely in her waistband, blousing her shirt to cover the grip that was sticking just above her waistband. She grabbed the black leather jacket from the back of the chair, sliding her arms through as she stepped into her loafers…grabbed her keys and headed out the door.

It was about a twenty minute drive to the pub…not long, but long enough for Devon to think about what she was getting herself into…

Okay, McKinney…let's get this straight…you're going to a pub to meet a woman about a murder case…you have no idea who she is…or what she looks like. For all you know…she may very well be the killer! You've got no back-up…and nobody even knows where you are…are these the actions of a sane person? Hell, no…but then, neither is almost suck-starting a .357 magnum! Okay…maybe I should call Mike…just let him know where I'll be…in case anything happens…

She reached into the pocket of her jacket, finding her flip-phone. She turned it on and hit speed-dial 4.

It rang three times before Mike's voice-mail kicked on.

"Hello, this is Detective Mike Penaglio. I'm unable to take your call right now…please leave a message with your name, time of day, and call-back number after the beep. Thank you."

BEEP

"Mike…it's Dev…listen…it's 6:45pm, I've got a possible lead that I'm following up on…I'll be at Houlihan's Pub…I'll give you a call later on and let you know if I've got anything. See ya later…"

She pulled into the parking lot, finding a spot near the door, she backed the Caprice in, just in case she needed to make a hasty exit. She double checked her gun, tucked her phone back into her pocket, and headed into the pub.

The lighting was dim…the room filled with the smell of a combination of cigarette smoke and stale beer. Needless to say, Houlihan's wasn't exactly what you'd call a 'high-class' establishment. They were known for good beer, good burgers, and all of the peanuts that you could eat for free…just shuck them, eat them, and toss the shells on the floor…it wasn't much, but hey, it had ambience…

Devon nodded to the bartender as she walked in…this was not her first time here. She made her way past the pool tables to the back of the pub, selecting a booth, and sat down, facing the door. It was something that was a given for any seasoned cop…you never sit with your back to the door…that's just asking for trouble. The bartender brought over a glass, sitting it in front of her.

"Been a while, Dev." He said, smiling.

"Not so long…I see you still remember my favorite, eh?" She said, taking a sip of the drink.

"Not too many people that come in here order a VO Manhattan, sweet, not dry…heavy on the cherries."

"No...don't suppose they do..." Devon said, looking around at the other patrons, who were primarily drinking beer.

"So how you been, Dev? Haven't seen you in a while."

"Yeah...been busy..." Devon shrugged, taking another sip of the Manhattan.

"So what brings you here tonight...business, or pleasure?" He said, crossing his arms on top of his rather rotund belly...

"Boy...you're just full of questions tonight, aren't you?" Devon said, smirking at the barkeep...

"Hey...gotta look out for our boys and girls in blue!" he said, smiling. "I'll let you get back to work...let me know if there's anything I can get for you."

Devon nodded as he walked back behind the bar. She looked down at her watch...6:54 pm.

Okay...where is she? Is she already here? How in the hell am I supposed to be able to tell who she is?

Devon's eyes scanned the pub...it was filled with a mixture of regulars and faces she didn't know...but by the looks of it, they were members of some kind of fraternity and sorority...as some of them had sweatshirts with Greek letters on them. Suddenly, motion at the door caught her attention...

She was relatively tall...about Devon's height, with sweeping golden locks streaked with platinum that draped perfectly over her shoulders...her lithe figure hidden behind her long skirt and peasant top...features so fine that they were almost ethereal...there was only one word to describe her...mystical.

She looked around the room, her eyes locking onto Devon's as she made her way through the crowd...

"Detective McKinney?" She asked, speaking almost in a whisper.

Devon rose up off of the bench, extending her hand and motioning for the woman to sit down.

"Miss Morrigan, I presume…" Devon said, sitting back down…never taking her eyes off of the woman who was now sitting across from her.

"Please…call me Brid." She said, smiling softly.

Devon couldn't help but be a bit mesmerized by the woman's pale gray eyes…almost silver…and they had such depth…almost mercurial…like looking into a mirror…

Devon broke the gaze "…I'm sorry, would you like something to drink?"

"Um…sure…White Zinfandel?" she said, tentatively.

Devon waved the barkeep over to the table.

"She'd like a glass of White Zinfandel…and could you bring me a diet Cola?" Devon asked.

"You sure you want to do that?" Brid asked, still wearing a soft smile on her delicate face.

"Do what?"

"Drink that…they've been trying to get you to stop…"

How in the…?Oh…nice try…I see what you're doing…playing on the generalities…it's pretty easy to assume that someone would try to get me to quit drinking the soda. Okay…let's just throw you a bit of a curve here…

"Someone's been trying to get me to stop drinking soda? Huh…that's a new concept! Sorry to disappoint you…" Devon said, the sarcasm evident in the tone of her voice.

"Baseball's not your game…" Brid said, cryptically.

"What...?" Devon asked...not realizing what Brid was saying.

The bartender brought over the glass of wine, sitting it on the table.

"But curves just might be..." Brid said, reaching for the glass and bringing it up to her lips.
"Oookay..." Devon said, taking another drink of her Manhattan.

Okay...did she just flirt with me? I'm thinking seriously loony here...there's only a few letters that separate PSYCHIC from PSYCHO...

She sat the drink back onto the table, pausing to collect her thoughts before continuing...

"Now...Miss Morr...er...Brid...you said that you have information regarding a case that I'm working on?" Devon said, trying to move things along a bit.

"You haven't eaten supper yet, have you?" Brid said, taking another sip of wine.

"What?" Devon said, confused.

"I said supper...you haven't had it yet, have you?"

"No...but Brid...that's not why we're here...you said you..."

"Do they have salads here? No...of course they don't...I know this little Italian place not far from here that has the best Eggplant Parmesan..."

Holy shit! Psycho and A.D.D.! Why do I do this to myself? I can't get a friggin' word in edgewise!

Without thinking, Devon reached across the table, placing her hand atop Brid's, in an attempt to get her attention...Brid stopped talking, looking down at their hands.

"Let's take a step back here for a second, okay? Now...you said that you have information on the case...I really need to..."

Devon was once again interrupted, when Brid interjected "...eat first...I never work well on an empty stomach...come on, what are you afraid of? Take a chance..." Brid said, smiling devilishly.

Devon smiled...she knew she had been 'had'. Brid had hit her weak spot...she dared her, and Devon could never refuse a dare.

"Okay...just let me catch the tab and then you can lead the way..." she said, taking one last drink of her Manhattan. She got up out of the booth, walked to the bar and tossed three fives to the bartender. "Keep the change...thanks for everything."

The bartender nodded as she walked back to the booth...

"Shall we?" Devon said, motioning for Brid to lead the way.

"Definitely..." Brid said, making her way past the pool tables heading towards the door. Just before they made it past the billiards area, one of the young men wearing Greek letters walked over to Brid.

"Professor Morrigan?" he said, obviously surprised to see her in the pub.

Devon's eyes opened wide in astonishment.

Professor? She's a professor? Holy shit! I wonder what her degrees are in...probably something like 'Women's Studies' or 'French Literature' or something...I don't know...artsy-fartsy...that's it...Liberal Arts...gotta be!

"Michael! Nice to see you! We missed you in lecture Monday."

"Sorry about that...had a touch of the stomach flu..." he explained.

"Yeah...I've heard that was going around...I believe it's called the 'I partied too much on Sunday night' flu..."

"No! Seriously...I didn't mean to..." Michael said, stammering.

"Hey…it's alright, Michael…I was a student once, too, you know…" she said with a smile. "I'll see you in class on Wednesday." She said, continuing to the door.

Once outside, Devon reached into her pocket, taking out the keys for the Caprice.

"So…I'll just follow you over there…okay?" Devon said, walking towards the car.

"That will be kind of tough…for you to follow me, that is…because I'll be riding next to you…" Brid said, walking to the passenger side door of the Caprice. "Hmmm…four door, black, no-frills…not your personal vehicle, I take it?"

"Um…no…not exactly my style." Devon said, opening her door and hitting the power locks to unlock the door for Brid. "I tend to refrain from taking my own personal vehicle to meet strangers who may be involved in homicide cases…call me crazy."

"No…not crazy…" she said, looking over the hood of the car at Devon, cocking her head to one side "…just uniquely different…special." she said, climbing into the seat.

Devon paused for a moment before getting in…

Uniquely different, eh? Huh…that's interesting…

The drive to the restaurant was a short one…only a few blocks down the street.

"There it is…there…"Bella Luna'…" Brid said, pointing to the left.

Devon turned into the parking lot, once again backing into the spot.

"Getting ready for a quick get-away?" Brid asked.

I may need it, with you…

"Old habits die hard." Devon said, opening the car door and climbing out.

"Yes...other things, too..." Brid said, climbing out and walking to the front door.

Devon walked ahead of her, opening the door and motioning her through.

"Thank you!" Brid said, surprised by the gesture.

"Another old habit...you're welcome." Devon said, following her inside.

There was nothing particularly spectacular about the décor of the place, but it's checkered tablecloths and drippy candles did give it a certain ambience. Inside the door, the maitre'd stood at a podium...

"Good evening and welcome to Bella Luna...how many will be dining tonight?" he asked, smiling.

"Just two...non-smoking?" Devon said, looking to Brid...

Brid nodded in agreement.

"Very good...this way, please..." he said, walking into the dining room. He led them to a table for two in a rather crowded area of the restaurant.

"Um...excuse me, sir? Would you happen to have something a little more private? We'll be conducting business while we're here..." Devon said, passing him a ten-dollar bill.

The man took the money, nodding silently, as he led them to a secluded room in the back of the restaurant.

"Would this be more to your liking?" he asked Devon.

"This would be fine...thank you." Devon said, pulling out the chair and sitting down.

He moved around to Brid, pulling out the chair for her.

"Your waiter will be with you shortly." He said, walking back into the main dining room.

"Wow! This is really something! I thought you said you hadn't been here before…" Brid said, looking to Devon.

"I haven't."

"I don't get it…how did you know that they would have something like this…a private room, that is…"

"This place is 'family' owned…they have to have someplace to conduct business in private…"

"Oh…oh! I see…interesting." Brid said, just as the waiter arrived at their table.

He was a strikingly handsome young man in his twenties…tall and muscular with shiny black hair and chiseled features, topped off with a thick Sicilian accent…

"Good evening, ladies…can I bring you a drink this evening…some wine, perhaps?" he asked, placing the menus before them.

"Do you have a nice Chianti?" Brid asked.

"Absolutely…and for you, ma'am?" he asked, looking to Devon.

"I'll have a club soda with a lime twist."

"Very good…I'll be right back with your drinks." he said, disappearing into the other room.

"What…no diet Cola this time?" Brid said, chidingly.

"Don't get your hopes up…just in the mood for something a little more refreshing, that's all…incidentally…what kind of professor are you?"

"A good one." She said, smiling. "Forensic Anthropology…and I dabble in psychology. What kind of cop are you?" she asked, turning the spotlight onto Devon.

"Persistent. Homicide…Violent Crimes Unit."

"Sounds interesting…and…difficult." Brid said, her tone becoming decidedly more somber.

"It can be…both…I guess. But that's not why we're here…is it?"

"You tell me." Brid said, looking deeply into Devon's eyes.

"Information…plain and simple…if you've got it…I want it." Devon said, locking eyes once again with Brid's silvery orbs.
The waiter arrived with their drinks, sitting them on the table.

"Your drinks, ladies…have you decided what you would like this evening?"

Brid looked at Devon inquisitively. "No…I don't think we've decided on that quite yet…could you give us a few minutes?"

"Not a problem…enjoy your drinks, I'll be back shortly." He said, walking back into the other room.

"Guess we'd better decide what we want, eh?" Devon said, picking up the menu and opening it.

"I already know what I want." Brid said, looking intently at Devon.

Okay…what exactly is going on here? She seriously is not flirting with me…

"The Eggplant Parmesan, remember? That's kind of why we came here…"

"Oh…yeah…right." Devon said, somewhat relieved…but also a little disappointed, much to her surprise. "I guess I'll have the same." She said, closing the menu and sitting it on the end of the table. She reached for her drink, bringing it to her lips just as the waiter returned.

"So...are we ready, ladies?"

"Yes...we'll both have the Eggplant Parmesan..." Devon said, ordering for the both of them as she sat her drink back on the table.

"Very good choice...it's one of our specialties...and what kind of salad would you like?"

"I'll have the Caesar." Brid said.

"I'll pass on the salad for now, thanks." Devon said.

The waiter nodded, walking to the kitchen to turn in the order.

"No salad, huh? Got something against healthy food?" Brid asked, taking a sip of wine as she looked at Devon over the rim of the glass.

"No...not really...just not much on food of the green, crunchy variety."

"Okay...I'll have to remember that...no salad."

"You don't have to remember anything, Brid...I'm here to get information from you...once I get that information, you'll never have to see me again...well...unless we need you as a witness, that is."

"What if I want to see you again?" she said, rolling the wine glass back and forth in between her hands.

Why does everything always have to be so complicated?

"Brid...listen...I really appreciate you being interested. I mean...you're smart and beautiful...and interesting and all...but..."

"But what?"

"But I didn't come here for a date...I came here because you said you have information about the case that I'm working on."

Brid leaned over the table, looking into Devon's eyes "I think there's several reasons that you came out tonight...only one of which was information."

What in the hell is she talking about?

"Oh really?" Devon said, leaning over the table "...and exactly why do you think I came here tonight?" She said, trying to egg Brid on a bit.

Brid sat back in her seat...studying Devon's face for a moment before giving her answer.

"I think you came here tonight for answers...not just on your case...but on a lot of things...like why you can't sleep at night without taking something to make it happen...and when you do sleep...why you have the nightmares. They started about...four months ago...after you lost someone...but now they've changed...haven't they?"

Devon's mood quickly changed as anger rose up in her veins like an acid burning through her soul.

"What kind of shit are you trying to pull, here? Huh?! What did you do...run some kind of background check on me? Have you been stalking me?!"

"Calm down...it's nothing like that...I promise you." She said, quietly.

"Yeah? Well what is it like? Because I gotta tell you...right now...it's sounding pretty fucking sick!" Devon said, loudly.

"You need to just relax and listen to me...I know that things have been difficult for you lately...I can feel it...I can feel your grief...it completely surrounds you...and others can feel it, too. But there's more...the dreams...I know what you see."

"You said that before! What do you mean?"

"The dreams you've been having since you started on this case...they have the victims in them, don't they?"

"Yeah...but that's not that unusual. It's pretty bad...you know...seeing kids like that..." Devon said, not understanding quite where the conversation was going.

"I know...I see them too...the nightmares...but I think I'm seeing them from a different point of view..."

"What are you talking about? There's no way you could possibly know!"

"Please...just give me a chance to explain...alright?"

"Just how in the hell do you think you're going to do that?" Devon said, skeptically.

"Let me tell you about the dreams..." she said, just as the waiter arrived with their food.

Great timing...

CHAPTER 10

▼

"Thank you…it all looks great." Devon said as the waiter sat the food down in front of him. Actually…the timing wasn't that bad…it gave Devon a moment to calm down and collect her thoughts before continuing her discussion with Brid.

"Is there anything else that I can get you?" he asked, politely.

"I think we're all set…thanks." Brid said, dismissing him.

"Okay…tell me about the dreams…" Devon said, waiting for an explanation.

"The food is going to get cold."

"I'll have them nuke it for you." Devon said, sarcastically.

"Okay…fine…In the dream, there's two young girls…I'm seeing it from their point of view…we're in the woods on some kind of a path…not a road…but not really just a footpath, either…"

"Like a two-track?" Devon suggested.

"Yes…exactly…and the woods seems to go on forever…like a forest or something. Then an owl…like a Great Horned Owl or a Barn Owl…flies into a tree in front of us, watching us…I mean, the two girls…watching the girls…and that's when it happened…"

"That's when what happened?" Devon asked.

"The owl disappeared...and you appeared in its place...standing in front of a fork in the trail, watching us."

"What? I was there? That's not possible...we've never met before...have we?" Devon asked, not understanding how this woman...this complete stranger...could have had a dream with her in it.

"Tonight was the first night that we've ever actually met...but I've seen you in my dreams before..." Brid said, her tone suddenly becoming more serious.

"Before what? Before now?"

"Yes, it started a few months ago...and there's always an owl there...in the same dream...but you're never together. If the owl is there, you're not...and vice versa."

Devon had to admit...there's no way that Brid could have known about her dream...about the two murder victims...the fork in the road...

Okay...this is really freaking me out here...is she for real?

"Before...on the phone...you mentioned something about eyes?" Devon said, remembering their phone conversation.

"Yes...the last girl...her eyes were gouged out, weren't they?"

"You tell me..." Devon said, knowing full well that she could not divulge any of the details of the case.

"They were completely removed. You didn't find the actual eyeballs...just empty sockets." Brid said, looking to Devon for some kind of reaction...anything.

"Okay...you've definitely got my attention. So how do I know you weren't the sicko that did this? The murderer would know the details..."

"You don't know, Devon…and there's no way for me to prove it to you one way or the other. I was at my home, alone for the evening. Spent most of it grading papers."

"Great…so you have no alibi…but you have details of the killing that only the killer himself or herself would know. You know I should be taking you into custody right now, don't you?"

"Do you honestly think I would have called you and arranged to meet with you to give you this information if I was the one who did it?"

"Stranger things have happened…" Devon said…but her gut was telling her that Brid was telling the truth…that she didn't have anything to do with the murders…but how then, did she know about the eyes?

"True…they have and they do…but I promise you, Devon, I had nothing to do with this…" Brid said, hoping that Devon would trust her.

Devon nodded.

"Your Eggplant's getting cold…" Devon said, trying to change the subject for a minute…just to give herself time to let things sink in a bit.

"Nothing worse than cold Eggplant…" Brid said with a subtle smile.

The two sat in silence as they ate.

It had been a long time since Devon actually enjoyed a meal. She had basically been eating out of necessity only for the past four months…but tonight…she savored each bite.

She had just finished when the waiter appeared once again.

"How was everything?" he asked, looking to Devon.

"It was outstanding…thank you."

"Can I get you ladies some dessert this evening? We've got an outstanding crème brulle...tiramisu...chocolate cheesecake..."

"Oooh...chocolate cheesecake...definitely!" Devon said, surprising herself with her enthusiasm.

"I'll have the same." Brid said, her face lighting up...noticing Devon's excitement over her dessert choice.

"I love chocolate." Devon said, smiling sheepishly.

It was the first time that she'd smiled that evening...and it did not go unnoticed...

"You have a beautiful smile." Said Brid.

"What?" Devon said, not quite sure of what Brid had just said.

"You have a beautiful smile...you should show it more often."

Much to her surprise, and to Brid's...Devon blushed.

The waiter returned with the desserts...sitting them down and taking away the dishes from the main course.

"There you go ladies...enjoy!" he said, returning to the kitchen.

Devon swiftly picked up her fork, digging it into the chocolaty treat. She brought the tidbit of cheesecake to her mouth, slowly pulling the fork away. The chocolate delight melted in her mouth...spreading sweetly over her tongue...her eyes closing in a moment of pure ecstasy.

Brid watched in amazement.

"Goddess...you really do love chocolate, don't you?" Brid said, chuckling.

"Love is definitely an understatement...and did you just say 'Goddess?'" Devon said, barely swallowing before bringing the next fork-full to her lips.

"Yes…I did…say Goddess, that is."

"Kind of an odd thing to say…don't you think? I mean…most people tend to say things like 'oh my God' and 'oh God'…things like that…" Devon said, digging into the cheesecake once more.

"It's not odd, really…I believe that it is rather arrogant for us to just assume that the superior being…whoever it might be…is automatically a man…" Brid said, finally taking her first bite of the cheesecake.

"Huh…guess so…I've never really been that keen on the whole organized religion thing…seems a little stuffy to me."

"I think that a lot of religions have valid points…all of them, actually…but I don't really subscribe to one over another. They're all interesting to…"

The discussion came to an abrupt halt as Devon's pager went off once again.

"Damn…hold that thought." Devon said, reaching for her pager.

POSSIBLE CHILD ABDUCTION…2703 WINCHESTER…PD ON SCENE.

"Son-of-a-bitch!" Devon said, grabbing her napkin, wiping the traces of chocolate off her lips.

"It's another one, isn't it?" Brid said, solemnly.

"I don't know for sure…could be…I'm sorry—but we're going to have to continue this discussion later…" she said, putting the cloth napkin down on the table and waving for the waiter to bring the bill.

"Yes ma'am?" He said, addressing Devon.

"Sorry about this…but we're kind of in a hurry…can I get the check, please?"

"Certainly…would you like a box for your desserts?" he asked.

"Sure…a couple of them…if that wouldn't be too much of a problem."

"Not at all…I'll be right back." He said, walking into the other room to retrieve the items.

Devon looked at the message on her pager once more…her brow wrinkled…deep in thought.

It's you again, isn't it? I've got to stop you…I will stop you…I just hope I can get to her before you slaughter her, you fuck!

Brid reached out, gently laying her hand atop Devon's…

"You will get whoever is doing this…I know you will…"

Devon pulled her hand back, feeling rather uneasy at the physical contact.

"Yeah…I hope you're right…" She said, placing the pager back on her belt.

The waiter returned with the check and two white Styrofoam boxes, placing the desserts in them.

"Here you go…I can take that up for you whenever you're ready." He said, setting the black portfolio with the check on the table.

Devon opened it, reaching into her pocket and placing three twenties in the folder.

"Here you go…" She said, handing the folder to the waiter. "Keep the change."

"Thank you…have a wonderful evening. I hope to see you both again!" He said, smiling.

Devon slid off of her seat, standing up and grabbing her jacket.

"I'll drop you off at your car…and here…" Devon said, digging in the pocket of her jacket, pulling out a business card. "This has my pager number and email on it…our discussion is far from over. I may be out in the field for a few days…but I'd like to get together again as soon as possible."

"Just a second…" Brid said, digging through her purse. She pulled out a small piece of paper…writing her home and cell phone numbers on it, handing it to Devon. "Why don't you call me…with everything that's going on…it would probably be better that way."

Devon took the piece of paper from Brid, stuffing it in her pants pocket.

"Um…yeah…thanks. Ready to go?"

"Sure." Brid said, sliding her chair out and standing up.

Devon stepped aside, motioning for Brid to go ahead of her as they walked out of the restaurant. She walked around to the passenger side of the car, opening the door for Brid.

"Thanks…" Brid said, climbing into the car.

Devon walked around the front, sliding into the driver's seat.

The drive back to the pub was a short one.

"That's mine…over there…the red VW convertible." Brid said, pointing to a perfect vintage VW Bug convertible.

"Somehow, that doesn't surprise me." Devon said with a smirk.
"Oh really? And what exactly do you mean by that, Detective?"

"I don't know…it's just…unique…"

Unique…definitely unique…

"I'll take that as a compliment…" Brid said, opening the car door and getting out. She leaned back into the car, looking intently at Devon. "Good luck with everything…if you need anything…you know…talk…whatever…feel free to call."

"Thanks...I'll give you a call as soon as I get this situation taken care of...so we can finish our discussion..." Devon said, qualifying why she would call.

Brid nodded in agreement, closing the door as Devon began to drive off.

She didn't know why...but for some reason, Devon looked in the rear view mirror just as she was about to drive out of the parking lot. She could see Brid running after the car...

"Wait!" Brid yelled...running up to the driver's side window.

Devon pressed the button, lowering the glass...

"I need to tell you..." Brid said, breathlessly "...you can't just look...you have to see."

"What?" Devon said, her eyes widening hearing those words...the same ones that she had heard Chris say to her in her dreams...

"Just go...be careful..." Brid said, stepping away from the car as Devon threw it into drive, the tires squealing as she disappeared into the night...

Devon's mind was reeling as she made her way to the scene.

Okay...what in the hell just happened there? Did she say what I think she said...or am I finally losing it? God...McKinney...what the fuck is going on with you? Huh? You agree to meet a total stranger who may be involved in a very high-profile murder case...completely by yourself...and instead of questioning her...you end up taking her out for dinner and drinks! What is up with that?

Before she knew it, she was knocked out of her inner dialogue and back into reality by the site of a myriad of flashing lights...

Man...this is really getting old...

Mike was waiting at the end of the driveway. She parked the car and quickly ran over to her partner.

"Hey…we really need to stop meeting like this…people are going to talk." Mike said, trying to lighten the situation up a bit.

"Yeah…no kidding…so let me guess…another little girl?"

"You guessed…only this time…we're closer, I think…I hope…" Mike said, solemnly.

"So what have we got?"

"Michelle Findlay…Caucasian Female…nine years old. Last time anybody heard from her, she was walking home from the neighbor's house…she never made it. Neighbors said that she left about 7:00pm…nobody has seen her since then."

"What was she doing at the neighbor's? Devon asked, making mental notes to herself.

"Playing with the kids…Josh…who's seven…and Emily…who's nine…she's in Michelle's class at school. Apparently she had been there since a little after noon…the Schmidt's have a pool…the kids spent most of the day swimming…she stayed for supper…was going to walk home afterwards."

Devon looked around…Winchester Rd. was on the very outskirts of the city limits…beyond it was a series of fields, wooded areas, and ponds. If they were going to get Michelle back alive…she knew that they would have to act fast…

"Okay…let's get Jim on the line…I want him over here as soon as possible. Seal off the victim's bedroom so that we can get a clean scent article. With this large of an area…I'm thinking we're going to need more than one dog to cover it quickly…"

"We could get the Fire Department out here…do a foot search." Mike suggested.

Devon shook her head "Uh-uh…we get a bunch of ground-pounders out here and all their going to do is screw it up for the dogs…trust me…this is the fastest way to do this…"

"Okay…you're the dog-woman."

"I'm going to assume you meant that as a compliment…" Devon said, teasing her partner at his choice of words.

"Always…I'll give Jim a call…"

"That's okay…I'll call him…I want to get the Area Search K-9s out here, too." Devon said, grabbing her cell phone out of her pocket and hitting the speed dial number for Jim.

"Area Search?" Mike said, not familiar with the term.

Devon held her hand up, motioning for Mike to wait for a moment.
"Hello Jim? This is Dev…listen…we've got another possible abduction. I'm going to need you and Hoover…and I'd like to get the Area Search Team out here as well. There's a lot of area out here to cover…woods, fields, you name it."

"Damn…okay…I'll be out there shortly…give me an hour to get everybody rounded up. You gonna be joining the team in the field?"

"Yeah…definitely…once I get the command post squared away. Can you do me a favor? Stop by my house…inside the garage, there's a duffle bag marked K-9…grab that and bring it, will you?"

"No problem. I'll see you soon…go ahead and collect the scent article for me…it will cut down on time when we get there. When was the victim seen last?"

"About 19:00. I'll fill you in on the rest when you get here…Thanks, Jim." She said, closing the flip-phone.

"Okay…now what is this Area Search thing?" Mike asked.

"You know how trailing dogs use ground scent to find one particular person? Well…Area Search dogs are trained to use air scent and will find any human scent within an area…could be the person themselves, or it could be an article of clothing or something else with their scent on it." Devon explained.

"Okay...but we're only looking for one person...shouldn't we stick with the trailer?" Mike asked.

"We'll still use Hoover...but we need to cover a lot of area as quick as possible...that's where the Area Search dogs come in. They'll help us eliminate areas where she might be...narrow things down a bit. This kid has probably played all over the place in the neighborhood and the surrounding area...her scent is going to be everywhere. It may take a while for Hoover to sort things out..."

"Got it...okay...but Dev...we don't even know for sure that she was abducted...don't you think you might be going a little bit overboard before we know for sure what's going on?" Mike suggested.

"What?" Devon said, not quite believing what she was hearing.

"Look...all I'm saying is that the boys in accounting are going to be asking us the same thing...I want to be able to give them an answer..."

Devon was immediately infuriated.

"Look...if those bookkeeping bastards have problem with this...they can come and talk to me...better yet—I'll take them to talk to the parents of the kid...see if they can justify putting a price-limit on their little girl's life!"

"Whoa...I'm on your side, remember? I'm just trying to take care of everything so we don't get our butts in the wringer." Mike said, trying to calm his partner down. "So what do you want me to do?"

"Why don't you go ahead and start interviewing the family and the neighbors. I'm going to make sure everything is sealed off, then I'll get the scent article...we're going to need maps of the area...I'll call downtown and see what we can get..."

"What about the media? They're bound to show up...probably sooner rather than later, unfortunately."

She knew Mike was right...the press was ruthless when it came to getting the story that they wanted.

"Let's just make sure they stay outside the scene…we're going to use them to our advantage this time…but I want to make sure we control every bit of information that they are being fed. I'll call the station…get one of our PR guys down here to handle them. I've got a couple other calls to make…I want to get an alert out to all of the local counties…we're going to cast a wide net on this one…hopefully it will pay off…"

CHAPTER 11

▼

One hour later, the quiet community along Winchester Road had been transformed into a paramilitary operation…complete with an Incident Command and Communications Headquarters, mess tent, and a rest and rehabilitation area.

Devon had just finished talking to the PR officer when Jim and the rest of the K-9 Teams arrived.

"Dev! Got your stuff…" Jim said, tossing her the duffle bag.

"Thanks…give me a second to change and I'll be right out to brief you all on what we've got." Devon said, heading off into the R & R tent.

She sat the duffle on one of the cots, unzipping it and removing its contents…a pair of dark navy BDUs, her duty belt and equipment, her K-9 Team ball cap, a pair of thick socks, and her combat boots. She stood for a moment, looking at the items…

Damn…it's been a long time…

She slid out of her jeans and shirt, placing them into the duffle, grabbing the BDU's…

Huh…good thing I've got a belt in here…looks like I've lost a little weight.

Devon straightened the BDUs, tightening her belt to take up the slack. She grabbed the pair of boots, turning them sole side up, running her fingers along the hard bottom.

Damn...gonna have to fix that before we head out...

She reached into the duffle bag, pulling out one last item...her K-bar knife. The knife had been a present to her from her Uncle John. He had served in WWII, and had carried this knife with him throughout his tours of duty. He said that it had gotten him through some pretty rough scrapes...and that it would serve her as well. She always thought of him when she held the knife...he was bigger than life itself. She thought about how ironic it was, that this big bear of a man had made it through battles in Africa and Europe...had been hit with an unexploded tank shell and had survived...only to die many years later on from a post-operative infection.

It just didn't seem fair...but then again, nothing these days did...

She pulled the blade out of the sheath with one hand, picking up her left boot with the other...running the blade along the sole, scoring it deeply with six cuts...three in the foot portion, three in the heel. She did the same to the right boot...finally sliding her feet inside and lacing them up, blousing her BDU trousers over them. She wiped the blade on her pant leg, sliding it back into the sheath, securing it on her duty belt...grabbed her ball cap, and walked out ready to face the troops.

Jim had the rest of the K-9 Team ready as Devon emerged from the tent.

"Wow! I feel like I should be reviewing the ranks here or something!" Devon said with a smirk.

"Just wanted to be ready for you when you came out...so...what's the story?" Jim asked, always being the one to just cut-to-the-chase.

"Okay...we're looking for Michelle Findlay...Caucasian Female...nine years old...Mike's getting us a picture...we'll show it to you as soon as we get it. The PLS (point last seen) was over there..." Devon said, pointing to the house across the road from them "...the neighbor's house...she was going to walk home...she never made it. Neighbors said that she left about 7:00pm…nobody has seen her since then."

Just then, Mike arrived with copies of a recent picture of the girl, handing a copy to each of the members of the team.

"Listen up everybody…this is the most recent picture of Michelle that we have…she's roughly 4 foot tall, dark brown shoulder-length hair, blue eyes, slim build. She likes to be called 'Mickie'…not 'Michelle'. When she left the Schmidt's house, she still had an orange and pink bathing suit on, along with a 'Hello Kitty' beach towel. She's got a half-moon shaped birthmark on her left shoulder. Any questions?" Mike asked, looking at the group.

Devon stepped forward to give them the rest of the information. Captain Winters had just arrived on scene.

"Captain Winters will be the acting Incident Commander…he'll be running the show back here at the Command Center. I'll be taking operations command from the field. We've got a lot of ground to cover…woods, ponds, fields, swamp…you name it…Captain Winters will be assigning each team their sectors. Once you've completed your sectors, report back to base for reassignment. Captain Winters…is there anything you'd like to add?"

Captain Winters stepped forward.

"You'll be physically checking in each time you leave or return to base camp. I'd like you all to keep radio traffic to a minimum…the press is already on site and they have definitely got their ears on. It's gonna be a hot one out there when the sun comes up…make sure you're all drinking enough water. We've got a rehab station back here at the base camp…use it. You're not going to do us or Mickie any good out there if you get yourself sick. That goes for your dogs, too, people. We've got a veterinarian on-call if we need it. Let's hope we don't. Okay people…let's go get her."

All of the teams moved towards the Command Center to check in. Mike walked over to where Devon, Captain Winters, and Jim were now standing.

"Mind if I tag along with one of the teams out there?" Mike asked.

"Sure you want to do that, Mike? You're not exactly dressed for the part..." Devon said, referring to his khaki pants and button-down shirt.

"I've always got a pair of boots in the van...and it's no big deal if these clothes get wrecked..."

"Suit yourself, bud..." Devon said with a smirk. Mike wasn't usually into the whole 'physical' aspect of police work...he usually left that part of it to the younger, more physically fit officers. Devon suspected that this...along with Mike's longing for a 4x4, was all a part of a little mid-life crisis that he was starting to go through...poor guy. It was a phase...he'd get over it sooner or later...

"Okay then...I'll be right back...just going to grab my boots." Mike said with a smile, walking back to the mini-van.

Devon looked at Jim and Captain Winters, grinning like the Chesire cat...

"This is going to be interesting..."

"Ten bucks says he doesn't make it through the first day with us..." Jim said, laughing.

"Twenty says he doesn't make it through the first hour." Captain Winters said, smiling.

"You think?" Devon asked. She knew that Mike would have a problem keeping up...but she thought that he would at least make it through more than one hour.

"Okay...I'll take that bet...he can't be that bad!" Jim said, shaking Winters' hand.

"You forget who's doing the sector assignments...that swamp is going to be really tough to get through...lots of mosquitos...knee deep muck..." Winters said, grinning.

"Damn...think I've been had..." Jim said, chuckling.

Just then, Mike walked up to the group.

"Someone's been had? And I missed it?" Mike said, smiling...not knowing that he was, in fact, the butt of the joke.

"Oh...it's nothing...just a little bet that Winters and I have going..." Jim said, smiling.

Devon looked down at Mike's boots. They looked like they had just been taken out of the box. No scuffs, no creases, nothing...

"Boy...are you sure you want to wear those out in the field? You might get them dirty!" Devon said, razzing Mike.

"Hey now...I'll have you know that I bought these for just this occasion...I just haven't had a chance to break them in yet...that's all." Mike said, defensively.

"Here...put your foot up on here..." Devon said, pointing to a fencepost near them.

"Why?"

"Just do it...we've got to score your boots before you go out in the field." Devon said, pulling her knife from its sheath.

"Whoa! What are you going to do with that?" Mike said, taking a step back.

"I'm going to score your boots..."

"Score my boots?"

"Yes...I'll cut a few notches in the soles so your boot prints are easily identified in the field...that way, they won't be mistaken for a possible suspect..." Devon explained.

"Really? I never would have thought of that...you learn something new everyday, I guess."

"Oh…I'm sure you're going to learn a lot out there today…You're going with Jim and Hoover." Devon said, smiling. She knew what her partner was most likely in for…she had followed the trailing team on many occasions. It was one thing to trail through a residential area, but quite another to do so in a rural setting…

"Sounds good…Jim…what exactly do you need me to do for you in the field?" Mike asked, turning to the handler.

"Just keep your eyes open, stay behind me, and don't get in our way…and if you could map our trail…that would be greatly appreciated." Jim said, matter-of-factly.

"Okay…stay out of the way…I think I can do that." Mike said, smiling.

"Have you two got your ducks in a row yet?" Winters said, looking to Mike and Jim…

"I think we're all set here, thanks." Jim said, wryly.

"Let's get this thing started then…time's wasting." Said Winters, walking toward the Command Center.

Within the next twenty minutes, all of the teams had been assigned a sector and were heading out, with the exception of Jim, Mike, and Hoover…who would be starting at the point last seen and going wherever the trail took them.

Devon and Mitchell, the Area Search Handler that she was going to work with walked past Jim and Mike on their way to get their K-9 out of it's crate.

"Hey…be gentle with him, Jim…it's his 'first time'." Devon said with a wink.

"Well…he'll be losing his cherry on this one, I can promise you that!" Jim said, laughing.

"I wanna hear all about it when you get back!" Devon said, grinning. "Good luck!"

"Thanks...you too." Jim said, turning to Mike. "Come on, 'Cherry'...let's go get Hoover."

"Cherry...geezus..." Mike said, scuffing his boots in the dirt as they walked over to the Suburban to retrieve Hoover the wonder-hound.

Meanwhile, Mitchell and Devon had just let 'Sergeant' or 'Sarge' as he was normally called, out of his crate. Sarge was a beautifully sleek three year-old Belgian Malinois.

"You ever worked with a Malinois before, Dev?" Mitchell asked.

"Only once...when I was back in the academy. We did a little bite-work with one...but no search work."

"Yeah...they are pretty darned good at bite work...kind of like a miniature German Shepherd on methamphetamine!" He said, laughing. "One of my instructors always called them 'Maligators'...cute, huh?"

Devon knelt down, placing her hands on the sides of Sarge's face, ruffing him up. "Ohhhh...is he talking about you, baby?"

Sarge responded by quickly laying a line of Malinois kisses from Devon's chin to her eyebrows.

"I think he's taken a bit of a liking to you!"

"Yeah...I think so!" Devon said, standing back up, patting the dog's head.

"Just let me get his vest on him and we can head out." Mitchell said, reaching into his pack, pulling out an orange K-9 Search Team vest.

Ten minutes later, they were heading out into Sector 4...a heavily wooded area with interspersed patches of swamp. Sarge moved through the thick underbrush at an amazing pace, zigzagging across the area in search of any human scent.

The mosquitoes swarmed on them like a black, blood-sucking cloud.

Devon slapped the back of her neck as one sunk its hypodermic-like mouth into her skin once again.

"Damn! These fucking things are brutal this year!" She said, following the slap with a scratch over the newly formed welt.

"Yeah…that is one thing I always hated about warm-weather searches…can't use the bug dope." Mitchell said, his eyes trained keenly on the beam of his flashlight illuminating Sarge as he made his way through the brush.

"Yeah…remind me when we get out of here to invent a completely scentless bug spray that we can use around these guys that won't interfere with their noses…I could make a million with the southern search teams, alone!" Devon said, ducking under some pucker-brush, the thorns grazing her skin, leaving a small line of red in their wake.

"Wonder how the newbie's doing…" Mitchell said, chuckling.

Meanwhile, Hoover and Jim were working their way through some of the same type of thicket. Mike marveled at the way that Jim negotiated the veritable obstacle course of fallen limbs, pucker-brush, and peat bogs. He seemed to glide effortlessly through the area, his foot never staying in one place for more than a split second while he moved to his next foot hold.

"Geezus…you make it look so easy, Jim!" Mike said, breathlessly, trying to keep up.

"Ah…it's nothing…I'm just the dope on the rope…Hoover here does all of the hard work." Jim said, never skipping a beat.

Mike lifted his feet…imagining them becoming light and sure-footed, like Jim…making his way through the thicket like a rabbit…

I'm doing it! I can do it!

Until his foot caught in a wild grape vine, sending him face first into a puddle of black bog muck.

Jim heard the thud, turning around to find Mike still in the prone position with a layer of foul smelling goo on his face. He knew he shouldn't...but he couldn't stop himself from laughing at the sight...

"I'm sorry...really...I am...are you okay?" he said, trying to stifle his laughter.

"Yeah...I'm fine..." Mike said, wiping some of the sludge from his eyes "...just felt like taking a little nap."

The teams searched throughout the night, with no success. As each team checked back into the Command Center, they were assigned another sector.

It was a muggy summer night...and the rumblings of a summer storm threatened in the distance. Devon and Mitchell were working on a parcel of woods that adjoined a grassland.

"Looks like we might get rained on..." Devon said, looking off to the flashes of lightening in the southwest corner of the sky.

"Yeah...southwest corner, too...not good. You want to start working our way back towards the Command Center?" Mitchell asked.

"Probably wouldn't be a bad idea...but let's hit this last ten acres before we head in. That will pretty much complete our sector." Devon said, pressing her way through another line of vines.

Suddenly, Sarge became more animated, his tail wagging. His movements becoming more urgent...

"Hey...he's got scent." Mitchell said, pointing ahead at the dog who was now wearing a strobed collar. You could see the flashing light moving quickly through the woods ahead of them, back and forth...hitting the edges of the scent cone, working his way back in...trying to pinpoint the source.

Their pace quickened, trying to keep up with Sarge.

Something seemed odd...out of the ordinary. Devon sensed something had changed...there was no sound. The woods, which had previously been alive with the songs of the spring peeper frogs and the crickets and all of the other creatures of the night, now fell silent. The air was thick and still…as if time, itself had stopped…

"Hey Mitchell…do you feel that?" Devon asked, half jogging to keep up with the dog.

"What?"

"There's no sound…no breeze…everything's…dead."

"Man…look at him go! He's really in a big scent pool…there's got to be something out here…" Mitchell said, picking up the pace.

The woods seemed to be opening them up…swallowing them whole. They ran blindly behind Sarge…following the flickering light on his collar like a beacon through the night.

"Geezus…what in the hell is going on? It's like this whole place is one big fucking pool of scent!" Mitchell said, now at a dead run.

Suddenly, something swooped out of the sky, barely missing Devon…as the wind from it's passing nearly took her ball cap off…

"What the hell was that?" Devon yelled, still running as the creature flew across her path once again…

"Looks like an owl…must have gone for the motion…prey drive." Mitchell said, trying to keep an eye on the dog. "Shit! We're losing him!"

Sarge was running full tilt, ducking through what appeared to be a thick row of brush. Mitchell and Devon weren't far behind, getting down on their hands and knees, crawling through the small opening in the bushes. Mitchell made it through first, crawling out of the way, allowing Devon to slide through. They weren't prepared for what awaited them on the other side.

It was as though they had gone from darkness to daylight, as they found themselves on the edge of what appeared to be a rather lush wetland. The whole place seemed to have an odd glow about it.

Sarge stood up to his chest in water, pawing desperately at the vegetation.

"What the heck is this? I don't remember this being on the map..." Mitchell said.

"I don't know...but it looks like he's got something..." Devon said, pointing to the Malinois...whom they could now see quite clearly.

"What'cha got boy?" Mitchell said, moving closer to the area that the dog was pawing at.

Mitchell reached down under the water...feeling his way through the muck...his hands catching on roots and sticks...but nothing else.

"I don't feel anything down here..."

"The storm's moving in...it would be better to check this out at first light...maybe get another team in here..." Devon suggested, hearing the sounds of thunder again in the distance.

"Let's check in with base...see if they've got an idea when this thing's supposed to hit..." Mitchell suggested.

Devon reached over to her shoulder, keying the mic on her radio "Red team to base...Red team to base."

"Base...Go ahead Red Team."

"Do you have an ETA for this storm that's moving in?"

"We're watching it on radar...looks like you've got about 40 minutes tops."

"Copy, thanks. Red team out."

"Copy. Time out zero four twenty-nine."

Devon turned back to Mitchell… "What's say we take one more loop through the woods and head back in before the sky starts falling in on us?"

"Yeah…he's definitely hitting on something in here…but with this being so wet—it could be sucking scent from anywhere around the immediate area…"

"We'll come back in as soon as the sun comes up…I'll mark the area before we go." Devon said, reaching into the side-pocket of her BDU pants and removing a roll of orange flagging tape. She tore off a two-foot section, tying it onto a branch above the area that Sarge had shown interest in.

"All set…let's go."

"Good boy, Sarge…come on…let's go…" Mitchell said, directing the dog back through the thicket with he and Devon close behind.

The dog emerged from the thicket, taking off like a shot through the darkness of the woods. The strobe on his collar once again the only thing making him visible to his two counterparts.

"Damn! He's got scent again!" Mitchell said, scrambling to his feet, Devon right on his heels.

The two took off running, trying to keep up with the dog.

"Geezus…he's…really moving!" Devon said, weaving through the trees.

Without warning, Mitchell fell backwards, almost flying into Devon. She caught him just before he hit the ground in front of her.

"Whoa! Are you okay?" Devon asked, helping him up.

"What in the hell did you do that for?" Mitchell asked, angrily.

"What are you talking about?" Devon asked, not understanding why he would be mad that she broke his fall.

"You pulled me back!" Mitchell said, dusting the dirt off of his trousers.

"Mitch...I don't know what you're talking about. I never touched you!"

"Well somebody did! I felt somebody grab me...I swear!" Mitch said, emphatically.

"Shit...I lost Sarge...do you see him?" Devon said, scanning the darkness, looking for the flash of the strobe.

"God damn it. SARGE! COME!" Mitchell yelled, trying to call the dog back to him. "SARGE! COME!"

Devon reached for her flashlight, pushing the button to turn it on. Nothing happened...

"Shhhh...wait...I hear him." Devon said, hearing the fast beat of Sarge's paws hitting the ground, heading towards the grassland. "He's heading out towards the field. Watch out where you're going, my flashlight isn't working..."

"M'kay." Mitchell said as the two started heading out to the grassland.

Devon felt the air currents change around her just before the owl passed over her once again, circling above her.

"Damn...did you see that?"

"Yeah...that owl has some prey drive!" Mitchell said, continuing to walk towards the clearing.

The first owl was soon joined by a second and a third, as they circled ominously overhead...basically pinning the two team members down.

"What in the hell is going on in here? I've never seen them do something like this before!" Mitchell said, looking at the huge birds circling just above their heads.

Suddenly, the woods came alive with sound…crickets, frogs, and the other various creatures of the night raising their voices…creating a deafening roar…

Through the wall of sound, Devon heard a woman's voice…or was it in her head?

You can't just look…you have to see…

Devon brought her hands to her ears in attempt to drown out some of the noise…but to no avail.

You have to see!

"There's something here…" Devon said, thinking out loud.

The owls continued their flight path, creating a whirling breeze about their heads…

I don't know what you want me to see! I can't see anything! Are you here? Give me a sign…show me!

Out of nowhere, a flash of light zipped past Devon on her left. It happened so quickly, she wasn't sure if she had seen it at all…but perhaps it was, in fact, the sign that she had asked for…she closed her eyes tightly…screaming to the powers-that-be in her head…

I'll come back! I promise! I'll come back!

One by one, the owls disappeared into the night…and the woods became quiet once again…

Devon and Mitchell continued their trek out of the woods, neither of them saying a word.

They reached the edge of the grassland only to find Sarge lying prone in the weeds, panting nervously, waiting for them.

Mitchell walked over to the K-9, took the canteen from his side, pouring some water into his hand for his partner.

"You okay, boy?" he said, looking the dog over. It was obvious that the dog was under great stress…as he continued to pant excessively, his body shaking beneath him.

"Have you ever seen anything like that?" Devon asked, quite sure that he hadn't.

"No…never…but it had to be the storm moving in or something. That'll make animals act weird sometimes." He explained, petting Sarge, calming both the dog and himself.

"Yeah…you're probably right…it was the storm…" Devon said, her eyes scanning the tree line, coming to rest on an all too familiar silhouette in canopy…

CHAPTER   12

▼

Devon, Mitchell, and Sarge made their way back to the pick-up truck parked on the edge of their sector.

"Come on boy…go to jail!" Mitchell said, as Sarge hopped up onto the tailgate and into the dog crate in the back end.

"Go to jail?" Devon said, chuckling as she took her pack off, tossing it in the back of the truck.

"Yeah…seemed appropriate at the time…" Mitchell said, tossing his gear in the back and removing his canteen, giving Sarge another drink of water.

The lightening was becoming more frequent as raindrops started to fall randomly onto the hood of the truck…the wind picked up, making the trees sway in silent ballet.

"Looks like the storm's just about here…we should probably head back to the Command Center and wait it out there." Devon said.

"Yeah…probably wouldn't be a bad idea…" Mitchell said, slamming the tailgate shut, followed by the capper.

Devon slid into the passenger side seat. It felt good to sit down. She hadn't realized how tired she actually was. She wanted to talk about what had happened in the woods just then…she suspected Mitchell did, too. But neither of them uttered a word the entire way.

The rest of the teams had arrived ahead of them.

"Looks like we're going to be last in line for the food…" Mitchell said, hesitantly breaking the silence that had plagued them on the drive back to the base.

"Yeah…you go ahead…I'll be there in a few minutes…I've gotta make a call." Devon said, reaching into her pocket for her cell phone.

She looked at her watch…

5:45 am…I'm probably going to wake her up…but hell…I should make sure she got home alright, shouldn't I? I mean…we did have a few drinks and all…Besides…I need to get a hold of her and set up a time so we can finish our discussion…

Devon scrolled down the memory on her cell phone, finding Brid's number. Hesitating momentarily…

BEEP! BEEP! BEEP! BEEP!
The sudden noise made Devon jump, as she reached down into the side pocket on her BDU trousers, pulling out her pager.

Geezus! Talk about giving somebody a heart-attack! Who in the heck would be paging me at this hour?

She pressed the message button on the pager…the number looked familiar, but she couldn't quite place it. She dialed the number, waiting for it to ring.

A female voice answered before the phone even rang.

"Hello?"

"Yes. This is Detective McKinney returning a page."

"Devon…it's Brid…are you okay?"

"Um…yeah…fine! Is everything alright…I mean…why did you page me?"

"Okay…not exactly the reaction I was looking for…"

"Sorry…I didn't mean that…I was just surprised that you paged me this early…it is early, you know." Devon said, backpedaling.

"I didn't wake you up, did I?"

"No…nothing like that…actually, I've been up all night…out with the K-9 Unit."

"Any luck?"

"No…not really."

"Are you sure you're okay?"

"Yeah…pretty much…why?" Said Devon. Trying to her best to sound nonchalant.

"Did something happen tonight?"

"When?"

"When you were out with the K-9 Unit."

"I don't know…" Devon said, not really wanting to talk about what had happened in the woods. She was still trying to sort out exactly what had taken place…trying to rationalize it. Most things in this life can be explained scientifically…at least that's what she had always believed…but this…this was different. *"You don't know…or you don't want to talk about it?"*

"It was just a weird night…I don't know…"

"You saw something, didn't you?"

Devon paused, unsure of what to say. How was it that this woman that she barely knew could be reading her like an open book? It didn't make sense...but then again, what did these days?

"...it was probably nothing."

"If you're still thinking about it...it's obviously something..."

"You still didn't tell me why you paged me." Devon said, trying to change the subject.

"Changing the subject won't make whatever you saw go away..."

"Now who's changing the subject?"

"Touche'...okay...what would you say if I said I think I had another dream about this case?"

"Okay...I'm listening..."

"I saw you...running through the woods...like you were chasing after something...but I couldn't see what...and whatever it was, it was always just out of reach..."

"Okay...now you're freaking me out..."

"Why? What happened?"

"It's a long story...lets just say that I spent the majority of the last couple of hours in my own little episode of the Twilight Zone."

"What do you mean? Are you okay?"

"Yeah...I'm fine...no biggie, really...it was just kind of...well...odd, for lack of a better term."

Static filled the phone lines as the approaching storm intensified. Each time the lightening would strike, the connection would momentarily be broken.

"Listen...this storm is getting pretty bad...I should probably let you go..." Devon said, looking out at the now horizontal rain bands running across the window of the pickup truck.

"Devon? Can you hear me? They're more than dreams..."

Brid's words were interrupted by a particularly close bolt of lightning, causing a prolonged bout of static on the line.

"Don't...look...you have to see! They're trying...tell you..."

"Brid? Are you there?"

No answer. The signal was gone. Devon moved the phone around, watching the signal strength bars on the LCD display...but to no avail. The storm had knocked out the tower. Devon sat there in the seat...contemplating the discussion that had just taken place.

God, McKinney! What in the hell was that?! You're talking to a possible witness...hell...a possible <u>suspect</u> in multiple homicides like an old friend or something! Better yet...you're actually contemplating believing her psychic-bullshit! Everything she was saying was general...like she had a dream about you running through the woods...but whatever you were running after was out of reach...Come on!

But she didn't know I was out in the woods...she didn't know where I was...My head is telling me not to listen to her...but my gut is telling me to listen...

Devon's inner dialogue was interrupted by her stomach growling...loudly.

Okay...I get the message...damn...hope there's something left...

Devon waited for a brief lull in the storm before opening the door of the truck and sprinting into the tent. Inside, the rest of the teams were sitting at tables, stuffing their faces with the pizza that had been provided by one of the local pizzerias. Devon walked over to the stacks of white boxes sitting on the end of the table, opening the top one and taking two pieces.

"Hey Dev…there's pop, water, and Gatorade iced down in the cooler over there…help yourself." Jim said, pointing to the corner of the tent.

"Got it…thanks." She said, making her way to the cooler. Sifting through the half-melted ice, she first reached for the diet cola…but left it in favor of the lemon-lime sports drink. Her drink and food in hand, she walked over to the table, taking a seat next to Jim.

"Nice of you to join us!" Jim said, sarcastically slapping her on the back.

"Yeah…I thought it was about time to grace you all with my presence." Devon said with a smirk. She looked over at her partner, Mike…who was slumped in the folding chair across from her. His clothes torn and stained with the telltale signs of black bog muck, his boots off, and his sweat and muck soaked feet propped on the chair next to him. It was obvious that Jim and Hoover had definitely made him 'earn' his first search…
"Mikey, Mikey…how's it feel? You're not a search-virgin anymore!" She said, grinning as she took her first bite of pizza.

"Gee…let me see…I have thorns embedded throughout my body…the mosquitoes have damned near drained every drop of blood out of me…I'm covered in Hoover—slobber…I've fallen down so many times that even my bruises have bruises…I'm wet…I'm tired…and…worst of all…I smell." He said, glaring at his partner.

Devon chuckled, looking to Jim "So…was it as good for you as it was for him?"

"You know…I've gotta say…me and Hoover have definitely 'de-flowered' our share of cherries…but I don't think I've ever enjoyed one quite as much as I did our Mikey, here!" Jim said, as the entire table, minus Mike, erupted in laughter.

"Ha. Ha. Ha. Thanks a lot, guys…glad I could provide your source of amusement for the night." Mike said, gathering up his things and walking away from the table.

"Awww…come on, Mikey…they were just kidding!" Devon said, trying to smooth his ruffled feathers a bit.

"Yeah…come on, Mikey! It always hurts the first time…the second time is always better…I promise!" Jim said, laughing.

Mike never said a word…he let his finger do the talking as he flashed them all the 'one-finger-wave'as he disappeared out into the rain.

"Boy…he's really pissed off, isn't he?" Jim said, trying to show some concern for his fellow officer.

"He'll get over it…he's just not used to hanging with the big dogs…that's all." Devon said, cracking the seal on her Gatorade.

Her eyes were drawn to the door of the tent as a figure appeared, dressed in yellow rain gear, carrying in boxes of doughnuts and pastries. The person sat them down on the table, pulling down the hood on their jacket.

"Hey Patrick! Come on over!" Jim yelled, motioning for the young man to join them at the table. "Dev…you remember Patrick Donnelly…don't you?"

The young man walked over to the table, smiling proudly at the thought of being invited to sit with the team.

Devon nodded, pizza still in hand. "Yep…Chief's son, right? I met your brother the other day, too."

"Oh really?" Patrick said, pulling out the chair where Mike had been sitting. "Where was that?"

"Over at the M.E.'s office…So what are you doing here?" Devon asked, as most of the regular uniformed officers had left the scene…allowing the search teams to take over.

"Actually…I'm on my days off…thought I'd stop by and help out a bit…you know…bring some food in…do the running for them…whatever needs to be done."

Devon smiled…it was something that she would have gladly done as a rookie on the beat. It was nice to see another person willing to give to her fellow officers without the promise of receiving anything in return.

"Ahhh…another rookie bucking for brownie points!" Jim said, teasingly. "Before you know it, we're going to have another 'McKinney' on our hands! What is it with you mics?"

"Hey now! The name is Scottish, I'll have you know!" Devon said, smiling.

"If I can do half as well as Detective McKinney, here…I'll be ecstatic!" Patrick said, raising his can of pop to Devon and nodding in respect.

Jim pushed his chair back, raising his feet a good three feet off the ground "Oh man! Save my boots! It's getting deep in here!" He said, laughing.

"Jealous?" Devon said with a smirk.

"HA! You wish! I think you've got yourself a badge buddy, Dev…" Jim retorted.

The smile on Patrick's face was replaced with one of embarrassment as the young man quietly got up and excused himself from the table…

"Way to go, guys! The kid is just starting out and already you've got him running away!" Devon said, getting up from the table and walking over to her young admirer.

"Hey…look…they wouldn't be razzing you if they didn't like you." Devon said, trying to offer the rookie a bit of comfort.

"I know…it's no biggie…I need to get out of here anyhow…" He said, flashing Devon an appreciative smile.

"Hey…hold on a second, will you?" Devon said, walking back to the table.

"Yeah…sure…" Patrick said, standing near the opening of the tent. The rain was still coming down in sheets.

"Hey...can you guys have one of the uniforms take that unmarked back to the station for me? I'm going to see if I can hitch a ride home and get some dry clothes while we're holed up for the weather..."

"Sure thing, Dev...when are you coming back?" Jim said.

"I'm just going to take a shower and grab some clothes, then I'll be right back..."

"What...don't like the wet and muddy look? It's all the rage this year!" Jim said, eliciting a laugh from everyone at the table.

"Nah...although it may be an improvement for you...I think I'll take the less popular clean, dry look..." Devon said, wryly...walking back to Patrick. "Hey kiddo...mind if I hitch a ride with you?"

"Um...no...I mean sure...if you want to...I'll go pull my truck up..." Patrick said, rushing out into the rain.

Devon followed the young man as he ran towards a blue Dodge Dakota 4x4. He reached in the bed of the pickup, taking out a folded tarp and starting to spread it over some garbage bags in the back end.

"Hey! Let me help you with that!" Devon said, running up to the truck and helping him with the tarp.

"Yeah...thanks...I've got the garbage from the mess tent in here...don't want it to fly out while we're driving...you know?" He said, pulling his end of the tarpaulin to the end of the truck.

"Do you have some twine or something to tie this down with?" Devon asked, squinting as the raindrops flooded her eyes.

"Bungees...just a sec..." he said, opening the driver's side door and reaching behind the seat, grabbing a handful of the cords, tossing half of them to Devon.

The two worked their way around, securing the tarp to the frame of the truck before jumping into the cab, soaked to the bone.

"Man! It's not letting up out there!" Devon said, wiping the rainwater from her face.

"Nope...supposed to clear up by late morning, though...so you guys should be able to get back out there..." Patrick said, turning on the windshield wipers before pulling away from the make-shift parking area.

"I hope so...we've still got a lot of ground to cover...and there's a couple of places I want to get a double-check team into..." Devon said, taking her ball cap off and running her fingers through her hair, separating the wet locks.
"So what areas have you guys covered already? Were you able to get much done?" Patrick asked, keeping his eyes on the road.

"We got a lot of sectors one through four done...which basically covered the woods closest to the two houses...but there's a lot more out there to cover. We've got a few ponds we're going to have to check out, too..." Devon explained.

"Oh yeah? The dogs can do that, too, huh? Find bodies in the water and all...because you know...they always say that the water throws the scent off..."

"Actually...that's the way that they show it on TV and in the movies...but it's actually quite the opposite...moisture holds scent."

"Okay...it holds the scent...but if the body is under twenty feet of water...how is the scent even going to get out?" He asked.

"Well...how do I want to explain this...when the body goes down into the water, depending on the temperature, it may sink...or it may float. Up here in Michigan, our lakes and rivers are pretty cold...so most of the time, the bodies sink..." Devon explained.

"So that's why they say that Lake Superior never gives up its dead..."

"Right. Lake Superior is really cold...usually not much above freezing...so the bodies sink right away...it slows down or prevents decomposition, too. You see...when the body starts to decompose, bacteria and gasses build up inside of it and are released in small amounts into the water...the dogs can smell this...along with another waxy-type substance on the body called adipocere. Using triangulation with the dogs, we can usually narrow down the area for the divers a bit…kind of streamlines the process a bit." Devon explained…even works on ice." Devon said, matter-of-factly.

"Seriously?" Patrick said, surprised.

"Yep…all you have to do is drill holes in the ice for the scent to rise…it's pretty amazing."

"Yeah…I never would have guessed…so you said you were going to have to double-check some areas that you already searched?"

"Yeah…it's pretty thick out there…just want to make sure we've got everything covered. I'm comfortable with saying sector one and two are clear…but the rest of them are really thick…best to have more than one team check it." Devon said. "Oh hey, turn here…sorry about that…I was so busy talking, I didn't bother to tell you where you needed to go…"

"No problem…actually, you don't live too far from my dad's place…I mean…he pointed it out to me once when we were driving out here."
"Yeah…that's true…the Chief's house is only about two or three miles from here…through the section, right?" Devon asked.

"It's over on Hunter's Ridge…"

"Oh yeah…I've seen that…it's really beautiful. Are you staying with him?" she asked.

"For right now…yes. Both my brother and I are. I've got an apartment lined up though…I'll be moving in next week."

"That's great…hey…you might want to slow down…my driveway is right up there, on the left…"

"Got it…" He said, turning in, following the rather long driveway back to the house.

"Thanks for the ride, kiddo…" Devon said, opening the door of the truck "…and don't let those guys get to you…like I said, they wouldn't be giving you the time of day if they didn't think you had potential."

"Thanks…" Patrick said, smiling.

Devon closed the door with a thud, running through the puddles leading up to her front porch…she reached down into her pocket, pulling out her keys, and turned to wave to the young man…but she was too late. He was just turning back onto the road…disappearing into the storm.

CHAPTER 13

▼

Devon barely made it inside the door before she kicked off her boots and started to peel off her wet, muddy clothing.

God…I should have done this in the garage…oh well, too late now!

As she dropped her trousers to the floor, her pager fell out of her pocket.

Probably should call her back…the phone call did end rather abruptly…Okay…I'm standing here basically naked…she can wait until I get out of the shower…

She continued removing the rest of her clothing, picking up the pile and walking to the laundry room, dumping it on top of the washer…continuing her trek to the shower.

Sliding back the glass, she reached in, turning on the water…adjusting the temperature before climbing in. Her skin already pruned from the constant dampness of her discarded clothing. She stepped into the shower, letting out a sigh as the droplets pounded her tired muscles…

Damn…that feels good…

She stood there, her hand planted firmly on the front wall, delighting in the feel of the warm water running down the curves of her body…

Okay…that's enough, McKinney…stay in here any longer and you won't be able to drag your butt back out to the field…

Five minutes later, Devon stepped out of the shower…only to discover that she had not taken a clean towel in with her. She walked out into the bedroom, still dripping, in search of something to dry off with…

Okay…think…towel would be nice…aha! Gotcha!

She bent down, grabbing the towel from the basket of laundry…drying herself off as she rummaged through the rest of her clothing, trying to find another pair of BDUs to wear out in the field.

Pulling on the clean trousers and a t-shirt, she headed back into the living room, dry socks in hand, sitting down on the couch. She reached over, grabbing her damp boots.

Ugh…wet leather…kind of defeats the purpose of dry socks! Oh well…

The pager was still sitting on the floor.

Okay…okay…I get the hint.

Devon reached over to the end table, grabbing the cordless phone off its base. She leaned down, picking up the pager and pressing the recall button…finding Brid's number, she dialed the phone.

"Hi…sorry I can't come to the phone right now. Please leave a message and I will get back to you as soon as possible…"

"Hi…this is Dev…um…Just thought I'd give you a call back…the storm…"

Suddenly, there was a clicking noise at the end of the line, followed by a familiar voice…

"Hey…I'm here! Hold on a sec…let me turn the machine off…"

"Okay…"

"Sorry about that…I was in the shower…"

"Oh…um…sorry…I can call you later…" Devon said, not exactly sure why she was stumbling over her words…

"No…it's fine! Really!"

"Hey…I just wanted to let you know that…earlier…I didn't hang up on you or anything…the storm cut off my cell-phone signal…"

"I kind of figured that…and…actually…I'm glad you called."

"Really?"

"Look…I'm sorry if I was pressing you earlier about what you saw out there. I know that it's police business…and I never should have…"

"Yeah…it is…but…No! I didn't mean…I really kind of did want to talk to you…"

Holy shit! What am I saying???

"…I mean…I need to get the rest of that information from you regarding the case."

"…and that's the only reason you called?"

"Well…like I said…I didn't want you to think I hung up on you."

"I didn't…"

"Good…look…as soon as I get things wrapped up with this search, we should really get together again…to talk…about the information…because it's not really something that we should discuss over the phone."

"True…well…just let me know, and we'll work out something when you're free…"

"That sounds good…um…look, I really should get back to the scene…looks like the weather might break soon."

"I have to go, too…I've got an eight o'clock class to teach at the university…"

"Okay…well, I'll call you then…"

"Hey, Dev?"

"Yeah?"

"You know…if you do want to talk or something…you can call…I mean…it doesn't have to be 'business'."

"Um…okay…thanks…I'll keep that in mind."

"I'll talk to you later then…"

"Sounds good…bye."

"Wait! Be careful…okay?"

"Always." Devon said, pressing the END button.

Okay…what in the hell was that all about? Why do I get the distinct impression that this is going to get complicated?

Devon sat there a moment before replacing the handset on its base. She grabbed her boots, slid them on…and headed back out the door to return to the search…

Half way to the scene, the rain finally stopped and the sun peeked out from behind the black storm clouds, slowly turning the rain-soaked woods into a natural sauna…

The teams were just getting ready to head back out as Devon pulled up.

"Hey Dev! Just in time!" Mitchell said, smiling as Devon climbed out of the SUV.

"Weren't going to leave without me now, were you?" Devon said with a smirk, walking over to Mitchell's truck, looking in the back to make sure her pack was intact.

"Nah…can't leave without my scout! Better stock up on the water…it's gonna be a hot one out there today."

"Yeah…it's starting to feel like a steam bath already…I'm going to go fill my canteens…I'll be back in a second." Devon said, grabbing the containers from her pack and walking towards the Command Center.

Captain Winters was standing amongst a series of maps and charts, carefully marking which areas had been covered and which had not.

"Hey Cap…how are we coming along?" Devon asked, glancing at the map.

"Nothing yet…we've covered a lot of ground, though. Even with the storm holding us up." He said, pleased with how the teams were holding up. This wasn't an easy search by anyone's standards.

"What kind of percentages did the handlers give on probability of detection?"

"Most of them gave me ninety percent or better…but there's a couple of places that we're definitely going to have to cover again…it's just too damned thick out there." He said, looking rather pensive.

"Well…I hate to say it, Cap…but with this heat…if there's a body out here…they way the temperature is rising…we won't need a dog to find it." Devon said, referring not only to the telltale odor of a bloating corpse…but also to the insect activity that would undoubtedly be taking place.

"You're thinking this is going to be a recovery operation." Winters said, dryly.

"Look…we both know that the odds are not in our favor here…She's been gone over what…eight hours now? You know with these cases, whatever is going to happen, usually does in the first couple of hours. Our chances of getting her alive after that decrease significantly…" Devon said, trying to be realistic.

She wished that the girl was alive…she prayed for it to be so…but the simple fact was that her gut was telling her differently. This was not going to end gracefully…it was going to be ugly…just like the others had been. The only difference is for whatever reason…whoever was doing this was going to drag it out this time…

"Well…let's just get out there and get the job done…and hope for the best." Winters said, trying to convince himself as much as Devon.

Devon nodded, walking over to the coolers of water, filling her canteens then walking back out of the tent.

One of the handlers, David, had his Black Lab just outside the tent. Devon turned to see Michelle Findlay's parents standing nearby. She paused briefly, not wanting to interrupt.

Mrs. Findlay knelt down on her knees, cupping the dogs face in her hands…leaning over and placing a kiss on the K-9's muzzle…

"Please find my baby…please?" She said, tears starting to flow down her cheeks. Her husband helped her up…guiding her away from the team, sobbing…

Devon walked over to David after the couple had gotten out of earshot.

"Hey…you okay?" Devon asked the handler. She knew how stressful situations like this could be.

"Yeah…we're fine…just feel bad, that's all. You know how it goes…" David said, scratching his partner, Tracker, behind the ears. "Some friggin' psychic told them it would be a black dog that found her…can you believe that?"

"Yeah…I can believe it. It's about the time when they start coming out of the woodwork. Just do your best, David…that's all anybody can ask. Remember, we're not part of the problem, we're part of the solution." Devon said, placing her hand on David's shoulder…giving him a comforting pat before continuing to Mitchell's truck.

"You ready to hit it?" Mitchell asked.

"Let's do it…" Devon said, climbing into the passenger side of the truck.

Ten minutes later, they were standing on the edge of a rather large parcel of woods.

"So David and Tracker covered this one yesterday?" Mitchell asked.

"Yeah…they said it's really thick in there…lots of pucker brush and swampy areas." Devon explained, securing her pack as Mitchell opened the tailgate of the truck, reaching in to open Sarge's crate.

The malinois came bounding out, bouncing with energy, even as he was given his command signal to sit.

"Looks like Sarge is ready and rarin' to go!" Devon said with a smirk, watching the dog silently obey the sit command, even though his entire body was shaking with anticipation.

"Yeah…probably more than me…" Mitchell said, reaching into the back end of the pickup for his gear.

Devon could feel the young man's apprehension…and she understood it completely. What they had experienced in the woods in those early morning hours was nothing if not intense.

"Look…about what happened…I know it was really…well…let's just say I've never experienced anything like it before…" Devon said, trying to find some way to lend a bit of comfort to the situation.

"Neither have I…and I've mulled it around in my head for several hours now…trying to come up with some logical explanation for what happened…and I can't."

"So what do you want to do about it?" Devon asked, knowing what her answer would be.

"I say after we clear this area, we go get a better look at that place in the daylight." Mitchell said, looking to Devon for her approval.

"Sounds like a plan to me…let's get this thing taken care of then." Devon said, looking towards their sector.

Mitchell secured the orange search vest on Sarge, leading him to the edge of the woods.

"What kind of wind have we got here?" Mitchell said, looking to Devon.

Devon looked up at the trees…there wasn't much movement. Everything seemed still.

"Boy…doesn't look like we've got much of anything…but I'm thinking it's still out of the Southwest from the looks of it."

"Southwest…looks about right to me…let's work it into the wind." Mitchell said as they began their trek around the perimeter of the woods.

Three hours later, the team emerged near the truck, tired and empty-handed.

"Well…I think I can say, without a doubt, that she is most definitely NOT in that section of woods." Devon said, examining the welts and scratches that now covered her forearms and face.

"I'll second that." Mitchell said, bending down to examine Sarge for injuries.

"You okay, boy?"

Sarge was panting hard. The K-9 had worked through the rough terrain like a trooper, barely pausing long enough for a well-deserved drink of cool water.

"I don't know if he's going to last another sector, Dev…I think we'd better put him up for a while." Mitchell said, finishing his examination.
"Yeah…he's looking pretty rough. Let's put him up and get back to base…see how the other teams have done."

"Sounds good…" Mitchell said, reaching in and opening the crate door.

"Come on Sarge…let's go to jail!" He said, tapping the tailgate with his hand. Sarge obediently hopped up and entered the crate, circling twice before finally laying down. "Good boy…" Mitchell said, closing the crate door and the tailgate. Leaving the back of the hatch open to allow more air to circulate.

Devon unbuckled her pack belt, swinging it into the back end of the truck, walking over to the passenger side, opening the door and climbing in.

"Man…it's hotter than Hades out there…let me crank the air…" Mitchell said, reaching down to the control panel.

"Hold on…let's keep the windows down and cruise around…see if we notice anything…" Devon suggested.

"You mean see if we can smell it, don't you?" Mitchell said, looking over to Devon.

"I'm just saying that if we have the windows up, we might miss something…could be something like her yelling…" Devon said, trying to remain optimistic for her partner's sake.

"You don't really believe that now, do you Dev?"

"We need to keep our options open, Mitch…I'm not ruling anything out at this point."

They continued the drive back to the Command Center, each sitting in silence, trying to heighten their senses to pick up on any possible oddities that they may notice.

Just as they were about to cross a small bridge that ran over a creek, the pungent odor of decay stung Devon's nose…

"Hold up for a minute!" Devon said, holding her hand across Mitchell's chest.

He immediately brought the truck to a stop.

"Back up a little…I just smelled something."

Mitchell threw the truck into reverse, creeping backwards slowly.

"Okay…stop right here." Devon said, hopping out of the truck before it came to a complete stop.
Devon walked over to the edge of the ditch, hastily sliding down the steep embankment to the creek below…following the all-too-familiar smell of decomposition that was growing stronger with every step. She walked near the creek bed, following the water upstream. She noticed an oily slick clinging to the surface of the water near a bend.

An annoying buzzing and chewing sound filled the air…it was one that Devon knew well…the sound of yellow jackets feeding on flesh. When she turned the corner, she saw the source of the activity…the large bloated carcass of a white-tailed deer laid stranded in the shallows.

Devon let out a sigh of relief…or was it disappointment? After all…she knew that the odds were stacked against them…and the sooner that they could find the girl, the sooner that her family could have closure.

Mitchell came walking along the banks, yelling down to Devon "Dev? You got something?"

"Dead deer…" Devon said, her back still to her partner.

"What?"

She turned around, facing him as he walked up. "I said, dead deer…"

"Ahhh…okay. Back to base, then?"

"Yeah…let's go." Devon said, walking quietly back to the truck.

The rest of the short drive was uneventful. They arrived back at the Command Center and checked in with Captain Winters, who was sitting busy pacing in front of a blown up map of the search areas.

"Hey Cap..." Devon said, approaching the table.

"Devon...Mitchell...how'd you guys do out there? Anything?"

"Nothing...but I can tell you this...if she or anybody else was out there, we would have found her. We covered everything..." Mitchell said.

Captain Winters looked to Devon, who seemed off in thought, "Devon...what about you?"

"What?" Devon said, snapping out of her thought-induced daze.

"What do you think the probability of detection would be for your sector today?"

"I think we covered everything...I'd give it a hundred percent at this point." Devon said, her mind fuzzy from a combination of lack of sleep and the scorching heat.

"Hey...you look like you need to cool off for a while, Dev...get some rest. Why don't you hit the rack for a few?" Winters suggested.

"I'm fine, Cap...really. I just want to double check that last sector that we covered before the storms set in..."

"Dev...I think Sarge has had it for a while...he needs a few hours up before we hit the field again." Mitchell said, knowing that the K-9 would not be effective in his current state of exhaustion.

"Okay...well...we can still go walk the area, Mitch..." Devon suggested, looking to her partner, hoping that he sensed the urgency in her voice.

"Sure...let me get Sarge into the shade and we'll go check it out." Mitchell said heading back out to the truck.

"You wanna let me in on what's so important about that sector?" Winters said, looking to Devon.

"I don't know, Cap…it just had a weird feel to it, that's all…" Devon said, hoping that this would be sufficient enough an answer that Winters would not pry further.

"Well…don't stay out there too long, Dev. I don't need my Ops Leader getting heat stroke out there…"

"I won't…we're just going to take a quick look around, that's all…then I'll come back and hit the rack for a while…promise." Devon said, smiling as she disappeared through the flap of the tent…

CHAPTER 14

▼

Devon and Mitchell stood in the grassland bordering the woods that they had searched just before the storm earlier that morning.

"Man…looking at it like this…in the daylight…I could have sworn it was bigger!" Mitchell said.

"That's what all you guys say!" Devon said, snickering.

"Ha. Ha." He said, dryly.

"Yeah…you're right though…it sure did seem bigger when we were running through it last night." Devon said, all kidding aside.

"That's for damned sure…I didn't think we'd ever get to the edge of it."

"Well…let's go take a look…" Devon said, walking into the woods.

The woods <u>was</u> different. Gone was the odd silence. Its canopy was filled with the sounds of life itself.

"This is a damned site different that it was in the dark."

"Yeah…no owls dive-bombing us, for one…" Mitchell said, following behind Devon as she walked through the trees.

"Good point...but do you feel it? It just feels different...and where's that hedge row that separated the woods from that weird wetland that we came up into?" Devon said, scanning the area for any signs of it.

"I don't know...wasn't that further to the West?" Mitchell asked, looking down at his compass.

"Yeah...maybe..." Devon said, turning and continuing her trek in a Westward fashion.

They continued walking for several hundreds of yards, finally coming to a thick line of brush and heavy undergrowth.

"This looks like our hedge row...now all we have to do is find that spot where we could get through..." Mitchell said, looking down for some sort of an opening...finally finding one large enough for them both to fit through.

"Find it?" Devon asked, seeing Mitchell drop to his hands and knees and crawling through.
"Yep...this is it...come on through." He said from the other side.

Devon dropped to her hands and knees, crawling through the small opening, coming up in a rather normal-looking swampy wetland. Mitchell reached down, helping Devon to her feet as they both looked around at the area.

Finally...Devon was the one to break the silence...

"Okay...it's official..."

"It's official there's nothing here?" Mitchell asked.

"No...it's official we're both crazy." Devon said, not believing that this place could be so drastically different than it had been only a few hours earlier.

"Hell...I don't think we're crazy, I just think we're overly tired...and a storm was moving in...and we're under a lot of pressure...and..."

"...we're mental." Devon said, partially joking, partially not.

Mitchell chuckled "Come on...let's go catch a few hours rest before we head out again."

"Yeah...guess it couldn't hurt." Devon said, kneeling down and crawling through the opening once more.

Thirty minutes later, they were back at the base camp. Mitchell had gone off to take care of Sarge while Devon made her way to the R & R tent for some much needed and deserved sleep.

Devon pushed the flap on the tent aside, happily finding that she had the place to herself. She closed the flap, walking over to the cot on the far side, nearest the window...sitting down for the first time since she had eaten hours earlier. She bent down, untying her burr-covered laces, extracting her feet from the damp leather boots. She laid back, resting her head on the pillow...not realizing how truly exhausted she really was.

It was only a matter of seconds before she drifted off into a deep, but restless sleep...

FLASH

Everything was moving in slow motion...

Devon sat up, swinging her legs over the edge of the cot. She stood up, walking towards the door of the tent...but instead of leading to the outdoors, it opened into the Command Center...

The tent is crowded...and Devon weaves her way through the people...Captain Winters...Mike...Mitchell...Patrick...and the other members of the team...making her way to the door...trying to find her way outside...

She finally reaches the flap leading outside...pushing it back and stepping out, she looks down at her own boot-clad feet...it is dark now...

"I couldn't have slept that long..."

Her eyes look towards the tree line that is now illuminated only by the full moonlight...perched on the branch of a large oak...stands the ever present owl...watching...

Suddenly, it spreads its wings, flying off into the night...

"Dev? Devon...wake up!" Mike said, laying his hand on her shoulder, only to be met with a swift hand reaching up and grabbing him by the shirt...holding him firmly while readying her other hand to strike out...

"Whoa! Dev! It's me...Mike!"

"Damnit, Mike...you know better!" Devon said, angrily...sitting bolt upright.

"Sorry, Dev...I didn't mean to startle you...Geezus, you're jumpy!"

"What are you doing here?" Devon asked, somewhat annoyed.

"Dev...they found the body."

Devon's face changed from one of anger to one of disappointment.

"Shit...when?"

"About twenty minutes ago. We got a positive ID from the father..."

"Goddamn it...where?" Devon said, sliding her feet into her boots.

"The sector that you and Mitchell covered right before the storm hit."

Devon stood up, meeting Mike eye-to-eye.

"There is no fucking way, Mike! We just walked that place again before I came in here for a break! She was not there!"

"Dev...there's more...your boot print was underneath the body."

"No...get out of my way!" Devon said, pushing past Mike and rushing through the doorway of the tent...barking orders the minute she hit the grounds...

"I want this place sealed off...NOW! Nobody leaves!" Devon said, running towards the Command Center. Captain Winters was standing inside with a couple of the K-9 teams.

"Cap...we gotta seal this place off, now!"

"Whoa, Dev...slow down! What are you talking about?" Winters asked.

"The son-of-a-bitch was here! He was here!" Devon said, acting like a caged animal...the rage inside her building with each passing second.

"Are you sure?"

Devon didn't answer; she just looked at him with a knowing glare.

"Get this place sealed off...now! I want road blocks up for a 5 mile radius and a list of everyone that has been in and out of this camp since the start of the search." Winters said to one of the Logistics people. "And I mean NOW!" Winters said, grabbing his cell phone, dialing central dispatch.

"9-1-1."

"This is Captain Winters...I need reinforcements immediately at the Winchester Street Command Center...I'm also going to need road blocks at Miller, North Eva, and Steel Roads...and get that entrance to the highway blocked as well."

"Okay...standby sir... 'Station One to all available units...report to the Winchester Street Command Center for immediate assignment.' Alright sir...they are en route...we'll get those areas blocked off for you."

Devon ran back outside...directing the troops on what needed to be done next. Patrick Donnelly ran up to her...stopping to catch his breath.

"Detective McKinney...I just heard...is there anything I can do to help?"

"Yeah...I want you to go door to door...get these people over here...I want all of them printed...and tell them not to leave the area until further notice."

"Right...I'm on it!" Said the young man, running off to the first house.

Devon's train of thought was interrupted by the sudden vibrating and ringing of her cell phone. She reached into her pocket, hitting SEND.

"Detective McKinney."

"Devon?"

"Brid? Listen...I can't talk right now...I've got to..."

"Listen to me...He was watching!"

"What?"

"He was watching you!"

"I know."

"The dream...your dream...I saw it."

"You saw it? How do you know it was mine?"

"I just know...trust me."

"Look...Brid...we'll definitely have to talk about this later. I have to get back to..."

"I know you do...just call me when you get the chance."

"Will do...thanks. Bye." Devon said, pressing END, hurrying back into the action going on around her. She ran to her SUV, jumping in and turning it on, stopping momentarily, rolling her window down...

"Mike! Get in here…let's go!" She yelled at her partner, who was standing among a sea of uniforms.

Mike ran over to the SUV, opening the passenger side and climbing in.

"Hey…thanks for the ride." Mike said, slamming the door shut just as Devon sped off.

"I want to get over to the scene before they start to process it." Devon said, not really hearing what he had said, her mind preoccupied with thoughts of her next move.

"Okay…got that, now you want to tell me what else is running through that head of yours?"

"Whoever is doing this…they knew where we had been…they knew where I had been…" Devon said, turning a sharp right onto a dirt road.

"Yeah…we kind of already established that…didn't we?"

"I don't want the CSU in there before I have a chance to get this area checked with an Evidence K-9."
"Dev, our Crime Scene Unit is great…shit…half of them have been trained with you looking over their shoulders! If there's something out there, they'll find it." Mike said, not understanding where his partner was going with this.

"Look, Mike…I've been all over out there. There is no way that our guys can cover some of the area thorough enough…it's thick. If we can get an Evidence dog in there, we'd have a better chance of getting something if it's in one of those areas."

"Okay…so why the hurry with getting out there before the techs do?"

"If we're going to use an Evidence Detection K-9, the less human scent in there, the better."

Devon reached for her cell phone, dialing Jim.

"Jim? Did you hear?"

"Yeah...heard they found her. Sorry Dev."

"Thanks. Listen, I want you to bring Mugs over here...I want to make sure that we find anything that's out there...without a doubt."

"Okay. He's back at the kennels. It will take me about an hour to get him and get back to the scene."

"Sounds good, we'll meet you over at Sector Four. Just look for my SUV...we'll be waiting for you."

"I'll be there as soon as I can, Dev. Just keep everybody out of there as best you can."

"Will do. Thanks." Devon said, closing the flip phone and placing it back in the side pocket of her BDUs. "Jim's going to meet us there in an hour. Let's get everybody out of there as soon as possible."

Devon pulled up to the scene, throwing the transmission into Park.

She jumped out of the SUV, walking over to the Crime Scene Unit's trailer, where the majority of the technicians were now standing.

"Hey everybody, listen up! I know that you were called out to process the scene here...but right now, I need you to just stay put." Devon said, her words being met by looks of confusion and mumbling from the group. Her eyes caught a glimpse of movement coming from the edge of the woods. It was Dr. Brown, the Medical Examiner.

"Doc!" Devon yelled, waving her arm to get his attention.

Doc looked over and, seeing Devon, waved back, walking towards the group.

"Hey Dev...I was wondering when you'd be showing up. I haven't moved the body yet...wanted to wait until you got here." Dr. Brown said.

"Thanks, Doc..." She said, turning back to the group. "Does everybody understand...no one...and I mean NO ONE is allowed in that scene until I stay otherwise...do I make myself clear?" Devon said, eyeing up the group.

The technicians answered each in their own way, some with a nod, others with a "Yes, ma'am".

"I'll stay back here and keep an eye on everything...you go ahead with the Doc, Dev." Mike said, trying to look as 'large and in-charge' as possible. He was thankful that she didn't insist on him accompanying her into the field. Death scenes—that was her bag, not his.

"Great...thanks, Mike." Devon said, giving him a pat on the shoulder, understanding exactly what her partner was up to.

"No problem...anytime."

Devon walked over to the M.E.'s van, taking out a pair of booties before walking over to the scene.

Doc was busily gathering his equipment, finally reaching in and grabbing a pair of new booties for himself. He discarded the ones he had worn into the scene previously.

"Shall we?" He said, looking to Devon.

"Definitely." She answered, motioning for him to lead the way. Stopping just behind the entrance to the scene, they put the booties over their shoes.

The two walked one behind the other looking out ahead of them for anything not indigenous to the area. The path that they were on was a well-worn deer trail. Devon and Mitch had used the same trail earlier in both of their walk-throughs of the area. Along the way, there were areas of dirt that had retained footprints quite easily. Devon carefully placed pieces of orange tracking tape around each print and one piece overhead so that the print would not accidentally be destroyed by those moving in and out of the area.

"How far back is she?" Devon asked.

"Actually…quite a ways…it's kind of surprising that he would have brought her in this far."

"He wasn't in a hurry…he knew he had time, because he knew that we had already searched the area and called it clear." Devon said.

"What? How?" Doc said, surprised.

"He had to have been around the base camp…listening in on our communications. He knew everything…what areas we had covered, when we searched them, all of it."

"Geezus."

"Yeah…nice, eh? I've got the place sealed off…we're printing everybody. Winters has got the roadblocks in place. Hopefully they didn't already slip through…"

"Okay…she's just up around the corner here…" Doc said as they neared a bend in the trail.

As Devon turned the corner, the body of Michelle Findlay came into view. The small girl laid on her back, completely naked, her legs spread widely at an almost unnatural angle. Her once flawless skin was now mottled purple with bruises from an obviously brutal beating. Her torso was one large gaping wound from her privates to her ribcage, the contents of her gut spilling out onto the ground. Her face shown all of the terror that she had obviously experienced in her final moments…and her assailant had taken the time once more to carefully remove her eyeballs. The body was quickly being overcome by large black ants…busily crawling in and out of every orifice of the child's body.

"Geezus…it's him." Devon said, taking in the full view.

"Yep. That's the first thing that ran through my mind, too." Doc said, looking at the body once more.

"Damn...he's definitely escalating. I've got to stop this guy...now." She said, her eyes viewing the extent of the ferocious attack that the girl had endured prior to her death.

"I would have to agree on the escalation. It looks like he beat her pretty good...that's new. This guy is obviously harboring some pretty big hostility towards these girls."

"You think?" Devon said, sarcastically.

Doc's hackles went up, as it became obvious to him that Devon's demeanor had changed significantly since the last girl had been found. He suspected that this was more than just another case to her...this was now personal.

"Dev...you okay with this? Because I can always have one of the techs come back and assist..." he suggested.

"I'll be just fine as soon as I catch this asshole." She said coldly. "Now let's get this done so we can get her out of here and let this area cool down before Jim gets here with the Evidence K-9."

"Okay then...let's get started." Doc said, removing a tape recorder and the camera from his duffle bag, handing the camera to Devon.

Devon moved to several different locations around the body, taking pictures at all different angles before moving in and taking the close-ups. Meanwhile, Dr. Brown pressed play on his tape recorder and started the preliminary examination...

"Subject is a Caucasian female...aged 7-12 years of age...large ventral laceration from the vaginal vault to the xyphoid process. Total evisceration. Multiple contusions...from position of body, sexual assault is suspected. Eyeballs have been forcibly removed." He said, pressing the STOP button on the recorder. "There's not much more we're going to be able to do from here."

"Okay...let's get her bagged and tagged so you can take her back and start the autopsy. I'm going to stay here on this one, Doc...but I need the report on her

ASAP…okay?" Devon said, reaching into his pack and removing the disposable body bag and two pairs of latex gloves.

"I'll personally take her back and we'll get going on her immediately. I'll call you on your cell as soon as we're done."

The two made sure that the area next to the body was clear of any possible evidence before laying the vinyl body bag out and unzipping it, preparing it for the body. They then pulled the gloves on…

"You ready to roll her?" Doc asked.

"Yeah…good to go here." Devon said, crouching next to the body.

"On the count of three…one…two…three." Doc said, as they rolled the body up onto its side.

The blood had started to pool in the back of the body; however, it was easy to see that the girl had also sustained quite a beating along her spine and ribs.

"The bastard really worked her over." Doc said, viewing the dark contusions on the girl's back.

"Yeah…by the deep discoloration, I'd say he did it shortly after he took her…kept her alive for quite a while afterwards…" Devon said. She knew that if the girl had been killed shortly after the beating(s), that the contusions would not have bled into the tissues as deeply and extensively as they had.

"Definitely…do you see any patterns?" Doc asked, as the two scanned the body for any shapes defined within the bruises that may give them a clue as to what type of implement, if any, was used.

"I don't think so…wait…this one here…" Devon said, pointing to the left buttock region "…kind of looks like a partial hand print, see…here's the fingers and part of the palm."

"Could be. We'll know better once I can get her under better lighting back at the shop."

"Anything else?"

"Doesn't appear to be. Let's go ahead and get her into the bag, then we can bag her hands and close her up. Watch out that we don't lose her entrails when we slide her." Doc instructed, trying to scoop the innards in his hands as best he could as they slid her body into the bag.

"Hand me the paper bags and bands, will you?" Doc said, reaching out to Devon.

Devon dug through the kit, taking out two lunch-sized paper bags and elastic bands, handing them to Dr. Brown.

He took the first from her, gently raising the girl's arm and placing the bag over her small hand, followed by the elastic band to hold it in place around the wrist. Devon repeated the process on the other hand. She then placed the girl's arms at her side, tucked them in, and pulled the flap of the bag over, zipping it shut.

"Let's go ahead and get her out to the van. I'll take her in and get started right away."

"Great…Jim should be getting here pretty soon, too. So this will work out well." Devon said, bending over to take hold of the handles on her side of the body bag.

The two lifted the bag, carrying the girl's lifeless body from the woods and placing her on the gurney before sliding her into the Medical Examiner's vehicle.

As they closed the doors on the van, the familiar sound of Jim's SUV hit Devon's ears.

He pulled the Suburban up to the edge of the scene, opened the door, and headed over to where Devon and Dr. Brown were now standing.

"Hey, Jim." Devon said, greeting her friend as he walked up.

"Just got her loaded up, eh?" Jim asked, looking towards the back of the Medical Examiner's van.

"Yeah…we're all set. How about you and Mugs?" Devon asked.

"He's raring to go…you know Mugs he's got a two-tracked mind…food and finding toys!" Jim said.

Devon laughed, "Gotta love those hounds!"

"Yeah…good old Mugs…he's not the sharpest tool in the shed, but when it comes to finding a needle in the haystack, he's your boy!" Jim said, proudly.

"Well…that's why you're here. I want this whole area checked. If this guy left anything out here…I want to know about it. If it doesn't grow out here…I want it bagged and tagged and turned in for examination. The techs will be standing by out here…you and Mugs are the main event." Devon explained.

"That's just the way we like it!" Jim said, returning to the Suburban to retrieve Mugs.

"Okay, Doc. You get her back there and let me know what you find as soon as possible, got-it?" Devon said, looking to Dr. Brown.

"You'll be the first one to know, Dev." Dr. Brown said, walking to the driver's side door, opening it, and climbing in.

Devon nodded as she walked over to the group of Crime Scene Technicians, who were still gathered around their trailer, waiting for directions.

"Okay you guys…listen up! Jim and Mugs from the K-9 Unit are going to be going in to do an extensive search of the crime scene. Your job is to make sure that everything…and I do mean EVERYTHING that is found by them is properly gathered, bagged, and tagged. I don't want anything screwing up the admissibility of possible evidence that we may find out there today…so make SURE you're following Standard Operating Procedures at all times. Myself and Detective Penaglio will be working between here and the Command Center…all decisions must be run through us…any questions?"

"Detective McKinney? Won't the dog contaminate the scene? I mean, what if it decides to retrieve the stuff or something?" One of the technicians asked.

"Mugs is trained to indicate with a 'passive' indication. When he finds something with human scent, blood or body fluids, or nitrates—like gun powder, he'll lay down and bark near the article." Devon explained.

"You're telling me that if he finds something like…say…a candy wrapper with half of a chocolate bar in it or something, that he won't eat it?" The technician asked skeptically.

"That's the idea, yeah. He's been proofed off of things like food…he knows that only his handler, Jim, can give him his food or treats. So I'll ask that all of you please do not pet the dog or offer him and treats while he's working."

One of the technicians turned towards the area where the suburban was parked. Jim had Mugs out and was walking towards the edge of the scene, waiting for Devon to give him the go-ahead to start the search.

A collective "Awwwwww!" emanated from the group as they got their first look at Mugs.

"Oh my God! That is the biggest Beagle I have ever seen!" said one technician in the group.

"Actually…Mugs isn't a Beagle. He's a Treeing Walker Coonhound." Devon began to explain.

"Looks like a Beagle to me!"

Hearing this comment, Jim stepped forward, speaking up. "Hey! Mugs here is a genuine Indonesian Fighting Beagle—and I wouldn't get too close if I were you!" He said, chidingly.

The comment elicited a chorus of chuckles from the crowd. Devon was glad—as it seemed to ease the tension a bit between the crime scene crew and the rest of them.

Mugs also seemed happy with the comment as his tail wagged excitedly like a whip from side-to-side…his mouth hanging open, tongue out in a full pant, looking very much like a grin.

It was true. The hound did look like a Beagle. His tri-colored coat and floppy ears made him look like an eighty-pound, long-legged version of Snoopy.

"Okay, okay you guys…just stand by your radios. We'll give you a call when we need you." Devon said, walking over to Jim and Mugs.

"All set?" Jim asked as Devon approached them.

"Good to go." Devon answered.

Jim clipped the long-line onto Mugs and gave him a pat on the head, "Ready to go, boy? Huh? You ready to go?" he said, scratching behind the hound's ears. "Okay boy…let's go find toys!"

The words 'find toys' were barely out of Jim's mouth when Mugs' body language changed drastically. It was as though someone had flipped a switch, changing him from a gangly, bouncing, happy-go-lucky hound to a well-oiled evidence-finding machine.

His nose went into overdrive, sucking in a myriad of scents with every breath, his expert mind deciphering their hidden codes one-by-one…using criteria known only to him.

Jim worked him back and forth, zigzagging as far as his long-line would allow. They broke the area up into a grid pattern to assure that no place would be overlooked.

Three hours later, Mugs had turned up three gum wrappers, two plastic shot-shells, and thirty-seven cents in change (one quarter, a dime, and two pennies).

Devon stood with Mike and Jim at the CSU trailer. Devon slowly ran one of the small plastic evidence bags through her fingers…

"I just can't believe that this is all we got." She said, half-heartedly.

"Dev...you can't find something if it's not there...that's the first rule of search work...you know that." Jim reminded her.

"I know...it's just that we have got practically nothing to work with here...and this guy's not going to stop...he's getting worse."

"Escalating?" Mike asked.

Devon nodded yes.

"Look, Dev. I spoke to Captain Winters...they've got everything under control over there...there's nothing more you can do here. Why don't you go home and get some sleep...you look like hell." Mike said, placing his hand on her shoulder.

Devon abruptly broke the physical contact with Mike, looking at him, her temper fueled by a persistent lack of sleep as well as the stress of the case...

"I'll get sleep when I damned well need it! Right now...I need to catch this fuck before he slaughters somebody else's little girl!"

"Dev...listen..." Mike said, trying to calm his partner down.

"No! You listen! Have you seen what he's doing to them? He's gutting them like fucking deer, Mike! Gouging their eyes out...and this one...he beat the piss out of her before finally killing her! Hell...killing her was probably the nicest thing that he did to her!" Devon yelled, gaining the attention of the technicians and other officers at the scene.

Mike and Jim knew that they had to get her out of there, before things got any worse...

"Dev...Mike's right. Just go home for a few hours, freshen up...take the case files with you, even...but get some sleep. You're not doing any of these kids any good by letting yourself get exhausted. You're gonna need a clear mind if you want to catch this asshole." Jim said, hoping to calm the situation a bit. He had always had an excellent repoire with Devon, ever since her academy days.

Devon noticed that all eyes were on her. She took a deep breath, trying to take a moment to calm herself. She knew that neither Mike nor Jim would steer her wrong…they were looking out for her, just like they always did…like big brothers looking after their little sister. But they didn't understand…they couldn't…they hadn't seen them…the bodies. Twisted and broken, sliced to bits—they didn't know what kind of a monster that they were dealing with…she did.

"Okay. I'll go back to the house for a while. Just let me get the files before I go." Devon said, turning to walk to Mike's van. After all…she could still work on the case at home…where she wouldn't have two sets of eyes watching over her like a pair of mother hens.

The files sat on the passenger side seat of Mike's van. Devon reached in and grabbed the stack of folders, turning and holding them up—giving Mike and Jim a sarcastic smile before getting into her SUV and peeling out onto the road, leaving a cloud of dust and dirt in her wake.

Mike and Jim watched as Devon rounded the corner, going past the road blocks…

"What do you think the chances are of her actually going home and sleeping?" Mike asked.

"About the same as the Lions winning the Superbowl." Jim answered, sarcastically.

CHAPTER 15

▼

Devon reached down deeply into the pocket of her BDU pants, pulling out her flip phone. She thumbed through the numbers finding Brid's and pressing SEND.

"Hello?"

"Brid…it's Devon."

"I've been waiting to hear from you…are you okay?"

"Yeah…I'm fine. Are you doing anything right now?"

"Just grading some papers…did you need something?"

"I need to talk to you…well…I need to finish our conversation…to get the information that you said that you had…" Devon said, stumbling a bit verbally.

"Definitely…did you want to meet somewhere? You could come over here if you like."

Devon paused momentarily. Going over to a complete stranger's house was not something that she had made a habit of doing in the past…but for some reason, she felt that this was going to be okay…after all, she knew how to handle herself.

"Devon?"

"Yeah! Sorry about that…that would be fine…if you don't mind, that is."

"I wouldn't have asked you if I didn't feel comfortable in doing so."

"Um…okay then. What's your address?"

"How familiar are you with the campus here at the university?"

"Pretty familiar…"

"Okay…you know where the Annex is?"

"I think so…it's across from the Art Barn, isn't it?"

"Exactly…there's a small subdivison just behind the Annex…East Campus Drive. If you turn right, I'm the house right at the end of the loop. It's 2223 East Campus Drive."

"Great…got it. Um…I should probably go home and change first…" Devon said, looking down at her rather dirty BDU's.
"Oh don't worry about it…it's no big deal. I'm sure you're just fine."

"If you say so…I'll be there in about twenty minutes, okay?"

"That's fine…I'll see you then."

"See you." Devon said, pushing the END button on the phone. She wasn't sure if it was the stress of the day, the lack of sleep, or her heightened senses…but something was making her feel rather…anxious, for lack of a better word.

It had been a while since she had been on the University campus, but she managed to find the Annex without much difficulty. As she turned onto East Campus Drive, the 'anxiousness' got a little more intense.

Geezus, McKinney! What in the hell is your problem? Take a nice deep breath and relax a bit. You don't want to look like some kind of spastic wreck in there, do you?

Her eyes scanned the numbers on the houses nearest the end of the drive, finally coming to rest on a mid-sized pale yellow Cape Cod-style house with a myriad of wind chimes and sun catchers hanging on the front porch. Devon couldn't help but smile when she saw them.

Why am I not surprised?

She pulled up into the drive, parking behind Brid's VW, climbing out and walking up to the porch. She was just about to knock on the door when it openened, revealing Brid standing on the other side.

"Huh…maybe you are psychic!" Devon said, smiling.

"Sorry to disappoint you…but I heard you drive in. We don't get a lot of traffic back here." Brid said, returning the smile. "Come in…" She said, stepping away from the doorway to allow Devon passage.

Devon walked into the door, stopping just inside the foyer, bending down to untie her boots.

"You really don't have to do that…you can wear them inside if you like." Brid said, politely.

"I don't want to get your floors all dirty."Devon said, continuing to remove her boots.

"They get walked on every day…"

Devon glanced over at the beautiful hardwood floors and light colored rugs. "Yeah…but not with boots covered in swamp muck, I'll bet."
"True. You've got me there." Brid said, walking into the kitchen. "Would you like some coffee or tea? Let's see…I have Lemongrass, Mint, Chai…"

"Do you have any diet Cola, by chance?" Devon asked.

"I thought you gave that up." She said smirking as she reached for the teakettle on the back burner, pouring the steaming hot water into a mug, dunking her tea bag in and out.

"Geezus…first I have to listen to Doc and Mike tell me about the evils of soda pop…now you, too?"

"Yes…it's all a big soda pop conspiracy! Someone's always watching…aspartame thing…very serious." Brid said, jokingly.

Devon laughed openly and it felt good. It had been a long time since she'd felt like laughing…hell, it had been a long time since she really felt anything. She turned her face down in an attempt to hide the fact that she was now actually smiling…after all…this wasn't a social call. She was here on business…serious business…a murder investigation for Christ's sake!

Brid saw the look on her face…she knew that Devon was embarrassed by the fact that she let her guard down…if only for a second.

"Hey…that was funny…it's okay to laugh, you know." She said, trying to ease the tension of the moment.

Devon looked up, her eyes meeting Brid's…green melding into silver, and a sudden calm warmth enveloped her—forcing out some of the stress and tension that had been building in her throughout the last few days. It felt good…almost too good. She hadn't felt anything like it since…well…Chris. The pangs of guilt forced her to break away from the eye contact…turning away suddenly from the situation.

"Look…thanks for the hospitality and all…I really appreciate it…but I'm really here to get the rest of that information from you." Devon said, trying to get her point across, but also trying to be somewhat sensitive in doing so.

"How about we go sit down in the living room and I'll tell you all about it." Brid suggested.

"Um…I really don't think you want me sitting on your furniture like this…" Devon said, her clothes somewhat muddy and wet from her earlier excursion into the woods.

"True…you've got a point, there…" Brid said, thinking for a moment "…why don't you just go hop in the shower and I'll get you some of my sweats to wear…then you don't have to worry about it, and maybe it will relax you a bit. You seem pretty wound up."

"I don't know…I don't think that would be such a good idea…" Devon said, feeling a bit awkward about the situation.

"It's no big deal…seriously. You need to relax, Detective…now I'll go get you the sweats and some towels…" She said, disappearing down the hallway.

"Brid…listen…" Devon started to say.

"I won't take no for an answer!" Brid yelled from down the hall.

Damn…she is seriously stubborn! What the hell am I doing? I'm supposed to be here interviewing her—and instead, I'm getting ready to climb into her shower?!

Brid reappeared walking back into the living room where Devon was standing.

"Okay…towels are on the sink, sweats are hanging on the back of the door…enjoy." She said, walking past Devon and into the kitchen.

Well…no point in fighting it. You need information—she's got it…so buck up, McKinney…get in there and take one for the team!

Devon walked down the hallway to the bathroom, emerging fifteen minutes later feeling refreshed and definitely more relaxed. She walked towards the living room, noticing a rather pleasant smell wafting in the air. She followed the scent into the kitchen, where she found Brid standing over the stove, spatula in hand, tossing the contents of the wok in front of her.

"Um…what are you doing?" Devon asked.

"Hey! I just thought you probably haven't had much time to eat or anything in the last couple of days…so I thought I'd make you something. Do you like Thai?"

"Yeah...love it...but you really didn't have to go to all of this trouble just for me."

"I didn't." Brid said, turning around, smiling. "I like to eat, too, you know." She said with a wink, turning her attention back to the wok and it's contents.

"Well...yeah! Of course you do! I didn't mean that you were just doing this for me or anything...you know?" Devon said, stumbling a bit over her own words. Her face feeling rather flushed.

Brid turned back around "I know." She said, smiling. Enjoying the fact that Devon was blushing a particularly deep shade of scarlet red. "Why don't you go sit down in the living room...I'll bring it out when it's ready."

"Is there anything I can help with?" Devon asked, feeling rather out of place.

"There's a bottle of wine over there on the cupboard. You could open the bottle and let it breathe a bit. The glasses are right above the cutting block."

Devon looked over to the cupboard area where a bottle of chardonnay sat with a corkscrew next to it. She picked up the tool, placing it on the top of the bottle-neck, working it down into the cork. The ears of the corkscrew slowly went up, only to be brought down once again as Devon removed the cork, sitting it next to the bottle on the countertop. The sweet smell of the Chardonnay blended sub-limely with the spicy smell of the contents of the wok.

"This is really...um...nice of you...I really appreciate it." Devon said, as she reached into the cupboard, taking out two cobalt blue wine goblets, setting them on the countertop.

Brid smiled softly, her back turned to Devon. "You're welcome." She reached over, putting the final ingredients into the wok, tossing them lightly. "I know it hasn't breathed much...but would you mind pouring me a glass of wine?"

Devon stood in a daze...she hadn't really paid much attention before...but Brid really was breathtakingly beautiful.

"I'm sorry...what did you say?" Devon said, shaking herself out of it.

Brid turned around, smiling. "The wine…would you mind pouring me a glass?"

"Oh yeah! Sure…sorry about that…haven't slept in a while…not real with it…" Devon said, reaching back for bottle, pouring each glass half-full with the tantalizing liquid. She handed one to Brid, keeping the other for herself.

Brid took the glass in her slender hands, swirling the nectar around within. Slowly letting her eyelids fall as she brought it close to her silky red lips, inhaling the smooth bouquet…her tongue jutting out briefly to moisten her pursed lips…leaving a glistening dew in it's wake.

Everything seemed to be moving in slow motion as Devon watched Brid's every movement.

Brid took a sip of the wine, letting it slide across her taste buds momentarily before swallowing. She opened her eyes only to find Devon watching her intently. "What?" Brid asked, smiling.

"Huh? Oh…nothing…sorry about that." Devon said, quickly averting her eyes and taking a sip of the wine.
"I hope you're hungry…I hate having leftovers around…" Brid said, sitting her glass on the counter before stirring the contents of the wok one last time.

"Yeah…actually, I am. It smells really good."

"Good…can you hand me a couple of plates from the cupboard?" Brid asked, pointing to the door next to where the glasses were stored.

"Sure." Devon said, reaching up and opening the cupboard door, taking out two dinner plates.

As she handed the plates to Brid, their hands touched briefly…sending a wave of fluttering energy throughout Devon's chest. She looked momentarily down at their hands, then suddenly broke contact when she knew that Brid had control of the plates. She had felt that feeling before…a long time ago, but now, it was accompanied by pangs of guilt.

Brid could see the confusion in Devon's eyes. Something or someone had hurt her beyond belief. She could literally feel the pain ripping through her soul.

"Are you okay?" She asked, looking at Devon with concern in her eyes.

Devon looked down, not wanting to make eye contact with her...hoping that if she didn't, the feelings would pass. "Yeah...I'm fine. Just been a long couple of days, that's all."

"Well let's get you something to eat and then we can talk." Brid said, dividing the mixture of vegetables, tofu, and rice noodles onto the plates. She handed Devon a set of chopsticks, taking a second for herself.

The two passed on the dining area, choosing instead to sit in the living room, where things were more comfortable.

Devon sat her plate on the coffee table while she sat down on the end of the couch. She picked up the chopsticks in her hand, trying to scoop up some of the mixture with them, however unsuccessfully.

Brid couldn't help but chuckle lightly. "Um...not having much luck with those, are you?"

Devon smiled weakly "You noticed?"

"Kind of hard not to...here...let me show you how." Brid said, taking her own set in her hands. "The bottom one goes here, in between your thumb and ring finger...like this." She said, placing the stick in the proper position in her hand, holding it up. She smiled as Devon mimicked her actions. "Then you hold the top one like you would a pen or pencil...then you can pinch the ends together like this..." She said, bringing the ends of the chopsticks together several times.

"Hey! I think I've got it!" Devon said, excitedly moving the chopsticks together, picking up some of the noodles from her plate and bringing them to her mouth.

Brid smiled, feeling good about the fact that Devon was letting her see this side of her...one that could laugh...one that could find pleasure in something as simple as being able to use chopsticks successfully for the first time. There was more to Devon McKinney than the dark, brooding Detective liked to let on.

"Mmmm...this is really good!" Devon said, tasting the spicy concoction.

"I'm glad you like it. Thai is one of my favorites."

"Well...it's quickly becoming one of mine, too! What's this stuff here?" Devon asked, picking up a piece of tofu with her sticks.

"That's tofu..." Brid said, popping some noodles and vegetables into her mouth.

"Huh..." Devon said, looking at it closer before popping it in her mouth "...it's pretty good!"

"It's a good protein source, and it basically takes on the flavor of whatever it's cooked with. I use it in a lot of things, actually."

"So what exactly is it?" Devon said, taking another mouthful.

"Oh...it's soybean curd."

Devon's chewing came to an abrupt stop. "It's what?" She said, a look of dread on her face.

"Soybean curd...they make it by curdling soy milk." Brid said smiling as she took another bite.

Devon's face dropped as she set the chopsticks down on the plate, struggling to chew what she already had in her mouth before swallowing.

Her actions did not go unnoticed.

"Is everything okay?" Brid asked.

"Um...yeah. Curdled soy milk?"

"Think of it as...well...as cheese. It's really the same kind of thing...only one is made from an animal's milk, the other from soy."

"Cheese, huh? Doesn't look like cheese." Devon said, picking up another cube of the firm tofu.

"Trust me...it's fine. You liked it before you knew what it was, didn't you?"

Devon nodded.

"Look...I'm sorry. This is great...it really is. Better than I'm used to, that's for sure! Hell...I find a frozen burrito in the icebox or a stale doughnut and it's like a feast to me!"

"Sounds like we need to get you eating better." Brid said, looking at the young woman compassionately.

"You sound like Mike and Doc." Devon said, taking another bite of the spicy-sweet concoction.

"Mike and Doc?"

"Mike Penaglio, my partner...at work. Doc is a friend of mine. He's the County Medical Examiner." Devon explained.

"sounds like you've got some pretty good friends, there."

"Yeah, they're good guys." Devon said, looking down at her plate, picking up a water chestnut and popping it into her mouth.

"So...you have a partner and a good friend...what about a significant other? Have you got one of them?" Brid asked boldly.

Devon stopped mid-chew, swallowing hard...not really sure what to say. She took a sip of wine, taking the time to try to compose herself.

"Dev? Are you alright? I'm sorry, I shouldn't have asked. I didn't mean to pry..."

"No…no. It's okay…really." Devon said, taking another drink of her wine. She sat the glass down, took a deep breath, exhaling slowly in an attempt to steady her nerves. "I…um…lost my partner six months ago. She was killed by a hit-and-run driver. We were both hit, actually…but I survived."

"Oh, wow…I am so sorry. Way to go, Morrigan! Open mouth and insert foot!" Brid said, chastising herself for having asked the question in the first place.

"Hey, you didn't know. It's not your fault." Devon said, trying to put her mind at ease.

Brid could sense Devon's pain. It was flowing off of her in waves. She wanted to do something to help her, but didn't know how.
"It was none of my business…"

"It's okay…seriously." Devon said. Suddenly losing her appetite, she laid the chopsticks down across her plate.

Brid noticed immediately, and the action only served to deepen her guilt for having brought the subject up in the first place.

"Hey, how about a change of topic? You came here to ask me questions about the case, right?" Brid said, trying to lighten the mood a bit.

"Yeah…I did. At dinner the other night…you started telling me about these dreams. You said that you were seeing things from the victim's point of view?" Devon asked, picking up her glass of wine, settling back into the couch, awaiting Brid's answer.

"I believe so, yes. The times that I've had them, I have been able to glimpse their faces…and they matched those of the victims from the first two homicides. But as I told you before, you were also there."

"That's what I don't get. How could you have been dreaming about me when you've never even met me?" Devon asked, skeptically.

"I'd never met the victims, either, yet I dreamed about them."

"Good point. So tell me again…what exactly did you see?" Devon asked.

"The first dream that I had…and I had it several times…had the two girls, the first two victims, standing at a fork in some kind of dirt path."

"A two track, right?" Devon asked.

"Yes…I guess that's what you'd call it. Something for all-terrain bikes or something."

"Okay…so you're sure that these girls were the victims, right?"

"Yes. I saw their pictures on the news, and that's when I put two-and-two together."

"But what about me? How did you know it was me?"

"I didn't for sure until I met you that night for dinner. I suspected it when we talked on the phone, though. I was getting some really strong vibes from you." Brid said, taking a sip of her wine and settling back onto the couch.

"Vibes? What do you mean?"

"Well…you know how you say you get 'gut feelings' about something? Well, that's kind of like vibes. Everyone and every living thing around us emits certain vibes…some good, some bad…it varies with everything."

Devon started to grin a bit. She was, after all, the born skeptic. Science, facts, logic…these were what she believed in.

"Hmmm…a bit skeptical, I see." Brid said with a smirk.

"Look, Brid…I'm used to dealing with facts, science, logical thinking. We have psychics and Bible Thumpers coming out of our ears when we have a high-profile case like this one. It's not that I don't believe you…I just do better when I have some tangible proof…something I can sink my teeth into."

"Well...sometimes you can't always have that solid proof. Let me give you an example..." She said, sitting her wine glass on the coffee table. "...you're looking at this glass. You can see it. You know that it's there. But if you weren't looking at it—would it still be visible? Or does it only become visible if someone is looking at it?" Brid said.

"...and if a tree falls in the woods, and there's no one there to hear it, does it make a noise? Yeah...I know all about the metaphysical stuff." Devon said.

"Well...you can't really prove that it is, in fact, visible when no one is looking at it; and yet, you believe 100% without a doubt that it is. So why couldn't some things, like psychic ability, visions, and the like be real, too?"

"I don't know..." Devon said, thinking that the whole idea was a bit far-fetched.

"Okay...how about this. Do you believe in God...or some kind of higher being?"

"Well, yeah. Of course I believe in God!" Devon said, crossing her arms protectively across her chest.

"Let's say I'm a non-believer...which, just for the record, I'm technically not...what kind of scientific evidence and hard facts can you give to me to prove that God exists and that I should believe in him or her?" Brid said, waiting for an answer.

"How about the Bible?"

"There are lots of books and documents on things like telekinesis, astral projection, and psychic phenomenon. The Bible is just another example of this type of documentation. Just because someone writes a book about something, doesn't prove that it exists." Brid stated, calmly.

She was in full-professor mode now.

"It's all a matter of faith...you have to believe."
"So basically, you're telling me that you have no proof that God exists. Aren't you?"

"Oh come on! Millions of people can't be wrong!" Devon said, hoping to gain some ground in the debate.

"Couldn't it be a simple case of mass hysteria?"

"No…it just…it just is! You can't see it…but you know that it's there. You believe that it's there."

"Exactly. So why are you so sure that these other things don't exist just like God and Christianity?" Brid asked.

"Okay…I'll say this much…that I can't prove that they don't exist. But likewise, you can't prove that they do. So I guess we'll just have to agree to disagree."

"Agreed. Okay…now that we've got that out of the way…like I said, I just felt that it was you when I talked to you on the phone, and then, when I saw you—I was positive of it." Brid explained.

"What about the owl. I remember you saying something about that." Devon said, not mentioning that the owls had been appearing in her dreams, as well as while she was awake. She didn't think that Brid would intentionally mislead her, but she also didn't want to give her any information to elaborate or build on.

"I've seen the owl several times…and when it is there, you are not—and vice versa."

"So what does that mean to you?" Devon asked. Truly hoping that Brid could come up with a believable answer.

"Well…the owl represents different things in different religions. Most of the Native American tribes revered the owl as being the 'Night Eagle'…and regard it's powers as a warrior, but also as magical and clairvoyant, very close to the spirit world. One tribe, the Mescalaro, fear the owl. They believe that it carries the spirit of the recently deceased to the Great Spirit, the messenger of death, if you will."

"Okay…" Devon said, still being somewhat skeptical.

"Now, the Celts, Druids, Pagans and religions like Wicca believe the owl to be a symbol of wisdom. They are the link between the unseen spirit world, and the world of light." Brid explained.

"The owl sees what others cannot—the essence of true wisdom. Seeing the owl in your dreams or in meditation would be telling you to use your powers of perception, your silent power of observation of the present situation."

"...and you seriously believe this?" Devon asked.

"I can't say that I don't believe it...I think that there is a lot to be learned from all of these religions. You have to keep an open mind, Dev."

"So...what are you saying?"

"I'm saying you need to be aware of these things...listen to them...or what they may be trying to tell you. Just don't close your mind off to the ideas. Be open about it. You never know what you might learn...you can't just look...you have to see. Do you understand what I mean?" Brid asked, getting somewhat frustrated with Devon's apparent close-mindedness.

The phrase... *"You can't just look, you have to see."* It was the same thing that Chris had told her...the same thing that Brid had also told her earlier over the phone. The realization sent a chill up Devon's spine, making the hair on the back of her neck stand on end. She didn't know why, but she felt that she needed to tell Brid what had happened in the woods that night with the owls. If there was something to be learned from this that would help the case, she would just simply have to bite the bullet and accept it, however unconventional it might be...

"Is there something you want to tell me?" Brid asked, once again, picking up on the uneasiness in Devon's eyes.

Damn it! How does she do that?

"Look...I can see it in your eyes, Dev. I'm not blind. Tell me what's bothering you."

"I shouldn't be telling you any of this! It's confidential…has to do with the case."

"I'm not going to tell anyone, Dev…I promise." She said, looking intently in Devon's eyes.

She wasn't sure why, but Devon trusted Brid. This woman whom she barely knew…who was into the whole mystic, magical, 'things really do go bump in the night' type stuff…had somehow gained her trust…and trust was not something that Devon handed over easily.

"I'd ask you to swear to God, but since you probably don't believe in him…" Devon said, jokingly.

"I didn't say that I don't believe in God…just maybe not as you do…and I swear on my life that I will not tell a soul." Brid said, placing her hand on Devon's knee to reassure her that she was, in fact, serious.

Devon looked down at the hand now resting on her knee. Part of her wanted to push away from the contact, to let her know that only one person had ever been allowed in her 'space'…and that person was gone. Yet, at the same time, she felt drawn to this woman…this stranger that had forced her way into her life.

"I can't believe I'm telling you this…but I do trust you." Devon said, softly.

"I think I'm going to take that as a compliment…" Brid said, smirking as she withdrew her hand slowly and eased back onto the cushions of the couch.

"It was. I don't trust too many people…so yeah, consider it a compliment." Devon said, swallowing the last few drops of wine from her glass.

"Would you like some more?"

"That's okay…I know where it is. I'll get it." Devon said, standing up from the couch. She took her plate in her hand, outstretching her other towards Brid.

"Can I take your plate for you?"

"Wow…not used to being waited on in my own house! Thank you." Brid said, handing the plate to Devon.

She walked into the kitchen, sitting the plates down on the countertop. Placing both hands on the edge, she took a moment to try to collect her thoughts. It wasn't easy for Devon to open up to anyone. It never had been. But for some reason, she felt compelled to do so with Brid. What was it about her?

After taking a deep cleansing breath, she grabbed the bottle of wine and headed back out into the living room.

She filled Brid's glass first, then her own, sitting the bottle on the coffee table. She eased herself down onto the couch once again, her back against the arm, her left leg folded under her right, facing Brid. She smiled nervously "I'm not really sure where to start."

"The beginning is usually a pretty good bet." Brid said, smiling softly.

"The beginning it is…"

CHAPTER 16

▼

The hours flew by like minutes as Devon told Brid about how the owl had been appearing to her in her dreams as well as during the search the previous morning.

"How long have you been seeing the owl in your dreams?" Brid asked.

"It started a little while after the first murder."

"You'd never dreamed about them before?"

"No…not that I can remember." Devon answered. "Hey…hello…Cop? I'm the one that's supposed to be asking all of the questions here!" She said, jokingly.

"I'm sorry…just trying to put all of this together…you know? Trying to figure out what it all means."

"Maybe it just means that the rumors are true and I really have lost it." Devon said sarcastically.

"You don't believe that and neither do I. They are trying to tell you something…we just have to figure out what that something is." Brid said, trying to reassure her.

"If you say so."

"I do." Brid said, getting up from the couch and walking down the hallway.

"Running out on me already? If you want to call 9-1-1 and tell them you've got a crazy woman in your house...the phone's out here!" Devon said rather loudly, chuckling to herself.

Brid reappeared as she walked down the hallway with a black case in her hand. She brought it over to the coffee table, sat it down, and unzipped the case. Inside laid a laptop computer and a series of power cords and cables.

"This will only take me a minute." She said, grabbing the cables and cords out of the case.

"Go for it..." Devon said, watching as Brid quickly matched and plugged in all of the cables needed. She sat back down on the couch, placing the notebook computer on her lap, finally powering it up.

"Sorry...I'm going into full research mode on you here." Brid said, waiting for Windows to power up.

"No need to apologize...I'll take all of the help I can get at this point." Devon said, gratefully.

Brid opened her internet browser, waiting for the modem to connect to it's dial-up connection. "Do you know what kind of an owl it was?" She asked.

"I'm not sure...but I think it was a Great Horned Owl."

"Just a sec...I'm going to pull up a bunch of pictures here, just to make sure. I know what I saw...but I want to see if we're seeing the same thing." Brid said, searching the net for an owl webpage with pictures of the different species on it.

Devon scanned over the images one-by-one, looking for the match.

"There...that's it. No doubt about it."She said, pointing to the image of the Great Horned Owl. "Is that what you saw?"

"Yes...looks like we're on the same track here, eh?"

"Guess so. What now?" Devon asked.

"Now the research starts. We need to find out everything we can about the mystical aspects of the Great Horned Owl. I'm not sure, but I'm guessing that it is one of your totems."

"Totems?"

"Yes…they're like…teachers, or guides." Brid said. She could see the confusion building in Devon's eyes.

"Okay…let's start from the beginning. We are all a part of the earth…animals, plants, insects…everything. We used to respect nature, taking only what we needed to survive. We didn't waste, we used everything that we took—and we showed respect by honoring and thanking the animal spirits for providing us with food, shelter, and comfort. We used to give thanks by wearing skins, singing praises, and praying to these specific animals. Doing this allowed us to remain linked to our animal spirit guides and accept the power and knowledge that they offer us in teachings, in life, and in death. Are you still with me?" Brid asked, hoping that Devon was grasping the concept.

"I think so…this sounds a lot like Native American beliefs."

"Exactly…and these animal spirits, these totems, still hold the power and knowledge that we can use. We just have to remember how to use it. We have to be one with nature. We are all one." Brid said.

"Okay, so why the owl? What does it want?"
"Well…that's what we have to find out. Animal spirits usually come to a person because they have a lesson that you need to learn or a power that they are going to share with you. Let's see what it says about the owl…" Brid said, typing OWL TOTEM into the search window and hitting enter.

"You know…now that I think about it. I've seen a lot of owls in my lifetime. More than usual, I think." Devon said, realizing just how many time she had come into contact with the 'night eagles.'

"Really?" Brid said, pausing momentarily to pay closer attention to what Devon was saying. There was something about the dark, brooding Detective that she found absolutely fascinating.

"Seriously! Growing up, I used to like to spend a lot of time in the woods behind our house…and I can remember several times when an owl would fly down close enough to me that I could feel the wind from it's wings running through my hair. This one time, I even got close enough to one of them to actually pet it…in the wild! It wasn't one of the big ones though…I remember looking it up at the time. I think it was a Screech Owl or something. It actually let me pet it!" Devon said, feeling oddly excited over the thought of her contact with these beautiful creatures of the night.

Brid smiled, the energy and exuberance projected by Devon was absolutely mesmerizing.

"That is so great! It sounds like the owl has been with you for a very long time." Brid said.

"Yeah…I guess it has. I wonder why I'm just noticing this now."

"Maybe you need it more now than you did before." Brid suggested.

"Because of this case?" Devon asked.

"Could be…or could be something entirely different."

"So what do you think it's trying to tell me?"

"Hard to tell at this point…it depends on what kind of totem the owl is to you." Brid said.

"There's different kinds?"

"Yes. There is your life totem or totems…you might have more than one. It's always there when you need its powers. It reflects your inner spiritual nature."

Devon shifted in her seat…making herself more comfortable as she got more and more drawn in to the conversation.

"You know what's weird? I remember when I was little, my dad and I were working in the barn and I found these little furry-like pellets…" Devon said, smiling as she remembered the moment. "…Dad laughed because I said something about the 'furry poopies' or something. He explained that it wasn't scat, that they were owl pellets. The owls eat their prey and then regurgitate the fur and bones—things they can't digest. I didn't believe him, so he cut one open with his jack knife and we looked at what was inside. This one had been feasting on field mice. You could see the fur and the little bones and everything."

"Sounds like your dad was quite the teacher." Brid said, enjoying the fact that Devon had opened up to her, giving her a glimpse of her childhood.

"Everything was always a learning experience with my Mom and Dad. Every summer, we would take a two-week long trip to somewhere in the United States or Canada." Devon said, taking another sip of her wine to wet her lips.

"We would hit every historical site along the way. Other people took their kids to Cedar Point and while we were learning the finer points of how the Union soldiers used to soften their hard tack bread by putting it in their sweaty armpits as they marched along."

Brid grimaced thinking about the sweat-soaked bread. "Really?" She asked.

"Yep…made show and tell a lot of fun! 'Hey Billy—tell us what you did on your summer vacation.'" Devon said, mimicking the teacher. "Well…first I rode on Demon Drop, and the kid sitting next to me puked and it flew up and hit the ceiling!" She said in her best little-boy voice. "…and then it was 'how about you, Devon?' Oh…I learned about an odd cult called the Shakers that didn't allow husbands and wives to live together. They picked up orphans and stuff and made them join and then they would all dance and shake until they passed out."

Brid tried desperately to stifle her giggling.

"Hey…you laugh! I was a real hit with all of the kids! You should have seen the look on the teacher's face." Devon said, trying to be serious.

"I'll bet you kept your parents and teachers on their toes." Brid said, chuckling.

She couldn't help being attracted to this woman…she had so many layers to her…brooding and dark, calculating and decisive, not to mention a sarcastically funny sense of humor.

"Hey, I'll have you know I was NOT a problem child." Devon said, trying to sound defensive in a humorous way. "I was challenging…that's all."She said, crossing her arms in front of her chest, smirking.

"…and you still are." Brid added, smiling seductively.

An awkward silence followed her actions, neither knowing what to say or do next.

"Um…yeah…well…I've been babbling on here. We should be getting back to this whole totem thing." Devon said, trying to change the subject. It wasn't that she didn't find Brid attractive, quite the contrary, actually—and that was the problem…the all-to-familiar pangs of guilt had reared their ugly heads once again.

"Of course…I'm sorry." Brid said, pulling back. She could feel the walls going up around Devon once again.

"It's alright…I just want to get back to what we were working on…the case, I mean." Devon said, trying to put the woman's mind at ease.

"So obviously the owl is trying to tell me something, the problem is we just don't know what it is, right?"

"Basically, yes. You probably won't know until the time comes. All that you can do at this point is use the gifts that your totem has given you."

"Which would be?"

"The ability to see what others cannot. The owl has the best stereoscopic vision of all of the birds, and depending on the type—some have better night vision, some daylight. The owl can't be deceived…it has the power to see through the deception." Brid said.

Devon flopped back into the couch, slumping and releasing a long sigh, frustrated with the whole situation. "Ugh! How in the hell am I supposed to figure all of this out? I've got nothing to go on!"

Brid laid her hand on Devon's knee. "You can do it. I know you can…I know you will. It's just a matter of time."

"We don't have time. This guy's not going to stop…"

"No. He's not. There's got to be something you're missing. He can't have done this and not left any clues, could he?" Brid asked.

"There's no such thing as the perfect crime…but this guy is coming pretty damned close. We haven't got really anything substantial at this point." Devon said, disheartened by the realization.

"Maybe you just need a second pair of eyes to look at them…" suggested Brid.

"I can't let you do that…these are police files, they're confidential, Brid."
"I understand that, I really do…but what if, say, you had the files with you here. You were going over them while eating dinner, and left them on the coffee table when you got up to use the restroom…and maybe I just decided to take a quick peek…"

"You are so bad! You know that, don't you?" Devon said, jokingly.

"Me? Never…I'm as pure as the driven snow." Brid said, trying to act innocent.

"Right…" Devon said, getting up from the couch and heading to the door.

"Where are you going?"

"I've got some files that I need to look over while I'm eating the rest of my supper…" Devon said with a wink as she disappeared out the door.

Brid felt a certain satisfaction that Devon had actually decided to go along with her suggestion. She got up from the couch and walked into the kitchen, placing Devon's plate into the microwave to warm it.

Devon returned a moment later, files in-hand. She was just about to sit back down on the couch when Brid walked in with her plate of food.

"What's this?" Devon asked as Brid approached her.

"The rest of your supper, remember? It's all part of my evil scheme!" Brid said, grinning.

Devon smiled, taking the plate. She knew that she had been had.

"Okay…you got me. Thanks." Devon said, sitting the files down on the coffee table.

She reclaimed her seat on the couch and began eating her food. "This is really good, you know. Thanks for doing all of this."

"No problem. I wanted to…help out, that is. Anything I can do…" Brid said, trying not to make it too obvious that she was, in fact, interested in more than just helping out with the case.

"So…you're a professor at the University, right?"

"That would be me…" Brid answered.

"What subject?" Devon asked, scooping another bite into her mouth.

"Subjects, actually…I teach a variety of Anthropology classes, as well as some religion classes."

"Really…religion? Like what?" Devon asked, quite interested at this new information about Brid.

"Oh…let's see…I teach a survey course that covers a wide range of religions, one on ancient cults, and also a course on death and dying."

Devon stopped mid-chew "Death and dying? I don't remember ever having a class like that when I was in college!"

"It's something that I actually originated here at this University. Not something that I created...just brought it here, to this school. It covers all different aspects of death and dying, the stages of grief, and how different cultures and religions view all of it." Brid explained.

"No matter how you view it, it sucks...death, that is. Just my humble opinion." Devon said, her tone turning decidedly dark.

"Everybody is entitled to their opinion."

"So what...you're saying that death isn't bad?" Devon said, not quite believing that Brid would be saying something like that.

"Death is only bad for those who are left behind. In some cases...I would even say death is a blessing..."

"A blessing? From who? God? How do you figure?" Devon asked, the emotion within her starting to boil.

"Well...how about a person who is terminally ill...with cancer, let's say. They go every week for their chemotherapy...which makes them sicker than they were battling the cancer alone. Their quality of life goes down considerably with each passing day. The chemotherapy doesn't work, but they continue to fight, day-in and day-out, in constant pain and seclusion because of their lowered immunity from the chemotherapy that is supposed to be saving them. Where is their quality of life? They have none. Would death not be a blessing to them? Putting them out of their misery, so to speak?"

"Okay...I'll go along with that...but it's different when the person hasn't been sick or anything...when they're taken before their time." Devon said.

"That's a tough one...but the way some religions look at it is that we are each assigned a task in life to complete. Once that task is completed, we are rewarded by being allowed to pass on to Heaven, or whatever your concept of Heaven might be…" Brid explained.

"Rewarded by being killed?" Devon said, not sure that she had heard correctly.

"Death is just the vehicle by which the reward is given…"
"So do you believe that?" Devon asked.

"Do I believe that there is something after death…yes, definitely." Brid answered. "What that 'something' is, I'm not sure. I think it's different for everybody based on their beliefs."

"So…you don't think that it's bad…death, that is."

"It's all a part of life, Dev. No…I don't think it's bad. I think it's just the next step in our transformation…kind of like growing up. We're constantly changing, growing…death is just a part of that change." Brid said. "The best way to honor those who have moved on is to live your life to the fullest…enjoy every day that you have before you make that transition to whatever lies beyond…no matter how tough that may be at times."

Devon thought about Brid's words and found some solace in them. Perhaps she was right…Devon hoped so. Feeling somewhat vulnerable, she decided to get back to the case at hand. Remembering the arrangement made earlier, she sat her plate down on the coffee table, getting up and walking towards the hallway.

"Is everything okay? Where are you going?" Brid asked, concerned.

"It's fine." Devon said, smiling, hoping to sound reassuring."Remember…I'm just going to the bathroom now…leaving the files on the table…aaahem!" Devon said, clearing her throat, chuckling to herself as she disappeared down the hallway.

Once Devon was out of sight, Brid reached for the files.

The stack, which was about four inches deep, contained several folders with statements, lab results, and pictures in it. Brid knew that it would most likely be very graphic; however, she was not prepared for what she saw as she opened the first folder.

The first thing that came to her was an unbelievable sense of pain…not just physical pain, but emotional pain as well—and not just from the victim, but also from the killer himself.

She looked at the label on the folder. It read: HINGERMAN, HALLIE.

She was the first victim.

Brid thumbed through the post-mortem report, as well as the interviews and backgrounds of the immediate family and other persons of interest. The whole time trying to be especially attuned to the feelings that she was experiencing while perusing the files.

One-by-one, she looked at each file. Reading the information, reviewing the pictures of the bodies and the scenes.

"Hey! Are you just about done in there? There's only so much a person can do in a bathroom…especially one without reading material!" Devon yelled from down the hallway.

Brid smiled, snickering to herself.

"Okay…I'm going through your medicine cabinet now…Hmmm…nice perfume! It does smell great on you!" Devon said, passing the time.

"Not exactly known for your patience, are you?" Brid said back to Devon.

Devon walked down the hallway, peeking around the corner into the living room.

"I'm a cop…not a doctor. I don't need patience." Devon said, jokingly.

"Good thing…or you'd definitely be coming up on the short end of things." Brid said.

"So are you going to hide out in the bathroom the whole time or are you going to come out here so we can go through this together?"

"I really shouldn't…"

"I really shouldn't be looking through these files, either…but I am." Brid said.

"Good point." Devon said, walking back to the couch.

"Slide over." She said, sitting down on the couch once more, this time close enough that the two women could look at the files at the same time.

Devon's skin tingled as her taut leg brushed up against Brid's. Both women looked down simultaneously.

"Ooops…sorry. Didn't mean to crowd you." Devon said, sliding over a bit, breaking the contact.

Brid felt a wave of warmth building within her very soul as her face blushed ruddy. "No problem…really." She said, suddenly feeling a bit nervous.

They sat for a moment, neither knowing what to say—both feeling the energy flowing between them. Devon was the first to break the awkward silence.

"So…did you find anything?" She asked.

"I'm not sure." Brid said, running her hand along the top of the Hingerman file once more. "I'm kind of getting something here that doesn't make a whole lot of sense."

"What do you mean 'getting something'?"
"Try to keep an open mind about this, okay?" Brid said, trying to ease into her explanation. She knew that Devon was a born skeptic, which was going to make things rather interesting.

"Okay…" Devon said, folding her arms across her chest "…let's hear it."

"Do you know what an 'empath' is?" She asked.

"Would you be shocked if I said yes?" Devon said, waiting for her reaction.

"No...not at all...well...maybe...yes." Brid said, rather surprised. "How?"

"You're going to laugh...but I was big into the whole supernatural thing as a kid...I read a lot about it. Some of it actually in comic books, believe it or not! I grew up on shows like 'the Twilight Zone' and 'Nightstalker'...so I guess it kind of sparked my interest in those things."

"Really?"

"Serious as a heart attack! I read everything I could get a hold of about it. So...what kind of an empath are you?" Devon asked.

"I can pick up feelings from people when I touch them, or if I'm in close proximity of them. I also get vibes from objects that a person has touched, or pictures of people or things."

Devon wondered if she had been reading her emotions...

"Haven't picked up on anything with me, have you?" Devon asked, sheepishly.

"I think you already know the answer to that question, Dev." Brid said, seriously. Her steel-gray eyes trained intently on Devon's.

"Yeah...kind of figured. So how long have you been able to do that?"

"Since I was nine." Brid answered.

"You mean you weren't born with the ability?"

Brid started to look decidedly uncomfortable. "No...I wasn't."

"Isn't that kind of unusual? I mean, everything that I've read...it's usually something that runs in families..." Devon said.

"Yes, usually." Brid said quietly. "So anyhow...I felt something kind of odd when I was looking at the crime scene photos."
Devon was not oblivious to Brid's sudden change of subject.

Huh...kind of touched a nerve there. Wonder what she's hiding...Whatever it is, she's doing a pretty good job of it. Looks like you're not the only one fighting with your inner demons, here McKinney!

"Okay...I'm not the psychic one here. Can't really read your mind..." Devon said, trying to break some of the tension.

"What?" Brid said, snapping out of an apparent daze.

"Are you going to tell me what kind of vibes you got off of those photos?" Devon said, pointing to the stack of files.

"Yes, I'm sorry. Got a little lost in thought for a moment. Here's the deal...the pictures of the first victim..." Brid began.

"Hallie Hingerman?"

"Yes. That's the one. When I hold those pictures, I feel a wave of intense pain." Brid said.

"Well yeah, that kind of stands to reason...I mean, hel-lo! She was gutted!" Devon said sarcastically.

"Obviously. But I'm not just talking physical pain...I sensed emotional pain, as well."

"Isn't that normal?" Devon asked.

"Not really. The victim's feelings are usually fear or panic...this is a deep-seeded emotional pain." Brid said.

"Well...it's not unusual for a killer to have some pretty hefty emotional problems, hence being a homicidal maniac and all..."

"Right. The thing is, when I hold the pictures of the other scenes, I get the physical pain, fear, panic…but the emotional pain isn't there. There's no regret. Nothing."

"That's interesting." Devon said, not wanting to put too much weight on it, but also not discounting it either.

"Did you find anything else?"

"Yes. Have you had a chance to look through the handler's notes?" She asked.

"No, not yet. Why?"

"When I was glancing through them, I found this one that mentioned a trailer in the middle of the woods…off from one of those two-tracks that you told me about." Brid said, shuffling through the stack of files, pulling out a hand drawn map. "Here…" she said, handing the map to Devon. "See? Right there." She said, pointing to the area on the map where the trailer was located.

Devon looked at the area on the map. She couldn't believe that it hadn't been thoroughly searched.

"They should have checked that out. I can't imagine the team finding something like this and not searching it. They had to have cleared it." Devon said, obviously troubled by this new bit of information. "Hand me their report for that sector, will you?"

"Sure…here." Brid said, handing the papers to Devon.

Devon scanned through the report, looking for any references to the trailer. She finally found the passage, it read:

12:35—   CAME UPON A SMALL TRAVEL-TYPE TRAILER. NO PLATES. APPROXIMATELY ONE MILE FROM POINT A, 150 YARDS WEST OF TWO-TRACK. VARIOUS SMALL MAKE-SHIFT OUT BUILDINGS NOTED. SIGNS OF RECENT OCCUPANCY. CONTACTED BASE TO INFORM AND WAS GIVEN NO-JOY COMMAND.

"Base gave them a NO-JOY command on searching the area." Devon said, obviously surprised, as it made no sense not to search the area.

"No-joy? What's that mean?"

"It means 'Do not approach—Do not engage'."

"Why would they do something like that?" Brid asked.

"I don't know…but you can bet your ass I'm going to find out." Devon said, an all-too-familiar look of determination spreading across her face.

C H A P T E R   17

▼

"Damnit!" Devon said, pressing END on her cell phone.

"Still no luck?" Brid said, walking back into the living room with a cup of hot tea for each of them. She handed the cup to Devon as she sat back down on the couch.

"Sorry…thanks…and no, no luck. I can't get a hold of Mike." Devon said, tossing the phone onto the coffee table.

"So what are you going to do?" Brid asked, cupping her mug of tea in both hands, bringing it to her lips for a sip.

"I'm going to go check it out. It should have been searched."

"Dev…you can't go by yourself!"

"I'll be fine. I'm just going to take a quick look around. If I find anything—I'll call for backup." Devon said, reassuring her.

"I don't think that this is a good idea, Devon…seriously. I'm getting a really bad feeling about it." Brid said, the concern coming through loud and clear in the tone of her voice.

"Look…it's probably nothing."

"If it's nothing, then why can't it wait until morning…or until you can get Mike to go with you?" Brid asked.

"Because."

"Oh that's brilliant!" Brid said, getting up and walking towards the hallway.

"Where are you going?"

"To change my clothes. I'm going with you." Brid said, continuing on to her bedroom.

Oh great! This is JUST what I need…

Devon stood up and started to follow her down the hallway, stopping herself just short of the bedroom door.

"This is ridiculous! You're NOT going with me!" Devon said, the tone of her voice sounding decidedly more aggressive than in the moments before.

Brid stuck her head out of the bedroom door, her steel-gray eyes meeting Devon's head-on.

"Okay, listen. I am NOT going to let you go out there in the dark, by yourself, and get yourself killed!" Brid said, matter-of-factly.

"And I am NOT taking you out there with me! You'll only slow me down…and besides, if something does happen—it will be twice as hard for me to get myself out of there if I have to worry about saving you at the same time!"

The thought of Devon thinking that she needed 'saving' infuriated Brid. If there's one thing that she could do—it was take care of herself!

"I don't need YOU or anyone else to take care of me! I've been doing just fine by myself for quite some time now, thank you very much!" Brid said, going back into the bedroom to change her clothes.

Devon leaned against the wall in the hallway, letting her head hit with a thud.

"Brid...I appreciate you wanting to do this...I really do, but I can't take you with me. I just can't. I do have something that you CAN do for me, though..."

Brid poked her head back out of the doorway, once again meeting eyes with Devon.

"Such as?" Brid asked.

"I'm going to leave the map with you and if you don't hear from me in say...two hours, I want you to call the station and get me some back up in there, okay?" Devon said, hoping that Brid would take her up on the offer.

Brid rolled her eyes at Devon, realizing that she was not going to win this debacle. She took a deep breath, exhaling loudly before finally relenting.

"Okay...but if you're thirty seconds late, I'm going to have every available police officer in the area in there looking for you." Brid said, sternly.

"I'd expect nothing less." Devon said, smiling. It was kind of nice to have somebody watching out for her...caring what happened to her, again.

Fifteen minutes later, Brid walked Devon out to her SUV. Devon climbed in, closing the door as the blonde leaned in the open driver's side window.

"Have you got everything that you need?" Brid asked.

"Flashlight...gun...extra ammo...cell phone...yep. I'd say I've got everything but the kitchen sink in here. You know where to send them if you don't hear from me, right?" Devon asked.
"I've got everything written down...along with the copy of the map." Brid said, holding the papers up for Devon to see.

"I gave you the phone number for central dispatch, along with the station-house, right?"

"Yes...everything." Brid said, nodding.

"Okay...well, guess I'll talk to you in a couple of hours then." Devon said, hoping that she wasn't jinxing herself by saying it. She turned the key in the ignition, feeling the hum of the engine throughout her body.

"Dev?" Brid said, laying her hand on Devon's forearm, squeezing gently.

"Yeah?" Devon said, her eyes meeting Brid's.

A million things ran through Brid's mind as she stood there for a brief moment, gazing into Devon's eyes...not sure what she wanted...just knowing that this woman was special. She had been hurt so much, Brid could feel her pain, and she didn't want her to be hurt any more...physically or emotionally.

"Just be careful, okay? Don't just look...see. Keep an open mind."

"I will." Devon said, smiling softly as Brid stepped away from the SUV. She pulled the transmission into drive, speeding off into the night.

Brid watched as the red glow of the taillights as they faded off into the darkness. She looked up to the sky, her eyes trained on the moon above.

Watch after her, Guardian of the Night...

Off in the distance, the Night Eagle took flight, gliding silently through the air...

Devon was actually surprised at how awake she was, given the lack of sleep that she had experienced in the past two days. She drove down the dirt road leading to the entrance of the two-track, mulling over what she was about to do. The sound of "Riders On The Storm" by the Doors echoing through her ears...

*"There's a killer on the road...his brain is squirmin' like a toad. Take
a long holiday...let your children play. If you give this man a ride,
sweet memory will die...Killer on the road..."*

Driving along the bumpy road, she wondered if this was the route that the killer had taken. Had he watched them as they searched the areas, waiting for the precise moment when he would be able to drop and position the body without being noticed?

As she approached the entrance to the two-track, Devon reached over, turning the volume on the radio off. She rolled down the windows on both sides and turned off her headlights. If someone was, in fact, squatting in the area, she didn't want to tip them off to the fact that she was snooping around. She knew that if there was someone back there, that they most definitely knew the lay of the land better than she did, and that could surely spell trouble.

Luckily, the moon was bright enough that she could see fairly well without the use of the headlights. The SUV slowly crept along the trail, Devon listening intently to everything that was going on around her. She looked down at the odometer, noticing that she was nearing the trailer area.

She found a small turn-around and parked the SUV, pulling the keys out of the ignition and sliding them under the mat on the driver's side. She sat there for a moment in the silence, listening to her heartbeat, finally deciding to open the door and step outside.

Making sure it was loaded; she tucked her .40 caliber into the pancake holster in her waistband, stuffing the extra clips into her pocket. Reaching into the cab, she grabbed her flashlight off the floor. Not wanting to announce her arrival, she slowly closed the door, waiting for the metal to make contact on the frame before quietly pushing it shut with a 'click.'

Damn…should have brought bug dope!

The mosquitoes were already swarming onto every bit of exposed flesh on her body as she took off walking down the two-track the last few hundred yards to the trailer area. The soft sand bogged her boots down as she continued down the path, her foot digging in deeply with each step.

She stopped dead in her tracks as she saw the soft glow of a lantern moving through the woods near the trailer. Taking a breath and holding it, she listened carefully…

Their voices were muffled, but decidedly male. Devon's hackles immediately went up, all of her senses sharpening as the adrenalin pumped into her system. She drew her gun from its holster, moving stealthily through the woods, trying to get closer to the out buildings.

The thorns from wild raspberry bushes tore into her flesh, leaving a stinging welt-like scratch in their wake as she moved closer. Two figures stood around the warm orange glow of a campfire. One was tall and thin, the other slightly shorter and heavy-set. The heavy-set one reached down into a cooler full of ice and pulled out what appeared to be a can of beer, handing one to the other man and then taking one for himself. The two sat down near the fire, laughing as they opened their beer...

"Did you see the ass on that one? Damn!" Said the stout man.

"Oh yeah...she was tighter than the security at Fort Knox!"
"Hell...what did you expect? She's only eight!"

Geezus...please tell me they are not talking about what I think they are...

Devon's stomach turned as she realized that they were, in fact, talking about children.

She looked around, noticing the silhouette of another person passing through the light inside the trailer.

Shit! That's number three...not good, McKinney!

Devon's heart was thumping hard inside her chest, her senses piqued as the adrenalin flowed freely now into her body. Suddenly, she caught movement from the corner of her eye. Fighting the urge to turn quickly, she glanced over the area, seeing yet another figure walking through the trees towards the campfire...talking on a cell phone.

Pretty damned hi-tech for a bunch of squatters...

"Hey...toss me a beer, will you, Dean?" He asked, pulling up a log to sit on.

The man sitting on the cooler stood up, lifted the cover, grabbed a beer and tossed it to the man who had been talking on the phone.

"Thanks." He said, popping the can open and taking a swig.

"So were you able to get a hold of him?" The thin man asked.

"Yeah...I've gotta meet him in town...he's going to bring the stuff with him."

"Can't he just send them as j-pegs to that blind email account you set up?" Said the thin man.

"He's pretty spooky...doesn't want to send anything over the internet. He said that he has a buddy that got caught that way."

"So what's he bringing, the actual pictures?"

"No...he's bringing a CD-ROM. As soon as I get it, I'll bring it back here and burn you guys a copy."

I'd like to burn you a copy of the child pornography laws, you asshole!

"Sweet! I can't wait to get a look at it...they are all supposed to be under ten."

Okay...as much as I would like to just stay here and shoot the lot of you—you sick fucks, I would also like to get out of here alive. Time to get the hell out of here and come back with the troops...

She turned quietly, lifting her foot, placing the ball of her foot down first, rolling back onto her heel so not to make a noise. Slowly she made her way through the brambles towards the two-track. Step by step, easing her weight down onto her foot, being careful not to make any noise that may give her position away. Just before she reached the edge of the trail, a small twig snapped under the weight of her step. She cringed as the sound echoed through the still night air.

Shit!

The sound caught the immediate attention of the men sitting around the campfire. Their heads turned, listening...trying to determine where the sound came from.

Okay McKinney...decision time! Try to sneak the rest of the way out of here...or run like hell!

She looked over, seeing the men rising up from their seats, heading into the woods.

Looks like 'run like hell' is the winner!

Devon took off on a dead run through the woods, trying to get back to her SUV before the group caught up with her. She could hear voices behind her as she crashed through the underbrush, finally reaching the two-track. Devon's feet dug into the loose sand, trying to gain traction as she ran down the trail towards the turn-around where she had parked her vehicle. She turned around briefly, looking behind her to see if anyone was nearby. Seeing no one, she continued to the SUV, grasping the handle, pulling the door open.

Keys...keys!

Devon frantically searched her pockets for the keys to no avail. Finally realizing that she had, in fact, stowed them underneath the mat. She bent over, flipping back the corner of the mat, revealing the keys.

Yes!

She reached forward, taking the keys in her hand, just as she felt a sharp pain in the back of her head.

What the?

The space around her seemed to collapse into darkness as everything went pitch black.

The figure of a man stood hovering over her body, the butt of a pistol visible in his right hand.

Meanwhile…

Brid looked down at her watch, it had been nearly two hours since Devon had left for the woods. She stood in the living room, pacing back and forth, waiting for the phone to ring…it never did.

Come on, Devon…call…please?

She looked down at the hands of her watch once more…five minutes to go.

Okay…I'm not going to panic. She's still got five minutes. Give her that five minutes…she'll call.

Brid glanced at the face of the watch once more…suddenly a sinking feeling invaded the depths of her very being…she knew in an instant what it meant…

Like hell, she'll call! Something's wrong!

Brid grabbed the phone and the list of numbers that Devon had given her, dialing the first on the list. It was the non-published number for Central Dispatch.

"Hello, my name is Brid Morrigan. Detective McKinney told me to call this number and tell you that she needs backup…"

Three hours later, Devon slowly began to open her eyes. The light was blinding, and sent a searing hot pain through her head. She squinted in an attempt to lessen its effects, however unsuccessfully. Where she was, she didn't know. What had happened? Also a big blank. But the one thing that she was sure of was that she was alive…because there was no way in hell that death could hurt this much!

"Mmmmmm…" Devon moaned, as she once again tried to open her eyes, her head throbbing intensely. Suddenly, through the blinding pain, she felt a calming touch.

"Shhh…just rest. You gave us all quite a scare, Dev." Brid said, wiping Devon's brow with a cool cloth.

"Wha...?" Devon said, trying to raise her head up. What should have been an easy task was much more difficult than she thought, as it felt as if someone had strapped a twenty pound weight on her forehead. Her head hit the pillow with a thud, sending yet another wave of pain through the lump at the base of her skull.

"Take it easy, there kiddo...you've got yourself quite the hema-tomato on the back of your skull. Lucky for us you're so hard-headed, if you'd been a human, you would have been dead!" Mike said, jokingly.

"Mike?" Devon said, looking up, squinting in the light.

"Yeah...Mike...you know...your partner...the one you're supposed to be taking with you on all late-night trailer-trash scum bag raids!" Mike said, partially kidding...partially not.

It wasn't like Devon to be so careless.

"You're lucky your friend here got a hold of us when she did." He said, looking at Brid.

"Mike...we gotta get somebody out there..." Devon said, trying to sit up once again.

"No...WE don't! YOU are going to stay right here and let this nice lady take care of you." Mike said, putting his hand on her chest, gently pushing her back to the bed.

Devon shot a glare in Mike's general direction. He knew how much she hated being told what to do...but he felt that in this case, he was in the right.

"Devon...listen. Mike is right. Let him take care of it. You need to rest." Brid said, trying to calm her down.

Devon pulled herself up by the railings of the bed, reaching over with her right hand, pulling out the IV that was in her left. Mike rushed to grab her arm, but he was too late, the needle was out.

"What in the hell do you think you're doing, Dev?" Mike said, placing his hand over the puncture wound where her IV had been, stopping the bleeding.

"I'm getting the hell out of here...I've got a trailer full of pedophiles, one of which very well could be the asshole we've been looking for!" Devon said, trying to lower the railing, deciding instead to climb overtop of it.

Mike caught her as her bare feet hit the floor, her legs wobbling beneath her.

"Dev...that's not your concern anymore." He said, supporting her weight in his arms.

Devon looked into her partner's face, searching for a clue that would help her to understand what he had just said, but there was none.

"We've been taken off the case." Mike said, knowing that Devon wouldn't want him to candy-coat it.

The look in Mike's eyes told Devon that he wasn't kidding.

"No!" Devon said, struggling to pull away from her partner. "They can't do that!"

"They can and they did, Dev. There's nothing you or I can do about it." He said, letting her go.

Brid stood back, folding her arms in front of her chest, feeling that it was not her place to get involved in the conversation at this point.

"Why?" It was all that Devon could think of saying. The words seemed to fall from her lips. Disappointment and hurt both evident in her voice.

"Come on, Dev...do you even have to ask?" Mike said, getting a bit irritated himself. "You go off half-cocked by yourself in the middle of the night to check out an area that had already been declared off-limits and you involved a civilian in the inner workings of a homicide investigation! You can't think that they wouldn't notice!"

Devon said nothing in response, she looked around the room, agitated.

"Where's my clothes?" She said, turning to Brid.

"Dev…I really don't think you should…" Brid began.

"Where's my fucking clothes?" she yelled.

"They're in a bag, in the closet." Brid said, trying hard not to let Devon's words sting too much. She knew how much this case meant to her, and couldn't imagine how she was feeling right now.

"Where are you going?" Mike asked.

"To get this case back…now do you mind getting the hell out of the room so I can get changed?" She said, gruffly.

There was nothing to say. He knew that she would not listen to him. She had her own agenda, and knowing Devon…nothing he could say would ever stop her. She was more stubborn and determined than anyone he had ever met. It irritated the piss out of him, but it was also what he admired the most about her. That stubbornness and determination was what had gotten her where she was in the department…but also, unfortunately…it had also gotten her where she was now.

He turned without saying a word, walking out of the hospital room, closing the door behind him.

Devon reached into the closet, grabbing the clear plastic drawstring bag, opening it and tossing her clothes onto the chair next to the bed. She reached behind her neck, trying to untie the hospital robe. The ties were knotted too tightly, and she quickly became frustrated that she couldn't get them undone.

Brid walked over to Devon, her slender fingers slowly untying the knots on the back of the gown.

Neither of the women could deny the electricity flowing between the two of them.

Feeling the tie release, Devon stepped away, putting some distance in between them to lessen the awkwardness of the moment.

"Thanks." Devon said, reaching behind to finish undoing the gown.

"No problem...I'll just step outside." Brid said, turning away from Devon. She didn't want her to notice the blush that was quickly spreading across her porcelain cheeks.

"It's okay...you can stay...I mean, I'm sure it's nothing you haven't seen before." Devon said, matter-of-factly.

"Actually...I should probably go get the nurse...we'll have to get you discharged." Brid said, hoping that Devon would buy the excuse.

"Papers or not...I'm going." Devon said, pulling on her BDU trousers underneath the hospital gown.

Brid nodded, smiling gently as she opened the door and slipped out of the room.

Devon took the hospital gown off, tossing it onto the chair and grabbing her own shirt, pulling it over her head.

They are NOT taking me off this case!

CHAPTER 18

▼

"Detective McKinney...I understand your wanting to go home..." the Doctor began.

"I don't want to go home! I need to go to my office...I've got a case to work on!" Devon said, angrily.

"Fine then...your office. Detective, you've sustained a pretty significant blow to the back of your head. You have a rather pronounced hematoma...if you leave the hospital now, we cannot guarantee your well-being..."

"Can you guarantee it if I stay?" Devon asked, sarcastically.

"Well...no...but we can look after you here, and should anything happen, the best of care would be available to you almost immediately." Said the Doctor, sheepishly.

"Dev, listen to the man...come on! You're gonna hurt yourself! It's not worth it!" Mike said, trying to reason with her.

"Mike...I'm going. You can either shut up and give me a ride to the station, or you can get the hell out of my way...either way, I'm out of here." Devon said, strangely calm.

"Okay...okay. I'll take you to the station." Mike relented.

"Detective McKinney...I'm going to need you to sign this form here. It simply states that you won't hold the hospital responsible should anything happen to you as a result of you leaving against medical advice." The Doctor said, handing her the form and an ink pen.

Devon took the paper, signed it, and handed back to the Doctor.

"Okay...let's get the hell out of here." Devon said, walking past Brid and Mike towards the elevator.

The two followed close behind. Devon walked up to the elevator, hitting the button several times, impatiently.

"I hear that makes them go faster." Brid said, smiling softly.

"What?" Devon said, turning towards Brid.

"Pushing the button incessantly...it makes the elevator go faster...common knowledge, really." Brid said, trying to lighten the tension a bit.

Devon looked back at the blonde, smirking.

"I know what you're trying to do...and it won't work. I'm allowed to be a bitch...it's my right."

"...and she exercises that right on a regular basis...just FYI." Mike added.

"I'll keep that in mind." Brid said, just as their floor number lit up on the panel, sounding an audible 'ding'.

"Looks like your number is up." Mike said, jokingly.

"Let's hope not." Devon said as the doors to the elevator slid open. She stepped aside, motioning for Brid to enter ahead of her.

Mike noticed the action right away, smiling to himself as he walked into the elevator, pushing the button for the first floor.

Huh…maybe she is starting to come out of the funk she's been in since Chris died. God, I hope so…

The three stood silent as the elevator descended to the first floor, coming to a stop before the door slid open. The three exited into the hallway. Devon turned to Brid, reaching out and taking the professor's hand in her own.

"Thanks for…well…everything. I owe you one, big time." Devon said, her voice taking on a soft, but decidedly serious tone.

"Not a problem…any time. I'll let you know when I plan to collect." Brid said with a wink as she slowly let go of Devon's hand, disappearing through the exit door.

"I like her!" Mike blurted out, grinning widely.

"What?" Devon asked.

"Seriously…she's got…spunk!" Mike said, continuing to grin.

"She's just a friend, doofus." Devon said, blushing slightly.

"Uh-huh…"

"Seriously!" Devon protested.

"Yeah…right. She told me all about you guys going out to dinner and all…" Mike said, trying to egg Devon on.

"She told you we went out to dinner?" Devon said, rather taken back by the thought that Brid would have volunteered this information.
"She didn't tell me…you just did!" Mike laughed.

Devon slugged him in the arm, kidding.

"You jerk! It's nothing. Seriously…we're just friends." She said as they walked out the door to the parking lot.

"Hey…I think it's great…I think SHE'S great…and it's obvious that she likes you."

"Can we not talk about this, please?" Devon said, now getting a bit annoyed by Mike's persistence.

"Okay…okay…sorry. I just think that it's good that you're at least being social again, you know?" Mike said, hitting the unlock button on the key chain remote, unlocking the doors to his mini-van.

"Oh God…the grocery-getter? You've gotta be kidding me!" Devon said, knowing that it would get Mike going.

"Hey…come on…not again." Mike pleaded, climbing into the van.

"I'll tell you what…you lay off on trying to fix up Brid and I…and I'll lay off on your little land-barge, here. Okay?" Devon said, closing the van door.

Mike looked at his partner, feigning disappointment.

"You drive a hard bargain, McKinney."

"Take it or leave it. That's my final offer…you lay off on playing Cupid, I lay off on making fun of 'mama's little mini-van'." Devon said, grinning…knowing that she had gotten the best of him.

"Okay, you win." Mike said, sliding the transmission into drive, pulling out of the parking space and onto the street.

"Where's my SUV? Did they tow it?" Devon asked, suddenly remembering that she had left it at the turn-around in the woods.

"No…one of the guys drove it back to the station. It's there waiting for you. The keys are in your office."

"Great, that way I don't need to go home before I get back out on the case." Devon said, not wanting to give it up just yet.

"Dev...there's nothing to work on...we're off the case. Chief Donelly's orders." Mike said, seriously.

"Yeah...well...we'll see about that." Devon said under her breath.

"I'm serious, Dev. He was furious...I've never seen him so mad."

"I'm going to talk to him, he'll understand." Devon said, confidently.

"You really think that's a good idea?" Mike asked.

"I'm not sure if it's good or not—but I've got nothing to lose at this point." Devon said, as they turned into the parking lot at the station.

Mike pulled up to the curb closest to the front door. Sliding the transmission into park, he asked, "You want me to go in with you?"

"Nah...I'm a big girl. Besides, no sense in both of us being in the hot seat." Devon said, opening the door and climbing out.

"Good luck...you're gonna need it." Mike said, forcing a smile.

Devon walked up the steps, still fighting the throbbing headache that she'd had since waking up in the hospital room. She reached up, rubbing the back of her head, feeling the large knot that had swelled up on her occipital region.

Damn...that guy must have been swinging for the fences! That's a helluva goose egg!

Devon made her way down the hallway to the Chief's office. His secretary was busy typing at her desk when she arrived.

"Hey Julie...is the Chief in?" Devon asked.

"Hi Dev. How are you feeling? I heard what happened!" The middle-aged woman said.

"Still got a pretty bad headache, but I'll be fine, thanks...about the Chief..."

"Oh…sorry about that. He just stepped out for a moment. He should be right back. He had some final things to take care of before he leaves on vacation. You can go on in and wait for him if you'd like." Julie said, smiling.

"Thanks." Devon said, walking into the inner office. The room smelled of pipe tobacco and rich cordovan leather. She ran her hand along the smooth surface of the over-stuffed hide of the chairs facing the burly maple desk. Pictures of his sons adorned the desktop and walls. Devon walked over, looking at the pictures.

Huh…wonder where the missus is. Divorce or death…it's got to be one of the two…

There were pictures of the boys when they were younger…playing baseball, soccer, graduating from high school. Devon picked up one of the few pictures that also included the Chief…one of the boys in the picture was holding what appeared to be a family pet…

"Detective McKinney…I'm surprised to see you out of the hospital so soon. How's your head?" The Chief said, walking over to the desk, pulling out the chair and sitting down.

"I've definitely seen better days." Devon said, frankly.

"Have a seat." Chief Donnelly said, motioning towards the chair behind her.

"Thanks, but if it's all the same to you, I'd rather stand."

"Suit yourself." Said the Chief, settling back into his chair.

"Devon…your record with this department has always been exemplary…until recently."

"Yes, well…it's been a hell of a bad year, but I've never let that affect my job performance." Devon said, trying to defend herself.

"I'm not so sure I would agree with you on that, Detective."

"Sir?"

"Devon, I know that Mike has probably already told you that I've taken you both off of the big case you've been working on…"

"Yes, he did mention it to me…and I know that I shouldn't have involved Ms. Morrigan in the case, but I thought that she may have had information that was pertinent to the case…" Devon tried to explain.

"Bringing Ms. Morrigan into the case is the least of your worries, Detective. Let me ask you this…because I'm really hoping that you have a good answer for me. Why did you decide to go and check out that area in the woods last night?" He said, tapping his pencil irritatingly on the desktop.

"I…" Devon began.

"Not only did you go into an unknown area without backup…but you also went into an area that you KNEW had been called no-joy!" the Chief said, becoming angrier each passing moment.

"That area should have been checked!" Devon said, emphatically. "It was well within one of the prime search sectors and had definite activity around it! The place is crawling with pedophiles, for Christ's sake!"

"That was NOT your concern! The area was to be left alone. Do you realize just what exactly you've done?"

"Last time I looked, my job!" Devon said, defensively.

Their discussion was interrupted by the intercom on the desk sounding.

"Chief…Special Agent Reynolds is here."

The Chief pushed the transmit button down.

"Thank you, Julie…send him in."

Devon turned her head to see a tall man, dressed in jeans and a button-down shirt enter the door. There was something oddly familiar about him…

Chief Donnelly rose out of his chair and shook the man's hand. "Hello again. Detective McKinney...this is Special Agent Scott Reynolds."

"Detective." Agent Reynolds said, reaching out to shake Devon's hand.

"Special Agent Reynolds is with the FBI. He's been working undercover for the past 16 months trying to break into a suspected pedophile ring that has ties from Michigan to Kentucky. He was just about ready to pull a couple of the major players into the sting when some hot-shot Detective decided to go off half-cocked on her own and walk in on them!" Said the Chief.

Devon felt sick with the realization of what she had done.

"Detective, do you have any idea how difficult it is to earn these scum-bags' trust? They are so stirred up now, I doubt we'll be able to bust them for another 10-12 months!" Agent Reynolds said, obviously not happy with what had happened. "By the way...how's your head?"

"I'll live...thanks." Devon said, sheepishly.

"You went down like a ton of bricks. I was afraid I hit you a little too hard..." he said.

"I thought you sounded familiar...look, I'm sorry for interfering with your operation out there. I didn't know."

"You didn't NEED to know. Your teams were given the no-joy order by the Incident Commander. If you had followed your orders as given, none of this would have happened." Agent Reynolds said.

"Gee, tell me how you really feel."
"I believe I just did, Detective." He said, coldly. "Chief Donnelly, I trust that this won't happen again."

"No, I can assure you that it won't. Detective McKinney is going to be taking a leave of absence..."

"I'm what?!" Devon said, not believing what she was hearing.

"…effective immediately." The Chief said, finishing what he had started to say.

"You have GOT to be kidding me!" Devon said, searching the Chief's eyes for some sign that perhaps he was just putting on a show for Agent Reynolds, but there was none.

Her stomach started knotting up at the thought of not only losing this case…but having the one thing that had been keeping her going since Chris had died, her work, taken away from her as well.

"I think that's my queue to leave." Agent Reynolds said, heading out the door.

Devon struggled to compose herself. She knew that losing control would only hurt whatever chance she had of getting the Chief to renege on the forced leave of absence.

Take a deep breath, McKinney…nice…cool…calm. A person who is in control of themselves is in control of the situation at hand…

She took a deep breath, letting it out slowly, hoping that some of the tension and hostility would go out with it.

"Chief, look…I understand that you're mad…and I agree that maybe I was a little out of line for doing what I did…and I don't really mean to sound cocky, but do you think that you can afford to take me off of this case right now? I mean it's not the kind of case that you can hand to a 'newbie'…"

"I seem to remember handing a certain 'wet-behind-the-ears rookie detective' her first multiple homicide not too long ago, and she did just fine. Stellar, as a matter of fact." The Chief said, referring to Devon's first big case in which a woman and her two children had been tortured and killed by an estranged boyfriend.

Devon remembered the case well. There were nights that she still couldn't get the sight of the woman and her two young children out of her mind. They had gone on a picnic in the woods behind their house, only to be cornered by the former boyfriend. He had tied the children, a boy and a girl, to trees using strands of barbed wire, and had raped their mother in front of them before killing them all. He had sliced their throats so deeply that he nearly beheaded them.

She knew that the Chief had taken a lot of heat for giving that case to her, and she had proven him right by overseeing the manhunt as well as the case, through the prosecution and sentencing...right to the end. All the more reason that he should trust her with this case now.

"I know that, and I really appreciate you having taken that chance on me. I proved that I could do it...and if you'll give me the chance, I'll prove it to you again." Devon said emphatically, trying to convince him.

"Devon, things have changed...you've changed. Back then, you were by the rules—all the way. I knew that I could count on you getting the job done, and doing it right." He said, getting up from his chair and walking over to a humidor that sat on the bookshelf.

He opened one of the drawers, selecting a cigar from his collection—lifting it to his nostrils and inhaling the rich scent deeply. His eyes closed briefly as he savored the aroma of the rum-soaked tobacco, a contented smile spreading across his face, fading to a more stoic look as his eyes opened once more, looking at Devon.

"But you're not the same person you were back then...hell, none of us are. Look at you! You're a loose canon...a ticking time-bomb waiting to blow up in the department's face...in MY face, for that matter! You're reckless, you're involving civilians in police business...I can't just sit by and let this go on!"

"Look...I know I've made some errors in judgment along the way, but..."

"Errors in judgment? That's putting it mildly, don't you think? I mean, you involving a civilian is just the tip of the shit pile, Detective! You single-handedly destroyed a very important federal sting—not to mention damn near destroying an agent's cover. That's something that I can't just sweep under the rug!" said the Chief.

"Alright, I get your point…and you can say what you want, but I did what any good detective would have done. I found a possible lead and I decided to follow it up!" Devon said, becoming more defensive.

I may not win this one, but by God—I'm not going down without a fight!

"You went off by yourself into an area that you KNEW had been called off-limits! I'm not going to discuss this any further with you." He said, moving back behind his desk. He looked Devon square in the eye, "Detective McKinney, you are on indefinite suspension with pay pending an evaluation by the review board and Internal Affairs."

"You've got to be shitting me!" Devon said, turning her back to him and heading for the door. Her blood pressure was rising to its boiling point.

"Devon, I'm going to need your gun."

Devon pulled her service .40 caliber from her waistband, dropped the clip and opened the chamber, popping the live round into her hand before placing it soundly on the desk.

"Your badge, too."

"Fine." Devon said, pulling the badge clip from her belt, tossing it on the desk, turning around to leave.

"For what it's worth, Devon…I am sorry." He said, half-heartedly.

"Yeah? Well why don't you ask the next girl's parents what it's worth when you're sticking their baby in a body bag!" Devon said, walking out the door, slamming it behind her.

Chief Donnelly watched as the glass in the door rattled.

He reached into his pocket, taking out a silver knife, clipping the end off of his cigar. He wet the end, sticking it in his mouth and lighting it, the end glowing a deep crimson red. He inhaled deeply, tasting the sweet rum tobacco smoke, holding it in to savor the flavor before exhaling…the corners of his mouth turning up with a smile of satisfaction.

CHAPTER 19

▼

She didn't know what time it was, or how long she had been driving. Somewhere along the way, she'd stopped at a party store and picked up a fifth of her old friend, Jack Black. It didn't take long for her to crack the seal and take a long swig of the smooth whiskey. She was surprised at just how easily it went down.

So this is what it's like...hitting rock bottom. Funny, feels like I've already been here once before, not too awful long ago.

She tossed back another mouthful of the whiskey and made a right-hand turn onto another street, cruising around in a haze. Suddenly, she heard a loud 'pop', and without warning, the SUV jerked hard to the right, sending her careening off the shoulder and into the ditch. She came to an abrupt halt when she hit the slope on the other side, setting off her driver's side airbag.

"Shit!" Devon said, taking a deep breath before unbuckling her seatbelt and turning off the ignition. Fighting her way past the airbag, she tried to open the door. Having no luck, she chose instead to climb out the driver's side window. Stumbling as she hit the ground, she took a few steps back, looking to see how bad things actually were. The front end of the SUV was buried in the soft dirt on the slope and a loud hiss was coming from underneath the hood. There was no doubt that the radiator had been damaged in the impact. The front right tire had blown completely off the rim, causing the SUV to veer drastically to the right.

"Son-of-a-bitch!" She said, slamming her fist down hard on the hood. She backed up, laughing at the absurdity of the whole thing…

"What? What the fuck did I do to you to deserve all of this? Huh?" She said, looking up to the heavens. "First, you take the one person who…who loved me, really loved me…you take her from me…just BAM! She's gone…and I'm left here behind…alone…again!"

Devon's temper rose with each passing second, she paced back and forth in front of the wreckage—spilling out a year's worth of frustration, pain, and loss to the night. "…and now…you take away the only thing I had left…the only thing that was keeping me going…giving me a reason to get up in the morning! I want it back!" She said, kicking at the driver's side door panel.

"I want it all back, now! You mother (kick) fucking (kick) bastard!" With the last kick, she lost her balance, falling back onto the ground. Devon pulled her knees to her chest and sat there, crying…finally letting out the months of pain that had been trapped inside her soul. She sat there, rocking back and forth, sobbing, and was still in that position when the pale blue beams of light from an approaching car lit up her face.

The small car pulled off onto the shoulder, aiming its lights down into the ditch and a figure climbed out. The figure stepped into the high beams.

She looked like an angel; this tall, slim woman enshrouded in a halo of light. Descending into the ditch, she placed her hand onto Devon's shoulder…

"Dev?" She said softly.

There it was. That voice again…that touch. Devon started to emerge from her teary haze.

"Dev, are you okay? Are you hurt?" She said, concern sounding loudly in her voice.

Devon looked up through teary eyes, snuffling back the sobs, trying hard to reclaim her tough exterior, recognizing Brid's golden locks and smooth voice immediately.

"No...I'm fine...just leave me alone, okay?" She said, turning away, not wanting Brid to see her this way.

"Come on, Dev...it's pretty plain to see that you're NOT okay." Brid said, placing her hand under Devon's chin, raising her face gently so their eyes would meet.

"Look, I don't know what happened, but I know that you're hurting, I can feel it. I understand, okay? Whatever happened, I'm here for you."

Devon looked into Brid's eyes, tears running hotly down her cheeks. It wasn't like her to depend on anyone...ever. The only person that she had ever allowed herself such a luxury with was Chris, and that was all taken away from her.

Almost as if she could read Devon's thoughts, Brid said softly, "I'm not going anywhere, Devon...I'm going to be right here with you. I promise."

Promises. Chris had promised to be with her forever, but it was a promise that she couldn't keep. Emotions welled up inside Devon once more. Pain, hurt, anger...and betrayal.

"Don't say that! You can't promise that, nobody can!" Devon said angrily. She quickly got up and dusted off her pants, putting some distance between her and Brid. "People say things like that all of the time...and it doesn't matter...they still go away. They are there for you...and...and...you think everything is going great...and then they're gone!"

"Sometimes they don't have a choice, Dev. They may not want to leave, but they have to...it's just their time." Brid said, trying to calm her.

"That's not true! It's not!" Devon said, the pain surging through her soul like a raging fire. "She could have stayed! She just didn't fight enough...she didn't! You won't either...you'll leave...or you'll be taken away—just like everything I ever wanted...everything that I've ever cared about!"

Brid thought for a moment. Caring, understanding, soft-spoken…this wasn't what Devon needed right now, and Brid knew it…she'd been there before herself, many years ago.

"…and you're the ONLY one whose ever lost anything that they wanted…anyone that they loved. Give me a break, McKinney…quit the pity party already!" Brid said, sternly.

Brid's change of tactics caught Devon unawares. She had not seen this side of her new friend before. It intrigued her and infuriated her all at the same time.

"Hey! I didn't ask you to come out here and save me, you know! What in the hell are you doing out here anyhow…stalking me or something?" Devon said, knowing in her heart that wasn't true.

"Ha! Don't flatter yourself! I was driving home from the University when I saw you in the ditch here and thought you might actually appreciate some help…but obviously I was wrong!" Brid said, turning and walking up the ditch bank towards her car, listening carefully for the footsteps that she was certain she would soon hear behind her…but much to her surprise, they never came.

Devon watched as Brid got into her VW, slammed the door shut, and pulled away—her taillights fading into the darkness.

Holy shit! She left! She actually left me here! I can't believe she just drove off and left me here! Damn…damn!

Devon leaned back against the front quarter panel of the SUV. Still rather stunned by Brid's actions.

How could she do this to me? More importantly—WHY would she do this to me? I thought that she wanted to help me…and instead, she leaves me out here alone? Wait a second…she said something about her knowing what it was like…she never said anything about losing anyone…did she? Or maybe she did, and I was just too wrapped up in my own crap to notice.

Great job, McKinney! You let her drive off like that! Geezus! Who knows what she's got going on...and you, being the selfish bitch that you are, thought of no one but yourself!

Now what am I supposed to do? Call a wrecker...that's a good start.

She reached into her pants pocket, pulling out her cell phone. Flipping it open, she noticed that the LCD screen had been broken when her leg hit the center console during the initial impact.
"Shit! Anything else you'd like to throw at me tonight—just for shits and giggles?" Devon said, looking to the heavens.

The words had barely left her mouth when she heard the distinct rumble of an incoming thunderstorm, hearing the first drops of rain hit the hood of the SUV with a 'ping'.

"I should have kept my mouth shut." She said, dryly.

Devon grabbed her keys and backup .45 from under her seat, tucking it in her waistband. She locked up the SUV, climbing up the ditch bank to the roadway.

Okay...pay phone. Can't be too far away, right? There's got to be a gas station towards town...

Devon headed off walking down the road in the same direction that Brid had gone just a few moments before. Her boots made a crunching sound with each step in the combination of sand and gravel on the side of the road. Hearing the thunder getting closer and the rain starting to fall more vigorously, she decided to pick her pace up a bit, switching from a leisurely walk to a slow jog.

This is just great. You could have been riding in a nice dry car right now with a pretty interesting, beautiful, and intelligent woman...but Nooooo...you had to open your big fat mouth and make her take off! Way to go, idiot!

Meanwhile, Brid hit the button on her electronic garage door opener, raising the door and driving in. She slid the transmission into PARK and turned the engine off. She sat there for a moment, pondering whether or not she had done the right thing by driving away and leaving Devon there in the ditch.

Maybe I shouldn't have left her out there. What if it all backfires in my face and throws her even deeper down that black hole she seems to be so insistent on spiraling down? Then what? I'll give her an hour and try calling her…see if she made it home alright.

Brid took the keys out of the ignition, grabbed her book bag, and went into the house.

The storm front hit with more intensity than Devon had anticipated. This was no run-of-the-mill thunderstorm; she recognized it immediately for what it was, a microburst. Michigan was notorious for such storms. They come out of nowhere and hit fast and hard, doing the majority of their damage with high-speed straight-line winds.

Shit…this is so not good! I've got to find someplace to get out of this.

Devon squinted as the water flowed into her eyes, clouding her vision. She was running full-speed now, hoping that she could reach some form of shelter before the worst winds hit. Noticing a turn in the pavement, she ran quickly to the right, hoping that she was either on a driveway or the entrance to a residential area. Suddenly, through the thunder and howling winds, she heard something in the distance…something familiar. Wind chimes. Could it be?

Lots of houses have wind chimes, McKinney…just get there, now!

The wind-blown rain stung Devon's face, making it impossible to see. She ran blindly, following the intermittent sounds of the chimes, hoping that they would lead her to a house or a business, anything to get out of the storm.

Meanwhile, Brid looked out the large bay window in her living room. The double-paned glass shook with each gust of wind, the rain pounding hard against its smooth surface.

Goddess…I never should have left her out there!

Brid ran to the table, grabbing her keys and purse and heading towards the door to the garage. Just as she opened the door, she heard a loud banging on the bay window.

What in the world...?

Brid ran back into the living room. The rain was still coming down in sheets, but she was able to make out a figure outside the window. It was Devon.

The wind caught the door just as Brid opened it, slamming it into the wall behind.

"Hurry up, get in here!" Brid yelled, reaching out and grabbing her by the shirt, pulling her into the house. Both women pushed against the heavy door, finally forcing it shut against the wind.

Devon was soaked through to the bone, her clothes clinging tightly to her body, accentuating every curve and muscle. Brid couldn't help but notice how striking the figure before her was.

Likewise, Brid was also quite a vision, her golden locks swept gracefully across her face, blown there by the wind when she opened the door for Devon.

Both women stood silently at first, each taking in the sight before them, appreciating the view. Brid was the first one to speak.

"I'm so sorry for..." She began.

"No, don't...I was the one who should be apologizing. I..." Devon said, interrupting.

"But I never should have left you..."

"I pushed you away, it wasn't your fault..." Devon said, cutting her off once again.
If there's one thing that Brid hated, it was being interrupted. Her face was starting to flush as her blood pressure raised with each interruption by Devon.

"Would you just let me finish what I was saying?! Goddess, you are stubborn sometimes!" Brid said, looking at Devon intently.

"Stubborn? You're calling ME stubborn? What about you getting all huffy and…"

"HUFFY?!" Brid said, crossing her arms in front of her chest defensively. "I was NOT being HUFFY! I'll have you know I have NEVER had a huffy day in my life! I'm quite known for my patience and understanding and…"

Devon silenced her in one fell swoop, stepping forward and placing her lips on Brid's in a rather passionate embrace. Much to Devon's surprise, Brid seemed very receptive, returning the kiss, bringing her hands up to Devon's neck and running her fingers through her rain-soaked hair.

Suddenly, Brid broke the embrace, pulling away slightly and looking Devon square in the eyes.

"Damnit! I HATE it when you interrupt me like that!" Brid said, grabbing Devon's wet shirt with both hands and pulling her forward to her waiting lips once more, this time deepening the kiss considerably.

Devon responded by placing her hands on the small of Brid's waist, resting them firmly, but gently, on her hips.

The two seemed lost in time as neither made the effort to pull away, both forgetting their pain, anger, and frustrations to luxuriate in the feelings that were coursing through their bodies.

Elsewhere, others were not as able to let those emotions go, and they were building up with each passing moment.

Not too far away, outside the doors to the root cellar of an old farmhouse, a man's voice was nearly drowned out by the pounding rain and thunder…

Do you realize what I've done for you? How much I've sacrificed for you? Geezus! I swear to God, you couldn't even wipe your ass without my help! You're pathetic! Do you know how many times I got my ass in a sling for you? How many times I limped home after getting the shit beat out of me by a group of kids, just because I was defending you? You mother fucking Mama's boy!"

FLASH!

Brid broke the kiss, but never the eye contact, as she held Devon's hands in hers, walking backward down the hallway toward the bedroom…

FLASH!

"What do you mean you can't take it anymore? YOU can't take it? You never could take it! I'm stuck cleaning up your mess, just like I always have!"

FLASH!

Devon pulled Brid closer, their hands entwined, kissing her as she backed her up to the bed. The back of Brid's long legs rubbed up against the bed as Devon lowered her back onto the softness below.

FLASH!

"Do you know what a fucking embarrassment you are to me? To Dad? To the whole family? Christ! Look at you!

FLASH!

Devon looked down on Brid, taking a moment to appreciate the woman's soft beauty before gently lowering her body onto hers, deepening their passionate embrace…just as the lightning struck once more, this time knocking out power throughout the area.

While passions raged, so did fury…both hidden by the inky black shroud of darkness that now enveloped the town…

CHAPTER 20

▼

Warm, soft…comfortable. These were things that Devon hadn't felt in a long time. Still half asleep, she wrapped her arm around the form next to her, running her hands along the curves, reveling in the feel of them.

A smile spread across Brid's face as she turned onto her back, seeing Devon lying next to her. Unsure if Devon was awake or asleep, she decided to 'test the waters'. Careful not to disturb her, Brid leaned over, gently placing her lips on Devon's.

"Mmmm…hi." Brid said, softly nuzzling Devon's neck.

Devon opened her eyes, the vision of Brid slowly coming into focus.

"Hi." Devon said, forcing a smile. Things had happened so quickly the night before that she really hadn't taken the time to think before acting. It wasn't that she didn't care about Brid…quite the opposite, really.

"Something not right?" Brid asked, picking up on Devon's feelings of discomfort.

"Everything's fine…why?" Devon asked, somewhat defensively.

Brid looked deep into Devon's eyes, there was something there…something that she'd seen before.

"You seem kind of...I don't know...distant or something." Brid said, running her hand up and down Devon's taut abdomen.

She was distant in a way, and very present in another. Every nerve in her body tingled at Brid's touch; however, her mind could not let her forget Chris.

Brid leaned over, pressing her lips gently against Devon's, slowly deepening the kiss.

God...this feels so good...WE feel so good! But it's not right! This just isn't right! Chris and I...we were supposed to be forever...and now I'm here...doing this...with her?

Devon broke the kiss, pulling away from Brid's embrace.

"I'm sorry...I just can't do this." Devon said, pulling back the covers and climbing out of the bed. She reached for her clothing that was lying in a heap on the floor; cast aside in a fit of passion the night before. The clothes were still dampened from the downpour during the storm.

Brid sat upright in the bed, clutching the sheet to her torso in an attempt to cover her nakedness.
"What do you mean you can't do this? Devon...wait!" She said, getting up from the bed and winding the sheets around her, fashioning a make-shift toga.

"I just can't do this right now, Brid...I'm sorry. It's not you, it's me." Devon said, sliding one leg into her BDU's. Goosebumps raised and a chill ran down her spine as the cold, wet rip-stop material hit her bare skin.

"Come on! At least talk to me...what's going on?" Brid said, watching Devon pull the rest of her clothes on.

"It's nothing. Just leave me alone, alright?" Devon snapped. Seeing the hurt in Brid's eyes, she softened her tone a bit. "Look...I'm sorry. I shouldn't have snapped at you. It's not your fault, really. I just...I just need to be alone right now...think things through. I'll call you later, okay?"

Suddenly, it hit Brid. Devon was feeling guilty...guilty for enjoying herself, for allowing herself to care again. She felt as though she was betraying Chris' memory. It all made sense; it didn't make it any easier to accept, but it did make sense.

"Whenever you feel like it...I'd appreciate that." Brid said, trying her best to maintain her composure and be understanding. She was hurt, there was no denying that; however, she did understand grief, and she knew that the only thing that could help was to give her the space that she needed to get over the survivor guilt that she was experiencing.
Just as Devon buckled her belt, her cell phone rang. She scrambled to find which pocket she had put it in, suddenly remembering as she grabbed it and flipped it open that the LCD screen had been broken in the accident.

"Shit." Devon said, exasperated with the situation.

"Aren't you going to answer it?" Brid asked.

"It was broken in the accident."

"Well, if it's ringing—you still might be able to receive calls on it."

"Yeah...good point." Devon said, pressing SEND on the phone. Although it took a moment for the signal to connect, she could hear a voice on the other end.

"McKinney here." Devon said, dryly.

Brid couldn't help but smirk.

Always the tough-gal...hehehe!

"Doc? Is that you?" Devon said, straining to understand the static-filled transmission.

"Devon? Listen...(static) know I'm not supposed to be telling you this...(static)...know how much this case means to you..."

"What are you talking about, Doc?"

"I know…(static)…took you off the case…(static)…got results on the hair…(static)…ferret hair."

"Ferret hair? The hair we got off of the Hingerman girl?"

"Yes…(static)…careful…(static)."

"I will Doc…do me a favor. I need you to keep these results to yourself."

"Devon…(static)…can't…"

"Please, Doc. Just give me a couple of hours to work this out, okay?" Devon pleaded.

"Two hours…(static)…that's all."

"That's perfect, Doc. Thanks!" Devon said, pressing END.

Brid waited until she was sure that Devon had hung up before speaking.

"Did I hear you say it was a ferret hair?" She asked.

"Yep…ferret hair."

"That's pretty rare up here, isn't it? I mean, I though Michigan had a law against having them." Brid said.

"Used to. They legalized them a few years ago." Devon said. Suddenly, it hit her. The picture in the Chief's office. The diener's nervousness during the one victim's autopsy…

"Holy shit!" Devon said, realizing the possibility of who the killer might be.

"What?"

"I know who it is! Oh my God!" Devon said, running around gathering her remaining items around the house and hurriedly putting them on.

"What do you mean you know who it is? What are you going to do?" Brid asked, watching Devon scramble around.

"I know who it is!" Devon said, pulling on her boot. "I don't have time to explain it right now—but trust me. I'm gonna get this guy...if it's the last thing I do!" "Devon...you can't just go off half-cocked! You've got to have some kind of backup! Remember what happened the last time you did this?" Brid said, reminding her of the trailer incident.

Devon swung her head around, glaring at Brid.

"Look...I don't need you to tell me what I should or shouldn't be doing!"

"Maybe not...but you do need my car to get you wherever it is that you're in such an all-fire hurry to get to." Brid said with a smirk.

Checkmate! Ha! Gotcha!

"Shit." Devon said, knowing exactly who had the upper hand at this point.

"Give me two minutes to throw some clothes on and we'll be out the door." Brid said turning and heading towards her closet.

Her keys lay in plain view on the bureau.

Devon's eyes picked up on them just as Brid turned around, snatching them from their resting place.

"Nice try." Brid said with a smirk, holding the keys in her hand while she grabbed a pair of jeans and a top from the closet.

Damnit! It figures! Why does she have to be so goddamned cocky about it! I'd like to wipe that smirk right off her face...but God help me, she is so fucking sexy when she flashes that little smirk of hers!

Brid held the keychain in her teeth while she slipped into the jeans and peasant top.

"Okay…" She said, taking the keys from her mouth "…let's go."

Brid and Devon headed to the door leading into the garage. Devon stepped ahead of her, opening the door.

Brid looked over at her smiling. "Thanks."

"Sorry…habit."

"Not a problem…shall we?" Brid said, walking over to the car.

Devon nodded as they both opened their respective doors and climbed into the VW, Brid behind the wheel.

Closing the doors, they sat briefly in silence until Brid looked over to Devon.

"So…are you going to let me in on where we're going here? Seeing as I am the one driving and all." She said, smirking once again.

"Just start the car, I'll tell you how to get there." She hadn't noticed before, but in the soft glow of the dome light, she noticed a faint scar on Brid's neck. It was barely visible, but there nonetheless.

Huh…never noticed that before. Must have been hidden under her makeup…just another one of the many mysteries of Miss Morrigan, I guess…

Brid hit the button on the garage door opener as she turned the key in the ignition. The little VW's motor was so quiet, you could barely tell that it was running.

They pulled out of the garage and into the darkness, the rain pounding on the hood of the small car.

Nearby, the blood-tinged water trickled down the drain in a miniature river of pink as the man meticulously scrubbed and rinsed the back of his vehicle.

You'll be clean enough to eat off from when I get done with you…Dad would be proud.

He turned the water flow off, laying the sprayer on the ground as he walked to the driver's side door, opening it and reaching behind the seat. Returning with a bottle of household bleach.

Ahhh...bleach. Simple but effective...and the 24-hour Car Wash? Where else can you wash your sins away for under five bucks?

He chuckled at the thought as he removed the cap off of the bottle, pouring its contents around the back of the bed of the truck. He scrubbed it thoroughly with the brush, knowing that the hypochlorite solution would render all biological evidence useless.

After giving the truck a final rinse, he cleaned the brush with the remainder of the bleach, sitting it back in the corner of the car wash stall. He gathered up the tarp and empty bottle and threw them into the dumpster.

Okay...vacuum time.

Reaching into his pocket, he pulled out three quarters, sliding them one-by-one into the coin slot on the power-vac and hitting the START button. The debris from the truck's interior made clicking sounds as it was sucked up through the vacuum hose.

It has a nice rhythm, but can you dance to it?

He smirked, almost laughing at his own thoughts. Inch by inch he went over the interior of the truck until it looked absolutely immaculate. He hung up the hose and climbed into the truck, a smile of satisfaction on his face as he disappeared into the night.

Later on, Devon and Brid were nearing the edge of a long driveway.

"Okay...slow down, we're almost there. Can you turn your headlights off?" Devon asked.

"I think so...hold on." Brid said, locating the proper control on the panel.

"Got it." She said, turning off the headlights.

The house looked dark with the exception of one room in the ground level on the west side.

"Nice house...looks like somebody's awake." Brid said, observing the soft glow in the window in the distance.

"Either that or they just forgot to turn the lights off."

"True. It's pretty early...or late, however you want to look at it." Brid said, wondering just whose house this was, and what Devon was planning on doing.

"Here's the deal. You stay here in the car and I'm going to go take a look and see if anybody is home...and check and see if they have any security systems. I need to get into that house, whether I'm invited in or otherwise."

"Are you sure you should be doing this, Dev? What if you get caught?"

"Hell, I'm already suspended from the department...its not like they can do anything else to me." Devon said, matter-of-factly.

"It's not what the department can do that I'm worried about! What if that psycho is in there! Geezus Dev, do you have a death wish or something?" Brid asked, a sound of concern and helplessness in her voice.

"Look, I don't have a fucking death wish, alright? I just want to get this guy before he hurts anybody else! I'll be careful, all right? The first time, I admit, I was a little careless...I should have waited for backup. This time, I have no choice, I've got to do it this way. If I call anybody I'll be in deeper shit than I already am. I'm sorry, but I've got to do this. If you don't want to be a part of it, I understand."

Brid looked deeply into Devon's eyes, seeing the sincerity there. She knew that she was Devon's only lifeline if something should go wrong inside...and she also knew that backing out now would not prevent Devon from doing it. Devon's mind was made up, she was seeing this through to the end, come hell or high water.

"I'll be here…whatever you need me to do." Brid said, putting her faith and trust in this woman that she barely knew, but longed to know better. Trust was not something that Brid Morrigan gave lightly…but she knew, somehow, she just <u>knew</u> that Devon would not betray it.

"Just sit back, watch and listen. If you notice anything out of the ordinary, call 9-1-1." Devon said.

"By out of the ordinary, you mean?"

"Gee, let's see…screams, gunshots, someone begging for their life…you know, the usual." Devon said, sarcastically.

"Great." Brid said, anticipating the worst.

"…and if I'm not out of there in thirty minutes, you'll know something went drastically wrong…send the troops in."

"Thirty minutes…not a second more, understand?" Brid asked, sternly.

"I got it." Devon said, climbing out of the vehicle. She slowly pushed the door shut until it clicked, preventing any unnecessary noise…a lesson she'd learned as a young girl when she went hunting in the early mornings with her father.

"Please watch over her." Brid whispered as she watched Devon fade off into the darkness…

CHAPTER 21

▼

Hands moved shakily across the keyboard, words appearing on the monitor…

…I NEVER WANTED TO DISAPPOINT YOU…AND NO MATTER HOW HARD I TRIED, THAT'S ALL I SEEMED TO DO. NOTHING WAS EVER GOOD ENOUGH. DAY AFTER DAY…THE TEASING, THE TAUNTING…AND NOW THE FEAR…FEAR OF BEING CAUGHT. I COULD NEVER MAKE IT ON THE INSIDE. YOU ALL KNOW THAT. SO BETTER THAT I TAKE CARE OF THIS NOW, WHILE I HAVE THE MEANS TO DO SO.

HOW IRONIC IS THIS THAT EVEN MY LAST ACTIONS ARE GOING TO BE A DISAPPOINTMENT…THERE IS NO WAY TO PLEASE ANY OF YOU. AT LEAST THIS WAY, I WON'T HAVE TO LISTEN TO IT ALL ANYMORE.

REGARDLESS OF WHAT YOU MAY THINK…I DO LOVE

ALL OF YOU.

A somewhat small hand pulled open the desk drawer, reaching into the darkness, searching for an end to all of the pain…and it found it in the form of a .357 magnum snub-nosed revolver. He laid the Smith and Wesson on the desktop and studied the gun, so smooth, so cool, hard…it was nothing like him. He smiled to himself at the notion that something so small could end a life's worth of torment, and he cursed himself for not thinking of this sooner…

There was engraving on the body of the gun, he read…

Smith and Wesson Model 37 Airweight—'Chiefs Special'.

Ha! Can you believe it? It figures…irony is so ironic sometimes!

He reached back into the drawer, finding the box of ammunition. He opened the end, sliding out the cartridge holder. Hollow points…guaranteed to leave the maximum path of destruction in their wake. He set the bullets on the desktop with the gun, before reaching for a white plastic shopping bag behind him.

Inside the bag were two disposable plastic tarps and a roll of duct tape.

I'm going to make it as easy and neat for you as possible…don't want you to come home from your precious vacation to a mess…

He spread the tarps out over the furniture and the wall, securing it all with duct tape before returning to his seat in front of the computer.

He picked up one bullet, running it through his fingers, feeling the smoothness of it. After a moment, he released the cylinder and swung it out, giving it a spin as he did so. He began sliding the bullets in one-by-one, comforted by the knowledge that it soon would be over.

Devon slowly made her way through the wooded edge of the property, the soft glow in the window guiding her towards the house. As she approached, she scanned the area for motion detectors, spying one on the side facing the road and another on the west side of the house.

Okay McKinney…if you go at it from the corner, you should be able to stay out of the beam.

Keeping an eye on the window, she ran quietly across the open part of the lawn to the corner of the house. None of the exterior lighting activated.

Made it! Okay…just going to take a peek and see if the coast is clear…

Devon slowly rose up, careful to stay in the shadows as she looked in the window where the light was emanating from. She could see the glow of a computer screen and a figure sitting in front of it, slowly raising what appeared to be a pistol to his temple...

Holy shit! He's going to off himself!

Not knowing how to stop him, Devon knocked soundly on the window, hoping to distract him if only momentarily.

The figure froze, pausing briefly before turning around to face the window.

Devon's suspicions were confirmed as the person turned around...it was none other than Frank Donnelly.

The look on his face was one of desperation. He had things all planned out...had the solution to his problem. But now, he had been interrupted. All of the pain that he thought that he would leave behind him came rushing back in, flooding him with emotion. Tears flowed freely down the young man's cheeks as he looked at Devon almost pleadingly.

Should she stop him? Maybe she should just let him go ahead and blow his brains out. After all, he did deserve it, didn't he? It would definitely save the taxpayers money...or was it just too easy? Why should she give him a break? He certainly didn't show any mercy to those girls!

But there was something in his eyes, and Devon knew it well. It was pain, pure and simple pain. Not physical pain, something much worse. The pain that shreds the core of your soul, tearing at the very fiber of your being. She had felt it herself not too long ago.

Frank cocked his head to the side, tears flowing down his face, as he raised the gun back to his temple.

Devon had a split second to make her decision.

Justice had to have its chance to prevail.

"No!" Devon yelled as she crashed through the window, setting off the perimeter crash alarms. The glass shards piercing the flesh on her bare arms as she cleared the frame.

"Leave me alone!" Frank pleaded.

Devon reached out towards Frank, wincing as a sharp pain shot up her arm from one of the lacerations.

"Listen Frank…you don't want to do this. Put the gun down…let's talk about it."

The sound of glass breaking cut the silence like a knife, startling Brid as she waited for Devon in the VW.

"Shit!" She said, her body jerking from the shock. She reached for the cell phone, not noticing the approaching headlights in her rear view mirror.

Meanwhile, Devon was trying desperately to talk Frank Donnelly out of blowing his brains out…

"Talk about what?! What is there to talk about?! I don't want to talk…I'm sick of talking! Just leave me alone!" Frank yelled, crying as he held the gun in place, just wanting the pain to end.

"Frank, come on…I know what you're feeling…and I know what you did…but you have a chance to make it right. Turn yourself in, Frank…don't do this. It's the cowards way out…you don't want to be a coward, do you?" Devon asked.

FLASH

"What are you gonna do about it, huh?" The girl said, pushing a young Frank Donnelly to the ground while others laughed. A somewhat older boy steps forward, helping him up.

Frank stands, brushing the dust from his clothes.

"Geezus Christ, Francis! Why do you have to be such a friggin' sissy mama's boy?" The boy said in disgust.
The rest of the children standing by in the playground join in chorus..."Frankie's a chicken! Frankie's a chicken!"

Frank sobbed remembering how he'd been branded a sissy and a chicken by the children at school...the boys, the girls, even his own brother...

"You kn-know what I'm feeling?! How could you EVER know h-how I feel?" Frank yelled, spit flying from his mouth as he spoke in between the sobs. "Look at you! Everybody r-respects you...my b-brother idolizes you, for Christ's sake! What could y-you possibly know about any of it?"

"Frank...listen...I haven't always fit in. Hell...I still don't in a lot of ways!"

Frank snuffled, wiping his nose with his free hand. "Yeah...right." He said, skeptically.

"Seriously, Frank! Geezus Christ...I'm gay, Frank...do you know how many years I hid that from everybody trying to fit in?" Devon said, desperately trying to empathize with the young man, to develop a bond of trust.

"I'm n-not gay!" He said, seemingly more agitated. He started pacing nervously, still holding the gun to his temple.

"I never said you were, Frank...I never said that...I'm just saying that I know what it's like to be different...to feel like you don't fit in." Devon said, trying to calm him down.

Sitting in her VW, Brid turned her cell phone on and was just about to dial 9-1-1 when a flash of light from her side view mirror temporarily blinded her.

"What the?" She said to herself, just as something tapped on her side window, sending her jumping off her seat.

"Ma'am?" A voice said from outside her car. "Are you alright?"

Brid turned slowly, looking towards the window. She let out a sigh of relief when she saw the police officer standing at her door. She quickly rolled down her window, smiling.

"Goddess, I'm glad to see you! I was just about to call 9-1-1!" She said, frantically.

The young man looked at her somewhat quizzically.

"Did you break down or something? You really should have your hazard lights on, Ma'am."

"No…I…" She started, trying to quickly come up with a story to explain why she and Devon were there at such an hour.

"…we're supposed to be watching the house while the owner's away…and my friend went up to check on everything…and I heard someone yell and it sounded like glass breaking! I really think that she might need help!"

"Okay Ma'am…just calm down. I'm sure it's nothing. Why don't we walk up there and I'll check the house out myself. Make sure everything is okay." He said, trying to calm the situation.

"That would be wonderful…thank you so much!" She said, as he opened the car door for her. She quickly climbed out of the VW and started walking with the officer down the driveway.

"So you said that you're watching the house for the owners?" He asked, walking beside her with his flashlight held off to his side, illuminating their path.

"Um…yes. Well actually, my friend is the one watching the house…I was just helping her…that's all."

"Oh, I see." He said, as they continued to walk.

Their soles of their shoes ground against the stonecrete of the driveway as they made their way toward the house. As they approached the cement stairs leading to the front door, he stopped.

"Why don't you wait right here while I check this out first, Ma'am…just to be safe." He said, holding his hand out, motioning her back as he walked up the stairs and tapped on the door with his flashlight.

TAP! TAP! TAP!

Both Devon and Frank were startled by the sound of someone tapping on the front door.

If he just turns his attentions away for a minute, maybe I can get the gun away from him…

The officer turned back to Brid, who was waiting at the bottom of the steps.

"No answer." He said, gently turning the doorknob to see if it was locked—it wasn't.

"I'm going to go in and take a look around…" he said, taking his sidearm from its holster. He carefully opened the front door, shining the light inside the foyer. The beam from the flashlight glared off of the white walls and highly polished hardwood floor.

Leading away form the foyer was a long hallway, and at the end, a doorway with a softly glowing light emanating from it.

After making sure that his path was clear, he cautiously stepped inside while Brid moved up the steps closer to the door.

The foyer was quite large with a vaulted ceiling, making it difficult to not make a sound.

The officer took his time moving quietly across the hardwood floor, pausing frequently to listen to what sounded like muffled voices. Brid stood quietly near the door, listening while the he moved down the hallway toward the room where the light was coming from.

Devon saw the movement in the shadows of the doorway that led to the hallway.

Please let that be my backup...

Unsure of what he was about to find, the officer carefully leaned around the corner of the doorway, using the jamb for cover if needed.

Frank realized that he may soon be interrupted once again, he focused once again on what he had intended to do in the first place. He held the gun tight to his temple, pushing in hard enough to dimple the skin with the barrel. Slowly he pulled the hammer back...first one click, then two.

As he stepped out of the shadows, Devon could now see who was coming to her rescue...it was Patrick Donnelly.

"Patrick..." She said with a sigh of relief, figuring that if anyone could, he would be able to get through to his brother.

Frank turned around to see his brother standing behind him, his gun still drawn.

"Frankie...what are you doing, buddy?" Patrick asked.

Still holding the gun to his head, Frank began to cry once more.

"I've gotta end this, Paddy...I can't d-do it...I'm not like you...I c-can't..." he said, shaking his head.

Patrick slowly made his way towards Frank. "It's alright buddy...it's all going to be over soon...everything's going to be okay."

Okay kid...take it easy...nice and slow. No fast moves. Just get him to put the gun down and we'll wrap this thing up.

"I can't, P-Paddy! S-stay back!" Frank said, swinging the gun toward Patrick, still sobbing as the tears ran down his face.

While Frank had his back turned, Devon took the opportunity to reach for her own weapon, pulling it out of it's holster, but keeping her hand down so not to draw attention to herself.

"Easy Frankie…" Patrick said, visibly nervous as a bead of sweat flowed ominously down his forehead.

"Geezus…I can't get her face out of my h-head!" he yelled, pounding his head in frustration with his free hand.

"Get out!!! Why w-won't you leave m-me alone!" He screamed, seemingly to his unforeseen specter. "How do you d-do it? How do y-you make them g-go away? Don't they b-bother you?! D-don't you see them?!"

Hearing the commotion, Brid's curiousity got the best of her.

What in the hell is going on in there?

Slowly she made her way down the hallway toward the room.

"I don't see anybody, Frankie…it's just you and me, buddy…put down the gun." Patrick said, his tongue running across his upper lip, licking off the salty-sweet beads of sweat that were now running down his face.

"I c-can't! We can't do it anymore, Paddy! Y-you've got to stop!"

"Put the gun down, Frankie! Put the fucking gun DOWN!" Patrick yelled. Stepping forward, he slowly squeezed the trigger on his .9mm, hitting Frank square in the chest.

Frank squinted as he looked at his brother, wincing before dropping to the floor in a bloody heap.

Devon holstered her weapon and ran to Frank's side, using her hand to apply direct pressure to the blood-spurting wound in the young man's chest.

"Get an ambulance!" She yelled, the blood pumping out in between her fingers with every heartbeat.

Patrick stood above his brother, his gun still drawn.

Brid stepped into the doorway, the sight before her causing the bile to well up in the back of her throat. She swallowed hard, bringing her hand to her mouth in an unconscious attempt to prevent herself from vomiting on the spot.

"Geezus Christ, Patrick! Get a fucking ambulance!" Devon screamed.

Frank struggled to breathe as blood filled his mouth. Every breath was a struggle...the liquid causing a thick gurgling sound as the blood trickled past his lips and down the side of his mouth.

"Shhhh...hang on there, kiddo. Don't try to talk." Devon said, trying to calm him.

"I-I tried to h-help her..." Frank said, struggling to get the words out.

Brid stepped forward "I'll call an ambulance." She said, her cell phone still in hand. She walked back into the hallway, dialing 9-1-1.

"I-I tried...b-but he s-stopped..." Frank said, using his last ounce of energy, he raised a bloody hand, pointing at his brother before finally slipping away.

Devon looked up at Patrick, his lips now trembling, and it all made sense.

The subtle differences between the Hingerman girl and the other victims, the bruises from CPR...someone <u>had</u> tried to bring them back.

Play it cool, McKinney...nice and easy. Maybe he doesn't know you're on to him...

Just then, Brid walked back into the room, standing near Patrick as she looked down to Devon for guidance.

"The ambulance is on it's way...what else can I do to help?" She asked.

Sensing that Devon was onto him, Patrick reached out, grabbing Brid.

Devon reached back for her gun, but Patrick had the upper hand and he knew it. He held Brid tightly in front of him, his .9mm pressed into her side.

"Ah-ah-ah, Detective McKinney…can't let you do that. Drop the clip and put your gun on the floor." He said, paying no attention to his own flesh and blood lying on the floor in front of him.

"Slowly…" he cautioned.

Devon slowly pulled the .45 from its holster, pressed the clip release, unloaded the chamber and placed it on the floor.

"Now slide it over here."

He's not going to give you any options, McKinney…this is it. You've got to come up with something quick, or you and Brid are going out of here feet first…he's not going to leave any witnesses.

Devon reluctantly slid the pistol over to him. He raised his foot, stopping it with the sole as it slid across the floor.

"Thank you…you know…I'm really sorry I have to do this…but you know I can't let either of you go."

"Patrick, listen to me…there's still hope. You can turn yourself in…you didn't mean to do all of this…it's all a big mistake…and mistakes can be taken care of…" Devon said, trying to reason with him.

Patrick actually laughed "Ha! You think this was a mistake? You think what I've done was a mistake? Those little bitches got exactly what they had coming to them…and so did Frankie, for that matter!"

"You don't mean that…" Devon reasoned.

"The hell I don't! Do you know what they used to do to him? You know…maybe you're right…maybe it wasn't their fault…maybe it was Frankie's! But hell! I took care of that one, too…so I'm golden!" He said, laughing as he looked down on his brother's still-warm corpse.

Come on, McKinney…think!

Devon's eyes met Brid's. She could see the desperation and fear in her steel grey pools…

You can't just look…you have to see!

What was that? Was it Chris? No. It wasn't…

You have to see!

Devon blinked, glancing down, she noticed a glimmer of silver sticking out from underneath Frank's pant leg…it was the handgun that he had intended to use on himself.

Devon looked at Brid once again for reassurance. She knew this was their only chance.

In once smooth motion, she reached down for the gun, cocking it in mid-swing. Brid saw what she was about to do and tried to roll out of Patrick's arm…but she was too late.

Devon and Patrick fired almost simultaneously.

Devon had aimed true. The .357 hollow-point had hit Patrick between the eyes, blowing the back of his head off, killing him instantly. His body fell on top of Brid as she hit the floor.

"NO!!!!" Devon yelled, seeing that Brid had been hit.
She rushed over, dropping to her knees and pulling Patrick's body off of Brid.

"No…no…baby…please! You're gonna be alright…you've gotta be!" She pleaded, gently repositioning Brid, examining her wound.

Tears welled up in her eyes as she saw the extensive damage that his shot had caused. The bulled had entered her side just below her left underarm. The blood was frothing around the entrance wound.

Devon sat in the pool of warm blood, holding Brid's hand, rocking back and forth sobbing uncontrollably…

CHAPTER 22

▼

The lights…the sirens…running alongside the gurney holding Brid's hand in hers.

Bad memories.

"Detective?"

"Brid…I'm here! You've gotta hang on, baby!" She said, running alongside the gurney as they rushed into the emergency room. "I'm here, Brid! I'll be right here…please hang on!" She pleaded through tear filled eyes.

Suddenly, an arm across her chest stopped her.

"Detective McKinney…I'm sorry, I know this is hard, but you'll have to stay out here." The nurse said, following alongside the gurney.

Devon watched as her life…a life she didn't even realize that she had, disappeared through the double doors of the emergency room.

This can't be happening again! Not again!

Everything seemed to go in slow motion, the following hour being nothing but a blur.

She stood silently alone outside the double doors, watching…waiting…until she felt a hand on her shoulder…

"Dev?"

She turned her head, finding her partner, Mike, standing next to her.

Her emotions on override, she threw her arms around him, sobbing on his shoulder.

"Hey…hey…Dev. It's gonna be alright." He said, holding her tightly, rubbing her back to try to comfort her.

As much as he wanted to give her a brow-beating for going off on her own again, he couldn't do it. Not now. Right now, all he wanted to do was take some of his best-friend's pain away.

"It's not gonna be alright…" Devon sobbed. "…she gonna die, just like Chris…and it's all my fault!" She said, pulling back from his embrace momentarily.

It was then that Mike got a good look at his friend. Her clothes and hands were covered in blood.
"Geezus, Dev…are you alright? Have you been checked out by a doc?" He said, frantically scanning her for any wounds.

"I'm fine…it's not mine…it's Brid's."

"Shhh…come on. Let's go sit down over here." He said, gently leading her to the seating in the waiting room.

Devon slumped in the chair, still sobbing uncontrollably.

Mike put his arm around her, reaching out with his other, taking her hand in his.

"Listen…it's not your fault…"

"How do you know? You weren't there, Mike! You weren't there!" She yelled.

"I know my partner...and I know that you never would have intentionally hurt Brid or put her in danger in any way." He said, trying to reassure her.

"But I did, Mike. I had her take me to a suspected murderer's house, for Christ's sake! She never would have been there if it weren't for me...just like Chris!" She said, breaking down once again.

"Is that what you think? That Chris' death was your fault?"

Devon's silence spoke volumes. Her head hanging low.

Mike reached up, lifting her chin so that their eyes met.

"Listen to me...what happened to Chris was not your fault. There was nothing that you could have done. Geezus, Devon—you got hit yourself trying to push her out of the way! This thing with Brid...from what I've seen of her...she would have ended up there on her own anyway if she knew that you were going to be there. It's pretty obvious that she cares about you, Dev."

"She shouldn't...look what it's got her...it's probably cost her life." She said, hanging her head once more.

Hearing the double doors open, she rose quickly from her seat, nearly running to the doctor that was coming through them.

"How is she? Is she..."

"She's going to be in surgery for a while. Do you know how to get in touch with her family? They really should be notified as soon as possible." The doctor asked.

"Um...I'm not sure..." Devon said, somewhat in shock. "...I don't really know. Maybe the university would have an emergency contact for her."

"I'll call and see what I can find out." Mike said, opening his cell phone.

"I'm sorry, Detective. You can't use cell phones inside the hospital, they interfere with the EKG's and other equipment." The doctor said, motioning to the sign on the wall—a picture of a cell phone with a red circle and slash over it.

"Right…sorry about that. Dev, I'm going to just step outside for a little while and see if I can get that information for them. Okay?"

Devon nodded her approval. She waited until he was through the doors before asking anything more of the doctor.

"Okay…how bad is she? Is she going to make it? I want to know." Devon said, trying her best to refrain from crying once more.

"I really shouldn't be discussing details of Ms. Morrigan's conditions with any-one but family members, Detective…you know that."

"I know…but I am…well…I'm her partner…her 'significant other'." She said. It was true, she was her partner. She had tried to deny her feelings and walk away, but they ran way too deep…much deeper than she had ever realized.

"Ah…I see…very well. Ms. Morrigan has sustained a significant gunshot wound to the chest. The bullet seems to have pierced the pleural space surrounding the lung, causing air to build up inside—which has caused her lung to collapse. It's called a tension pneumothorax. We've inserted a chest tube in the trauma bay which should reduce the pressure enough to allow her lung to re-inflate."

"Well…that's good then, right?" Devon said, hopefully.

"It will definitely help, there's no doubt about that. But she's still losing a lot of blood. That's why we're taking her into surgery right now. The bullet may have nicked an artery or possibly a portion of the heart. We really don't know for sure…and we didn't want to wait for the results of an angiogram. She's bleeding much too quickly. Exploratory surgery was our only option. We'll do our best to repair whatever we find." He said, trying not to candy-coat anything. This was definitely a life-or-death situation—there was no doubt about that.

"Doc…is she going to make it?" Devon asked, hesitantly.

"Let's just hope for the best, okay?" He said with a smile, heading back through the double doors.

Devon stood by, watching the doctor disappear down the hallway. That was exactly where Mike found her when he came back in.

"Hey…what did the doc say?" Mike asked.

"They put a chest tube in…she's bleeding pretty badly. They've got her in surgery now." Devon said, swallowing hard, trying to keep herself from breaking down again.

"I got a hold of the dean at the University. He's going to get her file and page me when he gets the emergency contact information from her file. He said it would probably take him twenty minutes or so. I got him out of bed."

"Hey…if we're not sleeping, why should he, right?" Devon said, trying to crack a joke to keep from crying. It didn't work, the tears started flowing down her cheeks once again.

Knowing that nothing that he could say would make things any better, Mike did the only thing he could thing of…he put his arms around his friend, holding her close, and just let her cry.

She was crying when a nurse approached them, carrying something with her.

"Detective?"

Devon wiped her eyes, turning around to face the nurse.

"Yes?" She said, sniffling.

"I've got a set of scrubs here for you…I though you might want to clean up and get out of those clothes." She said, holding out the scrubs, smiling softly.

"Thank you." Devon said, taking the scrubs.

"There's a shower in the resident's quarters, if you'd like to clean up. I can take you down there."

"Oh…I really ought to be here…" Devon started.

"Go clean up, Dev. I'll make sure that someone comes and gets you if there's any news." Mike said.

"Are you sure?" Devon asked.

"I'm sure…I'll be right here." Mike said, giving her shoulder a squeeze. "Now go get cleaned up. I'll see you when you get out."

"I'll be back in ten minutes." Devon said, walking with the nurse.
"Make it nine!" Mike said with a wink as she disappeared through the doors.

Seven minutes later on the button, Devon walked back into the waiting room dressed in a pair of green scrubs, her hair wet and pulled back into a ponytail.

Mike was sitting down, sipping a cup of coffee when she walked up.

"Did you hear anything yet?" She asked.

"I heard back from the Dean…it's kind of weird. Up until a few days ago, Brid didn't have anybody down as a contact." Mike said, blowing on his coffee, which was still just a bit too hot for his liking.

"You said up until a few days ago…so who does she have on there now?" Devon asked.

"You." Mike said, taking a sip of his coffee.

How could she have known that we'd…

Three hours later…

The doors opened once again as a rather weary Dr. Miller walked over to Devon, who was now sitting with her head propped precariously on her hands, in a twilight slumber.

"Detective McKinney?" he said, waking her by placing his hand on her shoulder.

Devon jerked awake, as did Mike.

"What? Oh…is she okay?" She said, almost afraid to ask.

"She's not completely out of the woods yet, but I think it's safe to say she's beat the odds this far—there's no reason to believe that she won't continue to keep surprising us." He said. "Would you like to see her?"

Devon felt like someone had breathed life into her body. She could barely contain her relief or excitement.

"Yes…please!" She said, smiling.

"Come on, I'll take you back. She's going to be in recovery for a few more minutes—then we'll be moving her to ICU." He said, motioning for Devon to join him.

"Go ahead, Dev. I'll be right here." Mike said.

The hallway to the ICU unit seemed endless. Seeing it's cold tiles, the smell of antiseptic hanging in the air…it all brought back even more bad memories of walking this same hallway once before.

After a maze of twists and turns, they arrived at the ICU room where Brid was being taken care of. Devon looked into the room, Dr. Miller still at her side.

Brid lay on her hospital bed, the head slightly elevated. The sound of the ventilator whirring along with the constant beeps of the heart monitor.

"She's not awake right now…but she can hear you." Dr. Miller said, guiding Devon into the room. "I'll have one of the nurses bring a chair in for you."

"Thanks." Devon said, hesitantly walking into the room.

Slowly she walked over to Brid's bedside. Her blonde locks stained pink with blood. It looked as though they had tried to clean her up somewhat, but there were still traces throughout her hair. Her porcelain skin once full of life, now looked pale and listless from the loss of blood. Devon reached down, taking her soft, slender hand in her own.

"Hey beautiful...it's me." She said, smiling...caressing Brid's forearm as she held her hand, careful not to disturb her IV.

"Excuse me, Detective...here's a chair for you." One of the nurses said, wheeling in a softly padded chair that was obviously from behind their desk.

"Thank you." Devon said, wheeling the chair closer to Brid's bedside, never letting go of her hand.

She sat there, holding Brid's hand to her cheek, remembering how it had felt only the night before...

"You know...you didn't have to do all of this, just to get my attention and all...you had it from that very first night. Eggplant parmesean, remember?" Devon smiled, remembering that night at the restaurant. She swallowed hard, feeling the lump forming in her throat once more.

"I'm so sorry that I got you into this, baby." She said, pausing to try to gain her composure.

"Last night...it wasn't that I though it was all a mistake...it wasn't like that. It was just...well...I felt more for you than I thought was possible...and it felt so good...so right...but I felt like I was somehow betraying Chris. Like I was betraying what we had...her memory."

You're doing just fine, baby...tell her...it's alright. I want you to.

Suddenly, Devon felt a sense of calm flowing through her...and finally, she understood.

"What I didn't understand was…that the best way for me to honor Chris' memory was to go on…live my life to the fullest…and to love again. I never thought it would be possible, but I do, Brid…I do love you…as crazy as it sounds, I know we barely know each other…but I do love you."

That's my girl…

With those words, Devon felt Brid's hand squeezing hers ever-so-gently and she knew that for the first time in a long time, everything was going to be alright…

EPILOGUE

▼

Three months later, Brid's wounds had healed. Unfortunately, the wounds that others suffered as a result of the Donnelly brother's actions would never heal.

Faced with the reality of what his sons had done, Chief Donnelly resigned from the police force.

Although her actions were condemned by a panel of investigators from Internal Affairs, Devon was reinstated as a Detective with Mike as her partner once again. However, the choices that she made would permanently mar her otherwise spotless law enforcement record.

It was a cool fall day. Brilliant hues of gold, umber, and crimson filled the trees, their leaves gently falling to the ground in a silent dance whenever a slight breeze would come along. Devon walked amongst the headstones, being careful not to step on any of the gravesites.

It had been almost a year-and-a-half since she had been to this spot, but she remembered the way without fail. She knelt before the pink granite headstone on Chris' grave, a bouquet of flowers in her hand.

"Hi baby. I know it's been a while since I've been out here…I'm sorry. I brought you something…" She said, laying the flowers by the headstone. "…forget-me-nots…your favorite."

She leaned forward, tracing Chris' name slowly with her fingers, a single tear falling down her cheek and onto the ground.

"I'll always love you, Chris…always…" She said, smiling softly.

Devon brought her fingers to her lips, kissing them gently and then placing them on the headstone.

"…and I kept my promise." She said, raising up, taking one last look at her past.

A warm, soft hand reached for Devon's, entwining their fingers together, and Devon turned away from her past, walking instead to her future with Brid.